SUGAR KIDS

SUGAR KIDS

A NOVEL

TASLIM BURKOWICZ

Roseway Publishing
an imprint of Fernwood Publishing
Halifax & Winnipeg

Copyright © 2024 Taslim Burkowicz

All rights reserved. No part of this book may be reproduced or transmitted in any form by any means without permission in writing from the publisher, except by a reviewer, who may quote brief passages in a review.

Development editing: Fazeela Jiwa
Copyediting: Kristen Darch
Cover design: Tania Craan
Text design: Lauren Jeanneau
Printed and bound in Canada

Published by Roseway Publishing
an imprint of Fernwood Publishing
Halifax and Winnipeg
2970 Oxford Street, Halifax, Nova Scotia, B3L 2W4
www.fernwoodpublishing.ca/roseway

Fernwood Publishing Company Limited gratefully acknowledges the financial support of the Government of Canada through the Canada Book Fund and the Canada Council for the Arts. We acknowledge the Province of Manitoba for support through the Manitoba Publishers Marketing Assistance Program and the Book Publishing Tax Credit. We acknowledge the Nova Scotia Department of Communities, Culture and Heritage for support through the Publishers Assistance Fund.

Library and Archives Canada Cataloguing in Publication
Title: Sugar kids: a novel / Taslim Burkowicz.
Names: Burkowicz, Taslim, 1978- author.
Identifiers: Canadiana (print) 20240305221 | Canadiana (ebook) 20240305256 | ISBN 9781773636757 (softcover) | ISBN 9781773636764 (PDF) | ISBN 9781773636771 (EPUB)
Subjects: LCGFT: Bildungsromans. | LCGFT: Novels.
Classification: LCC PS8603.U73776 S84 2024 | DDC C813/.6,Äîdc23

For my brother, Nishat Sherif.
For the times we tortured Mom and Dad by performing "Mama Said Knock You Out" by LL Cool J and charged them admission to watch us.

"I can live alone, if self-respect, and circumstances require me so to do. I need not sell my soul to buy bliss. I have an inward treasure born with me, which can keep me alive if all extraneous delights should be withheld, or offered only at a price I cannot afford to give."

— CHARLOTTE BRONTË, *Jane Eyre*

BEFORE

ONE

One day, I got the flu and Ravi didn't. It was September 12, 1988. We were ten. For the first time in our lives, he went to school without me. On the walk home my twin was struck by a car on a crosswalk. Hindus do not cremate saints, babies, or young children. These beings did not need their sins purified. Ravi was older than the typical age children are when they are buried. But despite my mother's protests that Ravi was as innocent as an infant, Ravi was not arranged to be buried in lotus position as a holy person would be. He was cremated.

On the eve of his funeral, I felt myself become buried with the same dirt he should have been. Heavy, cool, moist soil covered me, filled with worms, minerals, and decomposed animals. Whoever I had been when Ravi was alive sank deeper into the Earth's crust, and I swallowed all his boy traits in my sleep. The next morning, the blackened soil, laced with white dots of volcanic glass that looked like Styrofoam balls, wafted away from me like the ocean's waves. I sat up in bed, sure I had consumed Ravi's spirit. It was stored in me, like a genie in a bottle. I picked up Ravi's hat and his kid-sized skateboard, ready to go to school as both twins.

Instead, my mother came into my room, packed up the unisex clothes Ravi and I had worn and told me I should wear dresses from now on. As if what Ravi and I had together was a circus act. Ravi and I had used our twinhood to bypass our Indianness, climbing the ranks of popularity in a mostly white school. Together, we had won skipping rope contests dancing to Rob Base & DJ E-Z Rock. We had been as popular as Amanda Piper with her swimming pool–blue eyes, and golden Erik Danielson, who had been chosen for every sports team. But my mom was reshaping her reality, trying to squeeze Ravi out of me.

That very day, she transferred me to a different elementary school. At the new school, I wasn't someone anymore. The bullies spoke to me in made-up accents and put stickers between their eyes when they saw me. Girls pulled up my skirt and laughed at my Days of the Week underwear. I was nicknamed Tuesday. It could have been the ridiculous outfits my mother sent me to school in — sailor girl outfits and bumblebee dresses with sashes. Immigrant children's clothes, othering me from the get-go. That's also around the time my violent twitching started, like I was having seizures, and I really couldn't control when it would happen. Now, I was a twinless twin. I felt like I was missing a limb. Like I was barely alive. Ravi would never even return the last book he had borrowed: *Under the Night Sky*. Stolen library books became a comfort to me of sorts.

And that should have been the end of the Ravi's story; really, it should have been.

Instead, Ravi decided to visit me.

He looked exactly as he always did, black hair standing on end, dressed in plain jeans and a denim jacket, the last thing he had worn, and he calmly told me that we would still grow up together, just that he had to do most of his growing up some place else.

"I will visit you when I can, Baby, and if you tell anyone about me, they won't believe you anyway. So, let's just enjoy our time together, okay?"

"Okay."

Together, we thumbed through his unreturned library book, discovering the Leo the Lion constellation, which the ancient Egyptians used to design the famous Sphynx, located near the Great Pyramids of Giza. My parents moved apartments. And yet, Ravi found his way to me. He sat atop obnoxiously dangerous places like my bookshelf. We snuck out of my bedroom window to find an unencumbered view of the night sky.

Ravi and I became so interested in finding constellations we would map the stars out on a piece of onion-skin paper and line it up with the sky. Lying on an empty track field in our hometown in Burnaby we rested our heads on Ravi's penny board, the underbelly marked with scarred stickers. The synthetic rubber of the track massaging bits of small rocks into our backs, soon a pot with a handle appeared as if by magic, in the centre of the sky. The Big Dipper.

Ravi and I did grow up together, and he took up smoking. On his travels, Ravi also picked up a charming Camden Town accent. The tip of his spliff burning like some fiery, distant planet, he would say to me in his tight London way, "You know, Baby, with everything you see in the galaxy, you're getting a delayed look at things, innit. Even the sun you're looking at is what it was eight minutes ago. Nuffin's ever as it seems."

By way of dying young, Ravi was freed from all his religious duties. And I was forced to participate in Diwali, Holi, Navratri, Ugadi, Shivratri. What I hadn't factored into my system of playing along was that my mother herself wasn't up for it. Even her childhood pictures from Ahmedabad depicted her as a slight girl, with matchbox-stick legs and an odd-angled bob too big for her face. These photographs always appealed to me because I wanted nothing more than to be her mother when I saw them. But when I was sixteen, she had a stroke.

Just like with Ravi, I couldn't save her.

PART 1

WINTER 1995/1996

TWO

It had been a year since my mom died, and I had to attend a *shraadh* held by my grandmother to commemorate her death. We were smack in that magical little pocket of time after Christmas but before New Year's. My father and I had driven there together covered in a tarp of silence. All the traditional foods were present: coconut curry, *bhindi sabzi,* pumpkin curry, cucumber *raita,* deep fried puffed pastry called *kachori,* and a rice pudding called *kheer,* made with milk. I wondered if funeral *kheer* was made differently than celebratory *kheer* — perhaps topped with fewer nuts. Yet, there was not one small bowl of *gajar ka halwa* or *mutter paneer,* two of my mother's favourite dishes. That broke my heart a little. Her soul was supposedly visiting the house today, after all.

As the adults sipped too-sweet chai served from tiny cups, I tried not to make eye contact with my mother's portrait. Like a ghost, the milky caramel tea smell floated over the scent of the food. My boy cousins were wearing white Gap khakis and some variation of the white Club Monaco sweater. The girls, white Indian suits. Knowing this, I probably shouldn't have worn my cropped blue Yankees shirt (kid's size 5, nicked from the thrift store). To be fair, I no longer owned any *shalwar kameez* that fit me.

When one of the men my grandmother had hired tried to hand me the same sparkling waters my cousins were sipping, I refused.

"No, thanks," I muttered.

"One glass, have one," the waiter said.

"No." I wasn't trying to be rude. I just couldn't stand the idea of swallowing bubbles in water at that moment.

I felt one of my female cousins staring. I had shoved my long hair in a hat while she had one of those Jennifer Aniston haircuts, layered in steps and dyed a sandy colour, like an ancient Mayan ruin.

"Is that a baseball team or something?" she asked, pointing at my top.

I shrugged, pulling out my pager.

My grandmother's house was stupendously large, guarded by two stone carved lions. It was all white couches and marble floors. My late grandfather had owned a successful soda factory in India, leaving my grandmother money. My grandmother was used to hiring staff. In Ahmedabad, the servants would pummel your jeans and T-shirts clean with a stick and stretch them out to dry so they would grow stiffer over time, as if one day, they would be prepared to walk off the clothesline and leave you for another life. She'd always looked down at my father for being a bus driver and thought my mother could do better. And my mother, likewise, had wished for a house like this.

Carlie hadn't paged.

"Why did you come here dressed like this?" my grandmother said in her Gujarati accent, bringing with her a cloud of Eternity perfume. "People are talking."

"It's my mother, not theirs."

"This is about respect. Your mother liked you dressing feminine."

I wanted to say Ravi would approve of my clothes. Instead, I looked down at the translucent skin on my wrist, fascinated with the little blue highways rushing things to very important places.

"A girl without a mother needs guidance. Your father alone cannot control you."

"Why do I need to be controlled?"

"Today of all days, you should not wear vagabond clothing." She herself was wearing a white tailored Indian outfit designed to look Western, which modern hybrid Indian people thought made them look continental.

"She isn't here to say, is she?" I bit back. As I watched her lips curl, I started to feel my body shake. "Shame on you, Baby. I've had enough. Get out of my house. Come back when you have decency." This was my mother's one-year death anniversary. *My* mother's. Everyone looked on. Still, I did not move right away, trying to control my shaking. I thought of the options I had carefully recorded in my journal:

1. Run away.
2. Kill myself.
3. Do something so great with my life that what was left of my family would be proud.

"Fuck all of you," I said when my body woke up. Because if I didn't spit that out, I would have cried. And crying in front of these dickheads was pointless. I could never make them proud.

Quietly, without grand display, I picked up the skateboard sitting next to a wide vase filled with golden spray-painted twigs.

I never wanted to be like these people.

THREE

Despite the cold, as I walked my face grew hotter when I thought of how my grandmother had spoken to me. My shadow imprinted a midnight blue body upon a blanket of white crystals.

All I had on was a thin bowling jacket thrifted from Value Village. But in my state, I was more scared of crying over freezing. *Shame on Baby!* It could be a great name for a band, roaring in a satanic, heavy-metal voice, sticks hitting drums fast like staccato gunfire. My throat was all raw and scratchy, like it was lined with coarse brown sugar.

I had to keep on walking.

When I was really upset, sometimes Ravi would walk alongside me in his standard-issue denim outfit, no matter the weather. He would say, "Fuck you, mate," to everyone for me. But Ravi wasn't here. Instead, I had White Zombie's "More Human Than Human" raging on my Walkman, as I left zigzagged imprints in the snow with my skate shoes. It was too snowy to skate but carrying a board had become part of my identity. Something to show people who I was without saying a word.

At the high school I now went to, the kids didn't know about Ravi. At home, no one talked about Ravi, and even my own memories of him drifted like a bottle at sea with no shore to land on. I only saw one clearly. Ravi and I making movies, his hands and fingers forming the shape of a pretend camera, me jumping wildly. It was the hottest day in the summer. We hid inside our humid apartment so we could finish the next scene. Ravi had convinced me he was prerecording us with his hands and could transfer the film onto tape so we could watch it on VHS later. I had believed him, because out of the two of us, he always seemed sharp on how the world really worked. After all, he had been born first.

Because of the snow, it took more than double the usual time to walk from Granny's posh residence to our area. I stopped walking to consider my choices. Should I board a bus to Carlie's even though she hadn't paged? Or should I go home to an apartment where my dead mother's plastic bottles of pills would glitter like sea glass and jewels sitting at her bedside?

Instead, I stopped at the slummed-out Burger King, looking out at the bus loop and mall that sat across it. This was the central hangout in our ghetto-ass neighbourhood. I didn't want to go home. My mom's clothes still hung in her wardrobe. If Ravi had never died, she would not have had a stroke, and now my flu from 1988 had led to two deaths. Not counting my spiritually dead dad. The only two people he actually cared about were gone. I knew he had valued Ravi more than me. My mother used to say he made her eat more protein when she was pregnant because he was certain there was a boy in her belly. I was an afterthought. Unnecessary. After all, I couldn't carry the family name.

I stood back from the ordering counter and dug into my pocket for my pager. Still no page from Carlie Osborne, whom my mother, if she was able to rise from the dead, would have snatched me away from. Carlie's parents were what Indian parents stereotypically imagined poor whites to be: alcoholics living on food stamps, caring only for today, loving seventies rock, wearing dirty jeans. Much of this really did apply to Carlie's parents. They had epic parties. When they could afford it, they filled their fridge with beer, and everyone wore shoes on the carpet, just like on television. Carlie's mother Denise made us huge feasts when she was drunk and let us play with her makeup. Her dad Bill got us into card games.

When their money ran out, so did the liquor and that was usually when I left. Days later, Carlie would page me the code 555, which meant: *Welfare Wednesday, you know what THAT means!* Could be if I showed up, Denise would make a casserole with macaroni and cheese from a box topped with wild things like diced pickles, chives, and sour cream, and we all knew it would still taste good. Could be Denise would let us drink her boxed wine like it was cola served with our dinner. Or Carlie's older brother, Darren, would leave us behind a joint. Like us, they lived in social housing. We easily ignored the saggy, cigarette-burned carpets, the dipping walls, the black-rimmed windows. Her father rolled his own cigarettes and turned the ceilings yellow by chain smoking. It was dirty, greasy, and messy, but it was also the happiest place I knew.

Just then Burger King's graffitied door wheezed shut, and I saw an absolute vision walk in. I could smell her: raspberry cotton candy.

There had been gang fights at this location. Once, the cops were called when a boy had been shitkicked outside, and not one person had stepped in to help. A hundred teens had flooded the place to watch that curb stomping. This Burger King was one of the saddest places in the world. My jean cuffs were soaked three inches and my toes wriggled like slugs at the tips of my shoes.

She was completely out of place here.

Her long straight hair was the colour of a peanut shell, the lightest of browns, with eyes to match. Possibly Asian? She was wearing a puffy, marshmallow quilted white jacket and jeans with so many pockets a person could live out of them. A boutique shopper, she was not like the people from school, all of whom wore the same plaid cheerleading skirts and No Fear shirts.

I was embarrassed, suddenly, that I was about to order a kid's meal. Plain truth: I didn't have a lot of money. Some of the real hard-done-by kids in this area jacked cars, took them for joy rides, and then bartered parts. They sold acid or joints at the bus loop, made petty cash reselling used bus tickets, or pawned off single cigarettes to people who couldn't afford a pack. I didn't want to hustle or go to juvie.

The girl, oblivious to me, was already ordering. There was a chain clipped to her belt buckle which led to a sparkly blue wallet with a sultry cat on it. A bright, fluffy, fun-fur bag hung from her shoulder, which would look like a murdered Muppet on most women, but on her looked glamourous. I didn't feel so great about myself then. Wet with stolen coins in my bowling jacket. I wondered how I would look with a diamond in the crook of my nose. How I would look with expensive warehouse jeans. Next to her, even my badass best friend Carlie seemed homely, chubby cheeked with dyed wine-coloured hair and grunge clothes. Her style was meant to suggest a hardness, but to be honest made her seem more like a baker's wife.

Suddenly she was facing me with a tray of French fries. "Hey, you hungry? 'Cause this food'll make me gain, like, a million pounds. I only came here to get crowns. They made me order something to get 'em."

"Huh?" I managed, confused.

"D'ya, like, want my fries or not?"

"I mean, yeah, I guess."

We chose a booth. It should have been weird taking a stranger's fries. But it wasn't. She unzipped her jacket. I stared at the pale mint lingerie top she was wearing as outerwear. A thin rhinestone choker lined her neck. She was every vintage star, Liz Taylor, Rita Hayworth, Bette Davis rolled together, but the nineties version.

"There's a matching dressing gown that goes with this top. All fucking marabou feathers and shit. It's from the forties. They used to call 'em Husband Murderer Robes. I got the set from a thrift shop in LA."

"Oh."

She was talking as if shopping in LA was as casual as eating breakfast cereal. I got an image of her in that robe, feathers lining it like a layered cake, knife in hand, stalking around an old Victorian mansion.

"My pants though were manufactured at a local spot, you know, on East Hastings. They're the trademark feature of an acid house veteran. You must've heard of 'em. Laramy jeans?"

I had no clue.

"Anyway, what's your name?" she asked.

"Um," I said, pinching another fry. "It's Baby."

"Delilah." She gave me a light handshake. "Or Del. Hey, d'ya, like, know how to use that thing?"

I had quite forgotten about the battered skateboard I clutched in my lap, wheels and trucks borrowed from one boy and tacked onto another boy's deck. My Frankenstein creation.

"'Course." This was my time to act cocky. I knew how to do ollies, ride switch, and was working toward a grab. Most chicks didn't know the nose from the tail on a board. Mostly though, I used it for transportation. I squeezed a packet of ketchup on the tray liner and dipped another fry in. I licked the salt from my fingers. I regretted leaving behind the food at my grandmother's. Why couldn't I have accepted sparkling water served in shapely glassware with a wedge of citrus fruit? Why couldn't I have been someone else, if only for a day?

Delilah was playing with the rings on her fingers. Opals and amber flashed at me like animal eyes. "I have white rabbits, if you wanna drop some. I can get us into a party near Hastings."

White rabbits. I wondered what in the world she was talking about.

"Oh. I don't have a lot of cash on me."

I was surprised she'd offered. The whole "girl who skateboards" thing hadn't done much in my high school to get me into any cool group, except with two misfit skater boys named Stick Boi and Takeshi, who had taught me everything I knew. Takeshi's first name was Jed, but no one ever called him that. And Stick Boi, well, his nickname describing his looks had become a kind of honorific; even the teachers called him that. We ran together now, the three of us. Even Carlie was shocked I'd risk wiping out on the pavement to do tricks. But I had Ravi in me. Boy guts. I didn't care about ruining my nose or face, I didn't give a shit about makeup, and I sure as fuck didn't care about trying to fit in. Not anymore.

Last year, after my mother died, I started going to Value Village to get skate jeans and dress how I wanted to. Now, no one bothered me. Takeshi, Stick Boi, and I listened to Tribe, De La Soul, and Black Sheep on a ghetto blaster at school, next to the chain-link fence. We had no need for people like my cousins, listening to their radio chart hits. We made up our own tribe now, social deviants who had outsmarted the ranking system of coolness at school.

Carlie hadn't sent me any pages, and I didn't want to go home. Delilah must have seen indecision flicker on my face because she added, "You don't need money. I could use a pretty girl by my side."

I wiped my nose with my sleeve. When Takeshi and Stick Boi had officially let me hang around the skate area and pitched in parts for my board, it sure as fuck wasn't my looks that had gained their respect; it was the fact I almost broke my wrist trying reckless stunts.

"You're shaking," Del said.

"Um, I shake sometimes, it's nothing."

"But you're shaking pretty hard, dude. You're not still hungry, are you?"

"No," I lied.

"Good. 'Cause this food's trash. Hey, maybe you're cold. Your jacket's pretty fuckin' thin. Don'tcha have, like, a winter jacket or some shit?"

I didn't. My dad didn't buy me clothes. Fashion trumped functionality for the things I got myself. Trembling or not, I had to decide what I would do with my life. Run away, kill myself, or make something of myself. My trifecta. In my head, I repeated the mantra. I might have even started muttering it in the tattered booth.

"He-lloooo? Baby? You gonna come with me, or what?"

"Huh?" I said, just managing to steady my hands.

"To the party. Dude, not gonna lie, you look a little zoned out."

"I dunno," I found myself saying to Delilah dumbly, tearing a shred from the paper lining the plastic tray and folding it into a kayak. "I dunno what white rabbits even are."

Delilah smiled. "You've never been to a rave? You've never done ecstasy?" It felt like she was reading from an English grammar book for an ESL student. *You've never been to the Grand Canyon? You've never watched Star Wars?*

No, I hadn't. Despite living in this hood-rat area, all I'd ever done was smoke weed and drink.

"Well, tonight, Baby, you will."

FOUR

Delilah dealt ecstasy. She told me her pills were some of the most expensive in the city, going for thirty to even forty dollars a cap. Others went for a baseline of twenty-five, and if you paid any lower than twenty, you were getting speed, unless of course you were someone with incredible hook-ups. When the pills arrived from her dealer in capsules, she skimmed off the top. Meaning, she unscrewed them, took a little extra powder from each, and made new capsules. She explained how candy containers were the best place to hide E from the security people at raves.

"Hidden in plain sight," she explained.

I nodded, pretending it was usual for me to talk about drug dealing.

"My stuff is the best, Baby. You'll see. But sometimes, later in the night, you'll feel a trace of the speed kick in. That can't be helped."

We were on the Hastings Express. The sky was a slice of cantaloupe flesh. Darkness was coming. Snow looked like cotton glued to residential roofs by a television crew. The wheels of the bus dragged black slush. At some point I fell asleep, pager clasped tightly in my hand. No one had said they needed me to come back. It had been easy to put my life in the hands of a beautiful stranger. As I drifted off, I felt privileged that someone like Delilah wanted to be my friend. I inhaled her fresh smell of harvest berries and candy. I was enraptured. I dreamt of Ravi and I jumping on the couches, him filming me. But there was a third person jumping beside me now, and she had two nutty brown pigtails and a swirly lollipop.

Delilah shifted and I woke up. I looked out at the homeless people scattered down many city blocks. A police car drove by with sirens, blinding us briefly in fevered reds and blues. The bus drove silkily, used to navigating this route even when pedestrians dove in front without warning. Del pulled the string, and we got off on Hastings and Cambie.

Wedged in between Vancouver's famous and well-established drug corners was a huge fabric store named Dressew. Around since the sixties, it was known for selling ladies' tailored hats. Now, it was a wonderland of buttons, zippers, and fabrics. Styrofoam heads with blurred features bordered the floor of the dressing window, topped in an assortment of coloured wigs. Elmo-red fun fur and Big Bird–yellow feather boas hung from plastic body parts. Dressew was a circus of fun and horror, I figured. A place where you could transform into anyone you wanted.

"We should go take a look," Del said.

We pushed open the doors to "Where Is My Mind" by the Pixies. We raced down aisles, throwing bolts of fabric open. Gingham. Victorian lace. Crushed velvet. It felt like we were in Madonna's "Material Girl" video, rummaging through all the rhinestones, plumage, and hats from the pop star's on-set bedroom.

She fingered gold lamé. "Girlllll, can you imagine the wicked jumpsuit we could make outta this fabric?"

I nodded but I didn't know how to sew. Last year I had taken Carpentry 11 and had spent the year making a lopsided key holder and a wooden bowl that was too flat for salads and too rounded for flat breads.

"Look at these!" she squealed, stopping in front of coloured hair pieces on display, snow white, sky blue, and pink sorbet. I didn't like wigs. But Delilah said one would look good on me because contrasts of boy and girl mixed together were so sexy. "You need to amp up your touch of femininity," she was saying. Girls at my high school would never talk like this.

She made me try the frosted pink twenties-style bob. I put the Jackson Hole hat I'd snagged from Stick Boi back on top of it. She reached into her bag for a choker. Diamond crystals as large as pearls were embedded on a kitty collar.

"Don't lose the necklace; I use it to play dress-up at martini bars," she said, and without asking, fastened it around my neck. She didn't notice I had on another necklace, buried under my shirt. Takeshi had given it to me. Takeshi and I were almost something together. Once. But that moment had faded into something else. I still wore his necklace to remind myself of what had almost been. *A kind of pathetic thing to do,* I thought now, the Dressew overhead lights shining down on me. *A childish and fucking stupid thing to do.*

I'd never known anyone to carry around an assortment of fake diamond necklaces in their purse before. Stick Boi was notorious for carrying around half cigarettes and Takeshi sometimes had piña colada candies, but that was the extent of the pocket loot I'd seen. Del was the nineties version of Cinderella's godmother; she knew how to make me look like a cyber punk skate girl from some arcade video game. A modern-day Zelda Fitzgerald. I wondered what the kids at school would think. What my grandmother and cousins would think.

Suddenly, Del stopped and screeched, "I love this song! It's one of the queens of the scene, Norma Jean Bell. 'I'm the Baddest Bitch in the Room.' The Motorbass mix. It must be a pirated version. Ooh, clearly someone at Dressew likes their deep underground house!"

She started dancing while she perused the wigs and fabrics. Dispersed, scattered beats layered the track, and I bobbed my head. I was digging the sax and vocals. Del and I struck fierce poses for each other.

Del chose the white-blonde wig, which I thought was Dolly Parton–looking, but on Delilah it looked killer. She went up to the cash register and placed a roll of silver material on the counter. Told the cashier that she wanted three strips cut from it, and said not to worry, that she'd pay for the whole yard. Like it meant nothing to throw money away. Like life was more than shopping from sales bins. She tied one piece into her hair like a headband and teased her wigged hair around it. She looked legit. Like she should be on MTV or some shit.

"Fuck the Burger King crowns. I'm all in for this look."

I don't think Del paid for the wigs. We walked out and the girl at the counter kept smacking her gum, fabric shears still in one hand, looking bored. And that was that. It was like the scene in *Breakfast at Tiffany's* where Holly and Paul steal the cheap masks from the dime shop, and no one suspects them. Even though I was used to stealing clothes from the Value Village fitting room, I'd never taken something so boldly. There was a rush in committing an illegal act so obviously in plain sight, like walking out of Dior wearing one of their couture gowns.

We walked down the cold streets. We passed more homeless people on the way. Some had mental illnesses, some were addicts, and some were plain tired and hungry. Not one person, as I saw it, deserved to be that position. If we went in another direction and walked ten minutes, it was all pear-shaped diamond rings and Chanel quilted handbags with braided gold chains on display. Living in a small apartment with what was left of my family made me realize I fit into the category that would never buy brand-name anything, not even potato chips. I was briefly embarrassed by my bus driver dad.

But for tonight, I wasn't the girl living in social housing. I was the girl with the bubble gum–pink wig.

FIVE

On the way to the party, which was nestled somewhere between East Hastings and Water Street, Delilah told me about Jimmy. She said Jimmy would be at the rave we were going to with his new girlfriend, Eva. Eva was pronounced like Eh-va.

"Jimmy and I were an intense thing for a few months," Delilah was saying, as we walked quickly so the cold didn't have a chance to bite us through our clothes. "Like Bonnie and Clyde? I broke up with Jimmy because I was so in love with him. That sounds ridiculous, doesn't it? But when we were together, I felt like I was falling into quicksand. I hated that feeling. Unhinged. We'd do E and I would fall into his eyes, and he didn't fall into mine the same way, you know? Once, I found this photo album in his place. He had so many pictures of himself posing with hot women. They were all different nationalities, like fucking cake flavours in a bakery, Vietnamese, Jamaican, Puerto Rican. It made me sick, because the two of us had taken so many snapshots just days before with a disposable camera."

She rushed on, her breath moving in and out of her like dragon's smoke. "Now I knew where I was going to end up. Another ex-girlfriend in this photo album. A good-enough-looking half-Asian chick with a long torso and white teeth. An animal trophy on the wall of his hunting lodge."

Christmas was over but decorations were still up. Plastic Santa heads and garish gold garlands framing doors. Everything on this side of town had a cheaper version of the classic white and blue lights up on Robson and Burrard. Del hugged her arms around her puffy jacket. The tip of my nose was so cold I couldn't imagine how my body would ever warm up. I thought of how plants were stuck in soil, how lizards had to charge their bodies with sunlight. But humans were free to find their own forms of sun and water. I needed to find heat. We marched on. I tried to focus on listening to Del talk about Jimmy. It was the best way to get to know her.

"So, I panicked maybe," she said, picking out the white-blonde synthetic hairs that kept sticking onto her glossy lips. "I started feeling like pieces of glass were all over me, crushed into tiny sediment. It was in my eyes, filling my mouth, too, like I was chewing on diamonds. Maybe that was because I was doing too much E and grinding my fuckin' teeth right off, who knows? I decided to end things while Jimmy and I were still on a high."

"And then?"

She frowned. "And then he started dating Eva a hot minute later. And I ended up being the one stuck with the memories."

"Memories?"

"Yeah, like one time, we listened to that Chris Isaak song 'Wicked Game' when we were having sex and it was so incredible, you know? Like when you're high and you experience things in colours rather than what people ordinarily see?" I didn't know, but she kept going. "He cut us fresh watermelon after. Juice was dribbling down my chin and I didn't care; I was so thirsty, and I was mind-blown that these edible magenta triangles could give me such quenching satisfaction. It was like gulping down summer in every bite. I can't explain it, the fruit, our limbs tangled together, the haunting lyrics just dancing over us ... it was intoxicating."

"Hm," I said, wondering what to make of this. I could hear the Chris Isaak song in my head. I wasn't sure if I liked it or if it was creepy.

"He was too good at it."

"What?"

"Sex. It was formulaically too good. He knew how to please me because he knew how to be with women."

"Oh," I kicked my shoe against a pile of snow as we walked on, wondering how this was a bad thing and at the same time understanding how it could be.

"When I broke up with him, he didn't even try to stop me. He said, 'If that's how ya feel, Del.' Like I was asking to change detergents or something. I mean, I'm twenty-six, I don't want to fuck around anymore."

I tried not to act surprised.

"Fuck. You're just a kid, aren't you?"

"I'm, uh, seventeen, I guess."

She sighed, annoyed about something I had no control over changing. "Look, everyone you're going to meet at this party will be older. Just stick with me."

We seemed to have arrived because we had come to a full stop right where the street met an alley. She ran the back of her thumb under her eyes to fix her makeup, then pulled out a long, thin menthol cigarette and lit it. She was done talking about Jimmy. She was done showing me who she really was.

"'Kay," I said, as she blew blue smoke upward and I fiddled with my wig-hat combo.

The streets were so deserted we could have been in a Charles Dickens novel, what with the brick lanes of Gastown and the steam clock nearby. The lamplights reminded me of the 1800s. The doors to an Irish pub opened and drunk men spilled out, singing drinking songs. I half expected a boy in a newspaper cap to come shouting the news at us around the corner.

It was then I saw my twin Ravi across the street. I knew he was going to come after what happened at my grandma's, but not this late. He was wearing a scruffy denim jacket, the tongue of his high-top purple Converse sneakers jutting out because his pants were skinny all the way down to his ankles. In the world of baggy nineties fashion, Ravi was stuck in the jeans from *The Outsiders*. He was an anachronism punched into the Victorian setting of black skies, taverns with snow-lined roofs, and the yellow glow of square-shaped lamps. I was mad at him for not showing up earlier, and I turned my head away.

"What the fuck you shakin' your head at?" Del asked.

"What?" I said, and then recovered. "Nothin' yo."

"Stay away from the Jib Kids."

"Jib Kids?"

"They're the kids addicted to crystal meth, PCP, ketamine, poppers. They're sketchy as fuck," she tapped her cigarette, releasing an inch of ash that looked like a silkworm. "Sometimes Jib Kids dress like Candy Kids. You know who those are, right?" She didn't wait for my answer. "These fucking kids, they come to parties wearing plastic chains and baby toys fastened to themselves, sucking on goddamn pacifiers. They'll attach stickers on you, hug you, and generally annoy the living fuck out of you."

"What are you?"

"Who, me?" She smiled. "I like to think of myself as a Sugar Kid."

"What's that?"

"You'll find out soon enough. Maybe you'll become one yourself, who knows?"

"So," I said, wanting to steer the conversation to something I could compute, "Will you, you know, introduce me to your Jimmy guy tonight?"

Her face twitched. Like I did when I had my shakes, but her facial tremor lasted a microsecond. "He's with Eva now, remember? He's not *my* anything."

I chastised myself inwardly for bringing him up when she was clearly done reminiscing but a couple seconds later, she said, "Look, I can't say I don't miss the passion, but when I was with Jimmy, my brain was fucking eating itself with paranoia. I'd have never talked to you if I was still with him. You with your whole sassy tomboy act and flat stomach. Your whole young-and-confused thing would totally appeal to him, no offence."

Was that a compliment or an insult? *Sassy tomboy act,* I thought. *Flat stomach.* I'd never thought of my torso as having any kind of sexual value. Del made it sound like my whole persona was a comedy sketch I was performing on *Saturday Night Live.*

"At least now," she continued, her cigarette resting between two fingers while her other hand made sure hairs weren't meandering their way back into her lip gloss, "I'm recovering from Jimmy."

I was too inexperienced to reassure her as wise girlfriends seemed to do naturally on television. I could only fake my way through emotions. She threw down her cigarette and turned her foot on it. Where Ravi once was, now there was foggy mist. I only had a second to doubt whether ignoring him had been the best thing.

Delilah turned into the bend of the alleyway and knocked on a door I hadn't even noticed was there.

SIX

"'Sup, Del," said a Black guy when he swung open the door. He was extremely good looking. He pulled his headphones down around his neck. Souls of Mischief came pouring out. "What's crackin'?"

"This is Baby," Del said as a means of answering.

"You're actually called Baby?"

I nodded.

"That's one mean board you got there. Gotta favourite boarder?"

"Tony Hawk," I said, immediately wishing that I named someone less well-known, from one of the *Thrasher* magazines sitting on my nightstand. Stick Boi and Takeshi would have had way better responses. "I like Souls, too," I said, feeling childish as soon as I said it.

"I got a crate fulla records at home, some dope shit, girl. EPMD, Public Enemy, N.W.A, UGK —"

"If you're done spelling the alphabet, we should go," Del cut in.

Bryce wasn't bothered by Del. "D'ya wanna come by and listen to 'em sometime?"

I opened my mouth. "I —"

"Don't even try, Bryce. She's with me."

He smiled in a resigned way, accepting what Delilah said. He put his headphones back on and *93 'til Infinity* sunk into the chambers of his head.

"Look," said Del, lowering her voice as she steered me away. "I just saved you from the most boring guy in the rave scene. Bryce makes everything a Black-and-white issue. Whites are to blame with what's wrong with the world, and Blacks are the victims." She faced me. "I mean look at me, I'm half Chinese, and do I divide the world up like that?"

"No," I said automatically.

She nodded as if my response confirmed Bryce's stupidity. "Chinese people were also thought to be garbage back in the day, but I've moved on. Problem is, all Bryce wants to talk about is how Black people have a harder time getting ahead because of the past. But how can we be equals if all we focus on is how one group of people was once ripped off a long time ago? Oh, and, like, he thinks listening to rappers is somehow enlightening."

"I like rap."

"God, you would, wouldn't you?"

"Were you guys homies or somethin'?"

"Me and Bryce? Hell no. But I knew his ex, Athena well. We used to hang out a lot, Athena, Bryce, me. And Bryce was, like, totally obsessed with her. It's like I was invisible when she was there, you know? But I think he bores people with all his fucking political shit. She was such a free spirit. She lives in Thailand now. Probably moved countries just to get away from him."

I nodded, taking this info in and filing it away. Suddenly we were standing in a functional kitchen. The spot was immaculate. Plates stacked; stainless steel counters wiped. I could smell garlic. Like a cookbook without pictures where you could visualize the food perfectly; you could imagine what the place looked like in the day. *Penne arrabbiata* served by elegant staff delivering them to white-clothed tables; baked *ziti* with pesto eaten alongside bottles of merlot in the main dining room where everything glowed shades of gold. We walked to another door. This seemed to lead to a storage space, maybe somewhere wine bottles were stored. Del opened it. It was all dark and dungeon-like inside, the warmth of the restaurant gone. There were brick walls. Something smelled damp. A staircase. At the very bottom, a man was nodding off on a stool that was backed against a wall, a bare light bulb hanging over his head.

I felt like I was in the middle of a detective novel.

"Red," said Delilah, tapping the redheaded man. He was wearing a leather jacket that looked like it had seen some war in some desert. Metal piercings decorated his face like a studded leather purse.

"Hey Del." He gave her a long hug and then trailed a finger under his nose. "Go on through. Come see me if you want blow."

"Red's a folk hero," Del whispered as we walked. "Does so much coke he can fall sleep on it. Never makes me pay to get in though."

I stole a last glance backward. Red seemed like a character out of the movie *Labyrinth*. Del was opening the industrial doors. Puffs of coloured fog obscured my vision. I half expected the king of the goblins to jump out at me.

SEVEN

We were in the middle of an abandoned warehouse. Dripping ceiling. Concrete floors. Spotlights were rigged and scattered throughout, electricity generator–powered or stolen. There were glow-in-the-dark butterflies and dragonflies everywhere. And people. So many people. The music was so strong I could feel it in my throat and in my bones. A maple-syrupy voice cut through the smoky air, one that would make Carmen McRae envious. Hard beats dropped. My body vibrated.

This was unlike any place I had ever been. I saw two boys cuddling. A drag queen smoking a cigarette on the edge of the dance floor. A Black girl with an afro throwing her arms around a skinny white boy. A young man (who Del said was homeless) wearing patchy pants dancing in the middle of a circle, cheered on by spectators. There were girls in half tops, girls with low-rise jeans barely covering their hip bones, girls with pixie haircuts, and girls with silver-white hair. Glitter was everywhere. Pants were cartoonishly wide, with unique stitch patterns, pockets, and buckles, coming at me in an array of colours. Del was saying something about how the couture versions of warehouse jeans were made by JNCO or Kikwear but some people simply unstitched thrifted jeans at the outer seam themselves and sewed in extra material to widen their pants.

"It's amazing," my voice caught. "Everyone's allowed to …"

"Just be," Del filled in. "It's a Temporary Autonomous Zone." When she saw my blank face, she continued. "You know, like, a free space without anyone controlling who you have to be? It's a liberated area, as free as your imagination. We occupied this space and made it ours. Hakim Bey wrote a book about it. My dorky roommates probably have a copy of it."

"Wow," was all I could muster. Del humoured me, waiting patiently while I took it all in and the music got louder. It would have eaten my words anyhow.

"This is 'Beautiful People' by Barbara Tucker. The Underground Network mix," she informed me. The strong vocals cut through. A soulful gospel choir chanted.

It was all so enticing. Leaving behind all the world's stupid divisions at the door, this was like hippie mentalities but with streamlined techno. I even heard Indian music sampled into a track. Right then, I didn't want to worry about how ignoring my issues wouldn't make them go away. That the dancing guy would have to go back to the alley to sleep. That probably no one here was ready to protest in broad daylight. That part wasn't important. What was important was squeezing beauty out of life like droplets wrung from a cloth, in this fairy land of pixies and elves. After all, wasn't having secret parties in abandoned warehouses a kind of rebellion of sorts?

"Okay, Baby," said Delilah. "Let's go find DJ MouseCat. We can stash our stuff with him."

She rushed me up to the DJ booth. The guy spinning the records radiated when he saw her. He had a ginger beard and an odd red wig on that made him look like Ronald McDonald. Several beaded necklaces hung from his neck. We stuck our jackets and my board under the equipment table.

Del didn't speak again until we were inside a bathroom stall. "Open wide," she said. I stuck out my tongue, and she deposited a white pill stamped with a rabbit.

White rabbits.

She took one, too. I tried not to gag. I felt like I was going to throw up. I was probably retching a little when Del shook me.

"For goodness sakes, Baby. We don't vomit designer drugs!"

We were on some alternate wave of time and space even though it was too early for me to feel anything. She pulled out the silver fabric from her fun-fur bag. We took off our tops and she tied the aluminum bandeau strips around our chests. We looked magnificent. We were in that stall for an eternity. A lifetime. By now there were faint tracers, bands of light which sparkled and glinted off things. The toilet water seemed to be glowing iridescently.

When we exited the stall, we weren't the same girls anymore. Suddenly, I could read vibes off people. I could go up to virtually anyone here and give them a hug and it wouldn't be weird at all. I still didn't know how much time had passed, but my jaw had loosened. I felt airy. Weightless. Already colourful, everything was even brighter than it had been before. I felt brilliant. Delilah felt brilliant. She touched my face and I touched hers.

The music had changed to fast breakbeats. I was captivated by the melodic sultry words laced in, sweet, soulful, freeing. Then an unbelievable bassline dropped.

"CJ Bolland's 'Sugar Is Sweeter,' the Armand Van Helden drum and bass remix!" Del shouted. "I hear this at almost every rave I go to these days, even though it isn't officially released yet!" The music moved through me.

Del's face changed under the lights; she looked reptilian and then altered again. I realized with a slight panic that I had left Ravi standing alone in Gastown. Oh my god.

The wave of euphoria slipped away, and anxiety had filled its place.

"I want more," I found myself saying.

"No, you don't, hon. Doing too much E at once zaps the serotonin out of your spine, and you'll crash low tomorrow. We can space it out."

Her face morphed again into something that looked like a tropical fish. We were all swimming in a brightly coloured aquarium.

"Holy fuck. Jimmy," she said, barely exhaling his name out of her body before a man was standing in front of us.

"Del," said Jimmy. He was saying her name but looking at me. I felt something turn in my stomach. When I inhaled, a tickly sensation rushed down my throat as if I had swallowed a thousand pink, sparkly butterflies.

EIGHT

Del's ex-boyfriend didn't look like he was from our generation. He had a fifties pompadour, a cleft chin, and more fitted jeans than anyone else. All that was raver about Jimmy was that he was wearing a very yellow shirt under an unbuttoned bowling top. His energy was different, too. A kind of removed vibe that made you lean in to hear him talk.

"Hello," he said to me, somewhat formally. I nodded, mesmerized by untangling the connection he had with Del. Del was worldly and experienced and everything I wasn't. Why were my lips so dry?

Beside him was a girl who also looked like she was straight from Old Hollywood. She had fluffy, white hair pinned back in shiny barrettes and a mechanic's jumpsuit the colour of a glossy, iridescent seashell. "Hi-I'm-Eva." She was chewing rapidly on something, pulling at the zipper on her onesie.

"I'm Baby."

"Glitter?" she asked me, blinking fast. Her face was a furious shade of violet and pink due to the visual effects lighting. Transfixed by all the changing patterns on the walls, I was too stunned to say no. I waited patiently like a child getting their face painted as she smoothed glitter on my face. It felt wet because it was coming off some sort of eucalyptus-scented roller. The sensation was so blissful I closed my eyes, and suddenly Eva was massaging the fronts of my shoulders.

Delilah stiffened. I knew how she felt about Candy Kids, and though Eva didn't dress like one (she had no rattles or baby soothers hanging off her), she sure was acting like one. But I felt beautiful. Puffs of colour wafted around me; Eva's forearms glowed.

"Are you guys, like, having fun?" Del said rigidly. She wanted to leave, and yet she was frozen by seeing Jimmy and Eva together.

"Rabbit Hole is an okay event," Jimmy said offhandedly. But he seemed too cool to be here. He belonged at some LA studio party with edgy rappers, sipping an Old Fashioned next to a pool.

Garage house was playing; horns, liquid chocolate–coated vocals, smooth basslines. I stood, rooted to the ground, absorbing. "This is that track 'Gabriel' by Roy Davis Jr. featuring Peven Everitt," Jimmy said to Del as if she didn't already know.

"Do you guys, like, wanna go sit against the wall?" Eva asked us. I wasn't sure Delilah would agree, but the four of us, dressed in vibrant colours, went and sat mashed up against a cement wall, each of us connected with someone else's body part.

Del was probably too high to figure out her next move, and Eva's hand had felt reassuring, and I hadn't wanted to let go. Eventually, it did get weird when Eva and Jimmy started kissing, and I pulled myself up to yank Delilah away. There was an Asian girl on the opposite wall with green hair that was so bright it looked like a glow stick, kissing another girl. She was wearing big gangster clothes that swallowed her tiny frame. *I wonder what it would be like to be kissed by her,* I thought, surprising myself. I had never kissed anyone before. I watched how effortless it was for them to drown out the world around them.

Delilah, pale and ghostly, had something that looked like Aspirin in her hand. She bit into the pill with her canine, cracking the halves until they were two shark's teeth. "This half will make the high of your first pill come back, okay?" She slipped a sliver of compressed talc into my mouth before I could reply. Her voice was soft, all the fire and passion from before dissolved.

This time it was like the wave came within five minutes. We danced, and Del forgot all about Jimmy and Eva. Kids, which is what everyone called everyone, had begun clearing out, leaving behind a smaller group of kids who were just as high as we were. They matched our dance moves, hugging us. I wondered if this is what Woodstock felt like in 1969, only a little more than twenty-five years ago yet a lifetime away. Each generation was stacked on another like pancakes. The last movie I had rented from the video store and watched with Ravi had been *Age of Innocence*, set in the 1870s. I had to strain my brain to imagine the times: dirt roads, horse-drawn carriages, top hats, and dresses with bustles. And yet, maybe raving in 1995 would be something that future people would find as unimaginable. That blew my mind. I tried to say this all to Delilah, but my mind was spinning too fast for words to formulate.

So instead, I ran my fingers through Delilah's blonde wig and said, "I love you." Because in that moment, I was sure of only that.

NINE

Delilah and I exited the warehouse from the kitchen's back door and got hit with bright light. Through my squinting, I saw a woman walk by holding a purse my mom had once cherished, hanging off its strap like a tipped soda can. My dad had never been overly proud about being a bus driver, but sometimes he used to bring back things people had left behind. After the items had done their allotted time waiting in the Lost and Found, he'd present the goods to my mother as if they were treasures found in a chest. A new cookbook with the receipt still in the bag. No matter it was Jewish cooking. A stack of CDs from the pawn shop. Even though it was various metal and punk bands from the seventies and eighties. Once, a fake designer handbag with a broken zipper. This knock-off Louis was declared her favourite amongst all the odds-and-ends prizes.

It was definitely that purse this woman was holding. I was in a timeless daze, but I wondered briefly where this woman was headed so early on a Sunday. I could still hear what someone told me was "Alabama Blues" by St Germain playing (the Todd Edwards Dub mix), a garage house track with a kick of jazz. I loved this music with my whole soul, the way it made me feel. I wanted to know all the details.

By now Bryce was no longer guarding the door, and I wondered where his pretty face was. If I saw it, I would kiss him right on his mouth. Our pants were rimmed with inches of dirt, but with our coloured wigs and sparkly faces, Del and I still looked like we had climbed out of someone's magical attic. Parts of my body were shivering, and other parts glowed with warmth.

Delilah and I walked through places we normally wouldn't without fear; through alleys with dumpsters where people were openly shooting up. We were one with all. It wasn't sad looking at poor people or drug users as it usually was. There was a man drinking from a bottle. Delilah ran over and hugged him for a full minute, and he sobbed saying thank you, thank you. We had the gift of seeing the world upside down, in some post-apocalyptic movie.

At the same time, I felt empty inside, like someone had taken a straw and sipped away all the vitamins from my body. It might be hunger and thirst, we both decided, and Delilah said Subway was best because "it's got lettuce and healthy stuff. It'll, like, fuckin' rejuvenate us and shit."

We liked saying that word over and over, rejuvenate, rejuvenate, rejuvenate. As if the word itself gave the medicinal powers of restoration. House beats rattled in my head. Del had veered off into what I suspected by now was her favourite topic: how to stay skinny. She was saying how she usually avoided carbs but today, she would make an exception.

I didn't give a fuck about being skinny. Stick Boi and Takeshi and I practically lived off pizza. You couldn't be friends with two skater boys in high school and care about calories. But there was no pizza around us. Gastown was made up of odd shops that sold stuffed beaver toys and miniature maple syrup. These tourist traps were interspersed with Irish pubs but right now even their forest green, glass-plated doors were shut. And once you got out of the brick-paved, winding inner streets that folded in on each other like a pretzel, West Hastings was all about cryptic banking in futuristic skyscrapers that you couldn't get into unless you punched in a secret passcode.

We decided to catch a bus and get subs at a 24-hour Subway near where we met. Full circle. Right back near the goddamn bus loop and mall. Del, it turned out, lived near Commercial Drive, which was closer to downtown. But she was housesitting for her roommate Raz's cousin in Burnaby. Raz, the resident couch potato, hadn't wanted to do it. Living with two guys, Del wanted a getaway, so it was a win-win. Del and both of her roommates worked for a cooperative-run smoothie shop which she claimed attracted "annoying hippies who always wanted to talk about politics and shit" but "paid pretty well."

I didn't feel high anymore but from Delilah's eyes I knew I must have been. The thin rim of light brown surrounding her huge black pupils looked like fire agate gems. We had both ordered sandwiches, her turkey, me veggie. We fussed over the wrappers for what seemed an eternity.

"So, this stuff only happens on weekends?"

"Oh no," she said, between bites, "all week it's clubbing. Mini raves taking place in convenient, compartmentalized time slots. You know, in legal places."

"Oh. I'm too young for that."

"Bryce'll let you in, seeing as he works at most of them. Besides, I can score some ID off someone," she peeled back her wrapper and licked mustard off her thumb. "Lemme give a rundown of Vancouver club nights. Monday is Red Lounge. It's known for good hip hop. Wednesdays it's Ginger at Mars. Bit of a yuppie raver crowd there. Thursday, it's Sol at Graceland. That place has dope progressive house. Oh, and Sunday, it's The Chameleon, in this basement in a hotel — it's all about jungle. Backpack rappers dig that place, seems like your kind of crew. And The World is this after-hours place you go to when you don't want the party to end ... it's kinda desperate, though."

"Wait," I said. Everything she was saying was foreign. "My kind of crew?"

"Urban. Street. Whatever you call your, you know, look."

My look was based on what was easiest to skate in and steal. I picked a piece of processed cheese off the corner of my veggie sub and popped it into my mouth.

"Hey, stay away from Bryce, 'kay?" said Delilah, crumpling her wrapper into a baseball.

"I mean, gross," I replied. "He's, like, super old."

She shrugged. "I have no idea how old he is, but he got my friend so deep into politics that she stopped hanging out with me."

"The girl who moved to Asia?"

"Yeah. I think she's doing way better. She even scuba dives now."

"Wow," I said. Because, well, I didn't know anything about anyone.

"Hey, I thought you handled yourself well tonight, for a teenager."

I took a sip of water. "I'd have gone home and read if I hadn't met you."

"Read what?"

"I don't know." I dabbed at lettuce strings on my wrapper. They looked like something the Grinch would toss into a Christmas present. "I like psychoanalysts."

She looked at me blankly.

"Freud, Lacan," I continued. Seeing her expression, I didn't bother telling her about my love for Victorian gothic novels.

"Girl, like, why?" she asked, genuinely puzzled.

Because if I figured out what was wrong with me, no one else would have to fix me. Because sometimes Ravi talked to me. Because Ravi grew up with me even though he died, and he taught me things, and now he was a young man with an odd English accent. Because now my mom was dead, too. And because my dad would have never chosen me to be the one that he got stuck with.

But I couldn't trust her with all this. So instead, I said, "Hey, I'm still hungry."

"You know, if we did pure crystal tonight instead of E, you'd never be able to eat your sub. The best part about doing drugs is the skinny thing."

I instantly regretted saying it. We tossed our garbage away, and I remembered the food at my grandmother's house.

Saying goodbye, one pink-haired girl walked away from one blonde girl. I walked the rest of the way home. I slid my key into the lock and turned it. Every noise felt amplified. There was no need to sneak around because my dad must have had an early bus route. I set my board by the door. I imagined how terrible it would have been if I had gotten on my dad's bus that morning with Del. His empty coffee cup and plate were on the table. I thought it was odd how well functioning he was after my mom died, but I suppose he'd been self-sufficient for some while. When Ravi died, my mother had stopped taking care of the house. My dad had been making his own food and supplying the home with frozen foods for years. Maybe I should have helped out more around the house. That seemed to be what girl children were supposed to do. But my dad and I had both sort of navigated around the mess until he contended with it and bought more ready-to-eat groceries.

I locked myself in my bedroom. Tossed my wig and hat on my dresser. Stripped off my clothes. I fell onto my never-made-to-begin-with bed in my underwear and silver top. My body was buzzing. I pulled all the covers over myself. I felt like I had no skin on. I was so cold. I squirmed around, feeling the sensation of the sheets. Everything in my body felt achy and slightly off. I wanted to get more blankets to pile on the bed and make a nest, but I also didn't want to leave the safety of my own room.

I thought I would fall sleep, but I kept hearing techno beats and seeing horrible images in my mind. Halloween clowns and rabid raccoons. Dead rodents. People throwing large fish into hot pots in Korean restaurants. Competitive ballroom dancers with manic faces. For some reason, I kept visualizing Joey from *Friends* as being one of my cousins, and Fonzie turned into Jimmy. My mind would just not stop churning. I tried to concentrate on good things, wholesome things. Suddenly, my brain stopped on Eva.

Eva, with her angelic hair and beautiful spirit.

TEN

On Sunday, which was also New Year's Eve, Carlie and I watched a bunch of *90210* episodes taped on VHS. We didn't fast-forward the commercials. Just lay there after we smoked some of her brother's sticky chronic, sinking deeper into the sofa, melting and morphing into it. You'd need a spatula to peel us off.

I didn't love smoking at Carlie's, but now I was properly numbed from feeling things. The joint tonight mellowed me out from Saturday night. Or maybe, it kicked up something I already had in my system.

Even though there was often alcohol and freshly rolled doobs at Carlie's, she was pretty freaked out about hardcore drugs. I told her about the rave, and all she had to say about any of it was, "that sounds really weird, dude." Then she started talking about grad dresses, which I thought was more alien than the MDMA. Carlie hadn't struck me as someone into prom; she had always been more of a Marilyn Manson and Nine Inch Nails chick than Posh Spice. She was the girl who dyed her hair gothic plum while all the other try-hard wannabes at our school put streaks named after sundae flavours in their hair.

"I want something disco silver with gloves," she said.

A car commercial came on, and we watched a slick vehicle zigzag down a winding rainy road. "Yeah sure, disco gloves."

"No, not disco gloves." Carlie was getting annoyed with me. "You're so fucking out of it, you're not even listening to me, Baby."

"I am, I am. You're talking about prom. We just lit up, for fuck's sake. Why are you quizzing me? Can't we just chill the fuck out?"

She sighed heavily and turned off the television. "Well, what do you want to wear, huh?"

"Well, nothing disco," I said. I got an image of myself in a silly little silver dress going to grad. No way that was happening. "I'm not into dresses, you know that."

"Every girl imagines their prom dress, Baby," she said. As if I was being dramatic, like that time I'd almost refused to play along when she'd made us pick out our funeral playlists. She'd chosen "November Rain" and I had to list some random-ass songs for myself, even though I knew damn well better than anyone else that Hindus didn't play Guns N' Roses at their funerals.

"You know, Baby, the mall is giving away free teddy bear backpacks with grad dresses right now."

"Not really into the whole grad thing, dude."

"Just come check out some gowns. The backpacks are so freakin' cute. The brown bears are called Honey and the black ones, Licorice. Get your dad to give you money."

I sure as fuck wasn't excited about teddy bears that were named after candy flavours. I had just done a drug named after an animal, after all. I winced then, imagining how Del would see Carlie right now: baggy New Order rock shirt with fingers coated orange in Cheeto dust.

"I don't give a shit about grad," I said. "No offence, C." I turned the television back on and feigned interest in Brenda arguing with Kelly. It was so easy to fall into the alternate high school life of *90210*.

I ignored her hurt face. Or maybe, I was glad that I could hurt her.

ELEVEN

When school started up after Christmas break ended, I found Stick Boi and Takeshi hanging out by their lockers. They were planning on skating outside the art gallery on Robson. Robson Street's bougie-ass shops were still filled with last year's icy winter gowns. I preferred the alternative shops on Granville. Like the Rock Shop where you could buy any concert T-shirt you wanted, even if you missed the show. Or True Value Vintage, where once you walked down a windy staircase, you could buy cool finds pillaged from local thrift stores for jacked-up prices. I wanted to try on the sparkly barrettes that all the girls wore in their pixie haircuts at raves.

"Fuck off, Takeshi. Ya axe me to dye your hair like some punk-ass unicorn and then yer all mad at the *Sesame Street* references." Stick Boi was pulling out a nub of a cigarette he'd saved from earlier. It reeked. "Yo, you comin' downtown with us or what?" he was looking at me.

"Yeah, dawg. 'Course," I said.

"'Kay. Takeshi requested Cookie Monster–blue at the Beauty Shop first," Stick Boi told me, for which Takeshi punched him lightly in the belly. Takeshi's hair, a skater kid's version of a dishevelled blue mop, was skillfully crafted using Stick Boi's uncle's barbershop shears, bleach, and a jar of Manic Panic dye, all carried out in Stick Boi's bathtub. "After all I do, he got the nerve to act like a fuckin' sensitive beeyotch."

"Hey," I said, following the smell of nicotine out of the school doors. "You oughtta do something with my hair."

"I only do one style, yo," Stick Boi said in his Bronx way. "Suits Takeshi fine. He love looking like he about to perform a counting trio with Oscar the Grouch and The Count. *Van, Twooo, Treee.* Makes the girls swoon."

"Fuck off, white boy," Takeshi retorted, taking a fresh smoke from a pack tucked in his back pocket.

"I hardly think you oughtta swear at your hairdresser, man. 'Specially since you such a lousy tipper. The Beauty Shop may have another booking today, Cooks," Stick Boi winked at me.

"I don't mind the abuse. Pencil me in, I'll take Takeshi's spot," I jumped on my board and slid forward, leaving the boys to tackle each other behind me.

That afternoon, I sat on a stool atop a towel laid in a pink tub. Stick Boi ran his persimmon-coloured fingers, stained from cigarettes and doobies, through my hair, making me turn my head this way and that. Like a real fucking professional.

Stick Boi was raised by a single mom and two large Doberman dogs that resembled masked Mexican wrestlers. He was whiter than a full moon, probably due to iron and B12 deficiencies. His arms were covered in freckles, some of which were so close they looked like stratus clouds at sunset, painting streaks of orange across his wiry biceps. True to his name, he was as skinny as a straw. He had grown up in Burnaby but had an inner-city rapper's accent. Stick Boi's father was supposedly on crack and lived on the Eastside, and his mother, a recovered addict, worked night shifts.

After weeks of me occupying the edge of the skate turf, Stick Boi had eventually told me he had a learning impairment and had to attend special classes in a trailer parked next to the school in addition to his regular schedule, and could I possibly have a look at his English homework? I suppose he noticed that I wrote poems and shit in class, because occasionally the teacher made some deal about it. It was like he wanted me to know his biggest weakness before we became tight. Stick Boi used his time in special ed classes to design graphic cartoons depicting the adventures of the Purple Lynx (half man, half cat).

"You're not worried we're gonna look like twins with this hair? Like I'm robbing Takeshi of his special style or some shit?"

"The fuck do I care if youse two both look like Sonic the Hedgehog?" said Stick Boi, going to the sink to grab his scissors.

Takeshi was sitting on the closed toilet lid watching this, amused. "Baby, we don't look a thing alike." He was tall, skinny, and Japanese, and I was small and Indian. I watched my black hair fall around me in chunks.

Stick Boi, initially annoyed that a girl was hanging out by the school's chain-link fence — his skate turf — had now taken to spoiling me in little ways, like showing me how to nail skate tricks. Making tattoo ideas for me (all muscular cats, which I didn't feel suited me). I felt like an adopted kitten. Even the way he gruffly chopped my hair was done lovingly.

"Thanks for this," I said.

"You betta wait 'til you see whatcha look like before you go thankin' me." And then, catching me off guard, Stick Boi added, "Yo, you gonna take us to one of these rave things or what?"

I twitched for a second, hoping it wouldn't turn into a full shaking fit, which luckily it did not, and then winced at the smell of peroxide Stick Boi was now stirring in a cup. I hadn't looked at my hair yet; it would be too troublesome to inspect it before the bleach went on. This was no Yaletown salon. I realized then that I was embarrassed for the boys to join me in what I imagined as my and Delilah's pixie world. Takeshi and Stick Boi were too rough to loosen their bodies on ecstasy; I pictured them sliding down a wall and freezing there for the night when confronted with glitter and deep house. They'd get along better with Bryce outside, kicking it to straight hip hop. The bleach felt like it was sizzling my hair. It had to be completely stripped of colour before he would be able to coat the blue on. Stick Boi put his mother's flowered plastic shower cap on me. We waited.

"It won't be your thing," I said finally, turning to face them. "Everyone's all fucking happy and shit. They hug each other a lot.

They play breakbeats. It's like a mothafuckin' tea party scene."

Stick Boi nodded, taking this in. "And the E, what's that like? Compared to the time, say, you, me, and Takeshi did acid at the soccer field at night."

"But I didn't do the acid. It was you and Takeshi."

"Dayyum. Who was you talking to all night sitting by the goalie post then, huh?" he demanded, his words punctuated by nasally slang.

It was last year, and I had been telling Ravi about some of my poetry. He had been sitting cross-legged in front of me, head to toe in his customary outfit of faded denim jeans, jacket, and a Beatles shirt. A little suit made of jeans. We'd shared a joint. He'd told me about fun pubs he'd hung out at in England. Said I should go there sometime, that "London's, like, totally your jam, Baby." It had been a night of classic Ravi, him philosophizing about history and the gladiators. I had zoned out in his company, eventually spreading myself on the grass like I was making a snow angel.

"I wasn't talking to anyone," I said convincingly, trying to block out the image of my twin brother's ghost. "You two idiots were tripping the fuck out. You guys were talking to actual rocks, and you wanted to break into the school and graffiti the lockers. Luckily, I stopped you. Look," I said, scratching my ear, hoping it wasn't coated in bleach, "if y'all wanna go to a rave, you know your girl'll hook you up. Just give me a bit of time to get to know my way 'round things, okay?"

I saw them exchange a look, each checking to see what the other thought. They nodded at each other, processing what I had said. Boys didn't press too much once you gave them a reasonable answer. That's why I liked them. That's why Carlie could sometimes be a pain in the ass.

"Now, fuck off with the bullshit and concentrate on my hair already," I said. "I don't want you burning my goddamn scalp off."

TWELVE

Delilah paged me at nine in the evening. Stick Boi was landing his deck on and off a bench near the art gallery. It was cold as fuck, but the snow around the vicinity had been bitten away by pedestrians, the area crusted with blue salt. Lots of the veteran skaters had been chased away by the weather conditions, leaving the terrain to us desperate Burnaby teens. We'd just eaten ninety-nine-cent pizza, all green peppers and slippery cheese on a cardboard crust. But the smell of the hot dog carts was making me hungry again.

The boys stopped stunting to blaze on the steps, passing a gooey blunt between them. I sat a few steps down from them. I didn't want to get faded. I wanted to keep my mind clear for what might happen next. I lifted my hat off and combed my hands through my short blue hair, enjoying the lightness. Stick Boi had layered my hair and left the nape of my neck exposed in a way that had all my features looking more in focus. Refined.

I saw Ravi striding toward me. Takeshi was down to a roach. Stick Boi saved it in a cigarette pack, his little treasure box of half-smoked goods. They went back to doing tricks while I remained on the steps, staring outward.

"Holy fuckin' smokes. What did you do to your hair and shit," Ravi asked me in his clipped English accent, just as the two boys left. He sank next to me on the art gallery steps, all skinny jeans and purple Chucks. "You look like a proper li'l bluebird, innit, one of them flappy critters?"

"Wanted to do something completely different, Ravs." I put my hat back on.

"Shit, Granny gonna say you is a dyke for sure now."

"I ain't no dyke," I said, surprising myself with the force behind my words. I felt stunned that he had made me say this aloud. I scanned the area, but no one was looking at me. "Besides," I lowered my voice, "I don't plan to see her again. Or anyone else in our fucked-up family."

He yawned extravagantly. Pulled up a pant leg and scratched a spot. "That's your plan then, ey? Do nuffin'?"

"Nothing left to do. I got kicked out of Granny's party and that was that."

"Right. She's always been difficult," he shook his head. "Remember when she had that intervention with Mum? Trying to get me off the skip-roping witcha? Said it was too girly?"

I fiddled with my cap. "Yeah, man, she thought you were gay. She didn't like our matching hoodies. Little did we know, that would be the least of our problems. Hey, are you ripping pages out from my journal? I'm literally missing chunks."

"I'll tape them back in or some shit. Ya want my feedback, don'tcha? Hey, don't go and piss your life away on hardcore drugs and shit, Baby. Can't help you if you stop seeing me, na' mean?"

"If I get high on hardcore shit, I won't see you?"

"I mean, I dunno how it all works. All I know is last year you wouldn't even try acid with these fools. Now you is all wild and shit." He shook his hands in the air like a medicine man.

"I'm going to go to the Red Lounge with Del," I said, trying to sound nonchalant. I said it as if I had hung out with Del on every Monday for as long as I'd lived. When I looked up, Stick Boi and Takeshi were staring at me.

"It's pretty late, Baby," Takeshi said, shifting weight between his long legs. "Don't you want to come back with us?" He blew on his hands. "Better for us to go home together."

Ravi sat back, hands hooked in his belt loops, watching the exchange take place. His shoulder-length, curly hair was touching the edge of his denim jacket. Wasn't he cold always wearing the same damn outfit? His shirt was Pink Floyd's album cover, *The Dark Side of the Moon.*

I could tell Takeshi was worried about me. I wasn't sure if I was imagining the small crackles of electric currents running between us now. But I didn't want that to bog me down tonight. It was going to be hard to act cool around Del if I had to be a different person around the boys. I didn't edit what I said around Takeshi and Stick Boi.

I could see they were done for the night. Only I, with my manic hallucinations of Ravi, was lit with energy. Stick Boi and Takeshi had a long way home; they'd have to take the Skytrain to New West. They would chain-smoke bummed cigarettes, scaring all the ladies also waiting for the bus in front of the Salvation Army. No one wanted to be stuck near teenage hoodlums with skateboards. And Takeshi and Stick Boi, who were generally harmless, loved to play up the whole bad-ass act.

"I'm not tired," I said, my voice raw in the cold. I didn't need Takeshi to parent me. I knew how to travel home without getting jumped. It had happened once, a girl had tried to go for my red Filas at New Westminster Skytrain station, the one pair I had that weren't skate shoes. I had kicked her in the crotch, slid between her legs, and managed to catch the bus, which had arrived on time, just like out of a movie. She hadn't expected someone like me to fight back.

"You guys go on ahead," I added, standing up now. "I know my friend can get me in, but you guys'll need ID."

"I'm not feeling it anyway," said Takeshi, too quickly. And Stick Boi, never a fan of talking if someone else already did it for him, nodded in agreement.

They looked like hood rats; they knew it. No club was letting them in. Me too, but I was wearing the silver tube top Del had created under my hoodie, and with my wide skate pants and new hair, it would be enough. They gave me fist bumps and we parted ways, the sound of wheels filing against cement going in two different directions.

I held on to my hat and flew down the sidewalk, winding around pedestrians too shocked at me to be annoyed. I pushed Takeshi's disappointed look back in my head as far as I could until, finally, all I could see was the night ahead.

THIRTEEN

Red Lounge, which Del had given me a flyer for at the end of Rabbit Hole, was lit up the shade of a fire engine. It was too early for anyone to be guarding the door, and I slid in easily. The in-house DJ was warming up with Tribe. I realized Takeshi and Stick Boi would have liked it here; they loved to play the track "Oh My God" and fade out, and suddenly I felt like the world's worst friend.

Del's back was to me, her body upright, light brown hair separated into pigtails. She was saturated in red, as if she was sitting in the room that we processed photos in during Photography 12. A big, mocha, faux-fur jacket hung off her shoulders.

"Bay-beeeee," she said, coating me in the smell of lemon gin. I had shared a bottle once with Carlie and we drank the whole fucking thing in one sitting and now the smell made me gag. Yet on Del it smelled sophisticated. A Jennifer-Aniston-at-a-casino-in-a-white-pantsuit kind of smell.

The music changed to house, something with a reverberating bass loop that encapsulated the entire underground warehouse music sound in one complete experience. I leaned my board and backpack against the base of the bar. "What's playing?" I pointed questioningly at a speaker.

"Derrick Carter, 'Shock Therapy.' He's, like, only the best fucking DJ ever."

I set my hat on the bar. "Oh."

"Omigosh, Baby, your hair," she gushed, running her hands through my blue strands. "You look like such a teenager."

"Girl, you straight-up tellin' me I gotta a minor standing in my bar?" said a caramel-skinned man, too gorgeous to be straight.

"Ain't your bar, Ronny."

"She cute. Girl, you cute," Ronny said to me. "Sit, ignore the drunk white lady."

"She ain't that cute, Ronny," said Del, as I pulled up on the stool next to her. "Calm the fuck down."

"Del, you 'bout on your last chance with me. Acting like a goddamn queen when there can only be one of us up here in this joint. That five-dollar ratty coat ain't cutting it, neither. Someone's gramma wants it the fuck back," Ronny clapped back.

I wasn't sure if I should defend Del.

"She'd have never cut her hair before she met me. I'm like, you know, her mentor, or some shit," Del replied, unfazed by Ronny.

Del was sloshed. I didn't belong here. But Ronny put a pink drink in front of me. "If we're gonna stay here," I said to Del, "then I need to put my board somewhere, I guess."

"Board," Del guffawed. "Baby skates. Adds to the whole teeny-bop thing, right? Ronny, she reads books too, thinks that makes her smart."

"Reading does tend to do that," Ronny rolled his eyes up to the glasses hanging above the bar. "Drink's on me, kid, provided you get her the fuck out my bar."

Del tried to confront Ronny but slipped in the process. She stumbled, miraculously still standing. Her stool, however, hit the floor hard.

Ronny fingered a gold chain on his hairless, exposed chest and said to me, "Girl, get this bitch home. She cooked. I need her out before the actual paying guests get here. Her and her raggedy fur wouldn't last two seconds out on the town with me. Thinkin' she goddamn Liza Minnelli or some shit."

"Ronny, you're being dramatic," Del insisted.

Laughing dryly, he grabbed a paring knife and slid it through a lemon. The air was immediately punctuated with a sharp, citrus scent. He tossed the pieces into a jar filled with lemon and lime wedges. "Ain't got time for this shit, Del. You know I don't. It's about to get popping tonight. And I can see you rearing up to have a diva moment."

"So, you want us to leave?" I said, feeling my heart sink at the prospect of missing something "popping." I got up and righted the stool.

"Don't need her falling off the goddamn bar stools, you hear? And she wanted me to take her to a drag show," he pointed his knife at us. "Hell fucking no am I introducing her to anyone at Doll & Penny's. Y'all think I'm crazy?" His voice had raised to a high pitch. "Have a good night, bitches. Enjoy your sea breeze, kid."

I took out the little plastic straw and dumped the drink down my throat. Put my hat on and grabbed my stuff. Just then, that infectious Euro house hit by Todd Terry Project came on, "Put Your Hands Together" (the Café Americana mix). I knew that one because I had asked someone last time, memorizing the details even in my E-induced daze.

Dammit. I wanted to stay. I guided Del to the door.

Ronny saluted me. "Drag show, ma' ass, Del," he was shouting at her. "You ain't ready for ma' world, chile. Nu-uh. Baby? You come back anytime you want, and I'll make you your pink drink, you hear?"

My pink drink. But I was too busy trying to wrangle Del's body through the club to answer back.

FOURTEEN

Outside, Del handed me keys. She staggered toward the curb. "New plan. Fuck Red Lounge. You drive. To Stanley Park. There's a fashion show happening."

"Dude, I do not know how to drive."

"Gosh darn it, Baby," she said, shoving me toward a silver hatchback parked on the street. "You think you're so smart, right? Surely you can fucking drive a car."

I found myself sitting in Del's driver's seat on a school night. Lured by the video game sounds ping-ponging onto the sidewalk, Takeshi, Stick Boi, and I had played Daytona USA in the crappy arcade near the mall for hours. Had quarter lessons prepared me for real driving? Instead of being mad that Delilah had dissed me in front of Ronny, I was focused on impressing Del. Even though I felt a little stupid about it. But I didn't want to end up on Carlie's couch smoking Mary Jane talking about disco gloves for the rest of my year. *Fuck that shit.* I wanted another adventure story to tell Takeshi and Stick Boi.

There weren't a lot of other cars on the street on a Monday night, so with Del's instruction, I was able to pull out easily. On the main street, I pushed the gas and brake pedals intermittently. But by the time we got to Stanley Park, I had mastered the gas part so well we nearly bottomed out on a speed bump.

"Del?" I said, when she didn't reprimand me for scraping the metal underbelly of her car against the asphalt. "Why did we take a bus the first time we met?"

She might have fallen asleep. But then she spoke, "I left my car at the house I was watching for Raz's cousin. I'm no good at driving high."

"Oh."

"Now, you can be the one that looks after the driving bit."

"Sure, yeah."

"Look, I was planning on staying chill tonight, but Ronny kept making me doubles. No one'll get you drunker in this city than a drag queen working his second job. Red Lounge is fun, but it's the same every week. But this party will be something amazing. Hey, pull over, we're here."

Even from where we were, I could hear house beats travelling down to the sea. They sounded more expensive and sophisticated than the ones we had heard at the warehouse rave last weekend. White chiffon curtains blew from the windows. She climbed out of the Civic, pulling a skinny menthol out of her blue, leopard-print cigarette case. She offered me a smoke, but I shook my head.

"These pop-up parties are secret — no one knows the address 'til, like, a half hour before." Cigarette dangling out her mouth like a mob wife, she continued, "Tickets are hella overpriced. Vancouver fashion elites show up to prove they're relevant and shit."

She pulled her faux fur around her tightly, like a faded pop star. "The people from Le Chateau in Pacific Centre act like they run shit because they sell vinyl pants. The managers come here and do rails of coke off the bar talking about how they were once at a backstage party with Gipsy Kings. Like anyone gives a fuck. Tons of celebs film shit in Vancouver, and if anyone of 'em's a real raver, they'll find their way to this event. Alicia Silverstone showed up last year. She's a legit Sugar Kid."

"Ronny said I oughtta get you home."

"Ronny just wanted me the fuck outta Red Lounge. He likes to shine the brightest." She wobbled a little.

"You really wanna go to a fashion show?"

"It's more like a private rave. You'll get to know who's who. Like, Costello, the Black guy with the fabulous fun-fur hats and colourful bellbottoms? He's a riot. Janine, the older woman with a silver bob, pops so many pills I don't know how she's still alive? She owns a shoe store on Granville. It's where I got these." She pulled up her pants to show me silver, astronaut-inspired sneakers. "These people have the money to do premium drugs. Jimmy designs T-shirts; did'ja know that? He's gotta shop. Gets invited every fucking year. He's on the list for everything that's anything in this city," she confessed.

Jimmy. I didn't imagine him to be someone so together. I tried not to react.

She paused to light her cigarette, looking up at me through fake, sparkly lashes. She had on lowrider white bellbottoms. Her jacket, which had fallen open, exposed a scrap of metallic fabric.

She felt me staring. "Oh, you like my lashes? Hang on. Costume and dance shops have the best finds." She rummaged through her fun-fur bag until she produced thick eyelashes trapped inside a plastic box like they were pinned butterflies or valuable diamond earrings. Showing a more sober side when it came to makeup artistry, she stripped off the lashes and lined glue on them. Swaying, she eventually managed to press them close to my lash line, like a professional working at a swanky cosmetic boutique. The cigarette, still lit, hung outside her lips the whole time.

I tried not to blink but my reflexes kicked in. No one had done my makeup before.

"Hold still, let 'em dry, Baby." Remembering her cigarette, she inhaled and puffed. "Don't go batting your lashes like you're trying to fly away. Such a kid," she muttered to herself, letting out wafts of gin. It mixed with her scent of ripe raspberries. I leaned in closer, realizing why Jimmy had fallen for her.

"Jimmy stopped going to events when he met Eva. Surprised they even came to Rabbit Hole. All they ever want to do is get high at his shithole apartment. She's such a fucking flake, don'tcha think? We'll say we're with his T-shirt company, The Grape Monkeys, okay? We'll take his ticket and his plus one."

"You want us to jack his tickets?"

She made a face at me. "Jeez, relax, I do it, like, all the time. You know how many acts I've seen at The Roxy cause of Jimmy? I play the stood-up date to collect his unused tickets. The box office people tell me to 'go and at least enjoy the band even though your boyfriend pulled a no-show.'"

"Wow," I said, trying to imagine Del hanging out with washed-out rockers.

"There's two of us, so I can't pull my usual heist off. Just follow my lead. We work for Jimmy. Got it?"

We work for Jimmy, I rehearsed in my head.

We made our way down to the glass restaurant, which reminded me of a plant conservatory. It came with sweeping, all-encompassing views of the ocean, like a boat docked at sea. This party was full of real adults, with actual jobs and stuff. It was going to be a lot harder to convince people we were worth knowing.

FIFTEEN

"The Grape Monkeys!" Del was shouting. With her strawberry popsicle–stained lips, fat eyelashes, and sloppy coat, she looked exactly like she'd just been kicked out of a club.

"It's a T-shirt company," I said, in a calmer voice. "But we also make clubwear. Like this," I unzipped my thick hoodie and pointed at the silver top that Del had made us last time, when we had gone to Dressew. "Jimmy's the head of our company, but we're here on his behalf."

"Ain't no one making changes to the *list*, sweet pea," said a fabulous drag queen with a wig as puffy and pastel blue as cotton candy on a stick. Her skin was the shade of Lindt. Everything in this new world looked like sweet treats to me — hair, skin, clothes. "No substi-*tu*-tions, ya hear me?" She enunciated certain words and sounds, and I watched her, fascinated.

"Hey," Del tried again, "maybe you know Ronny? He goes by Cocoa Chenille?"

"Uh, uh, *uh*," said the drag queen, raising her finger. "You droppin' Cocoa Chenille like that bitch'll do you any good getting in here? Girl, please. But I do *like* the top," she was looking at me. "How 'bout dis? You mail me one to this *add*ress right here," she handed me a card, which Del snatched. "And I'll pretend like I see your names here. We clear, bitches?"

"As the day," said Del.

"Good. Go *on* through then. Two fun ride passes *on me*. Trust, I remembah every face in Vancity so don'tcha even *think* of fuckin' *me* ova."

"Wow," Del said to me as we sailed in. "We got lucky, but why are you wearing the same top again?"

"I don't have a lot of party stuff," I admitted, thinking of my kiddish cartoon T-shirts. "It's mostly a new crowd, right? I'm sure it doesn't matter."

"Didn't you hear that psycho queen? People'll remember us. You need to coordinate with me next time. I don't want people to think we're fucking amateurs and shit. And that weird, ancient-looking locket you have around your neck, Baby? It has got to go."

I felt tight in my chest when she said that, but I neutralized my face. She hadn't said anything the first time she had seen me with it, when she lent me her rhinestone cat collar. I slipped the necklace Takeshi had given me into the journal in my backpack. It was the safest, most meaningful place I could think of putting it.

When I looked up, Del was shouting excitedly. "De'Lacy's 'Hideaway'! The Deep Dish mix! Quintessential New Jersey garage house track!" The crystal-clear vocals and silky, groovy energy perfectly matched the scene. "This song is all the rage in Europe, but in Vancity, you can only hear it at underground places like this!"

I inspected the room. Tendrils from live ivy plants criss-crossed over the white walls. A sizable skylight marked the centre of the ceiling. People were wearing the most interesting blend nineties fashion had to offer. A woman in a latex catsuit with an embroidered choker. Two girls with linked arms had partitioned off a white men's suit: one wore the blazer as a dress, the other, the suit pants and vest. Two drag queens in dresses: one, Chinese-style with a mandarin collar, and the other, a Betsy Johnson–tea-party number, bright yellow with teal flowers. There were goths in vinyl pants and black lipstick. Artsy waif types in lingerie slip dresses. We could have been at any art show in any international city in the world. I felt like a dumb high school kid. Like everything Del had accused me of being.

Del turned to me. "Lawd, someone's a little dazed and confused, *huh?*" She was imitating the queen working the front.

"I just wish I could dress like these people. Are we … are we dropping E again?"

"I'm dry tonight. We need to find a new way to score. Hm," she said, squinting one eye at me. "The people near the bathroom are always the ones doing coke. Let's start with that."

Until we reached the bathroom sign, we did some sort of decoy dance to what Del said was the iconic house song "Push the Feeling On" (the MK Dub of Doom mix) by Nightcrawlers. The song's eerie, gibberish-sounding vocals made me feel feverish with excitement. One guy, wearing a shiny red jacket with a yellow T-shirt, stood out in the crowd. I'd only done E once, but now I had the ability to see the world in two ways; my high side saw him as a dodgy drug dealer, and my straight side saw him as a flashy dresser. People gave him money for sachets, then disappeared into the bathrooms.

I wanted to do coke, and I wanted to do it for free.

"Rich high people are super sloppy. I know where we can score," Del said.

"The guy dressed like McDonald's?"

"Nah. I literally have five dollars to my name. Follow me."

There was one stall in the women's bathroom. We went inside. My heart was pounding. Above the metal toilet paper dispenser sat a card advertising a rave. She lifted it. Underneath, white powder was exposed on the platform like freshly sprinkled snow.

"Nobody's more wasteful than rich people doing cocaine in public," Del declared. "They always leave a trail of breadcrumbs. Roll up your sleeves, Gretel."

Del and I started snorting what we assumed was leftover cocaine on top of a toilet dispenser contraption with a rolled up five-dollar bill. I copied her, licking my fingers and jamming the powder on my gums. It could have been a lot of other things, angel dust or maybe meth powder. But perhaps the people that made up the art and fashion scene really did dabble only in high-grade cocaine. Perhaps they all lived in pricey Mainland Street studio apartments, drank mimosas at brunch, and listened to Queen on Sunday afternoons. These were Vancouver's nouveau riche. And they liked their quality coke. The high was at best as if I'd drunk a few cups of coffee. The nicest feeling was the numbness of my gums. I didn't understand why people would waste more money on cocaine than, say, a gourmet espresso. But I wasn't as sophisticated as Delilah. She climbed atop a pedestal used by the models earlier to display clothing. She danced like she had been hired to be there. The colours from the disco ball above rained over her body, imprinting it with a thousand crystal diamonds.

SIXTEEN

The fashion party had a name, Moon Glow. Del and I were in a mood to party hard. The coke had done enough to boost us, but we started to feel it waning as we danced. And then smack in the middle of the dance floor, we ran into Jimmy and Eva.

Delilah stiffened immediately when she saw them. But after it became clear Jimmy had no notion of how we had weaseled our way in, Del relaxed. She told the story about promising to send the drag queen a silver lamé top she designed in exchange for entry. Del made herself the heroine, leaving me completely out of the tale. Del talked endlessly about her several effective ways for getting into parties. Either she knew someone, worked at an event to earn her free ticket, or told people she was shooting a documentary. She'd even dragged video cameras into raves, the size of small gerbil homes on her shoulders, borrowed from one of her roommates.

Jimmy looked tired, perhaps of Del's antics, perhaps in general. He offered all of us E, and Delilah didn't second-guess taking drugs from him. We each swallowed a cap, sharing a water bottle that had a neon glow stick in it. A wave of anxiety rushed over me, and I hurried to the washroom. Eva followed me. She rubbed circles on my back and then locked the stall door behind us. "You'll be fine, love. Do you wanna try and go to the bathroom? That always makes me feel better. Means the drugs are good."

After about twenty minutes, I felt the euphoria soothingly creep into every part of my being, the corners of my toes, and a part of my brain I didn't realize needed to relax. It wasn't weird at all being in a bathroom stall with someone I barely knew. It was like she had come from another planet to help me cross into the high world. Eva's arms were coated in a long-sleeved cotton crop T-shirt that had been softened by all the people who had ever worn it. Eva was the starlet wearing a T-shirt in a ballroom crowd. Judging from the looks of the worn letters advertising some softball team, it had come from the time when Ravi had Star Wars bedspreads and we'd filmed fake movies in our place.

By the time we joined the others, I had a huge grin on my face. By then, the polished house music had given way to drum and bass. The dirty jungle tunes, which I learned were influenced by reggae and derived from the UK and Ireland, were pinging syncopated, shredded breakbeats everywhere. Doc Scott's "VIP Drumz." Randall and Andy C's "Sound Control." DJ Dara's "RNA," a contraband version apparently, because it wasn't out yet. Someone had snagged a fresh-off-the-press copy of LTJ Bukem's new album *Mixmag Live Volume 21–1996*, and snippets were being sampled and meshed into the set. Jimmy knew his music and was rattling off trivia. Thoughts shot in and out of my head so fast I couldn't hang on to any one long enough to share it fully. I looked at Eva and wondered if by sheer osmosis my thoughts were penetrating her mind. She sighed and I sighed, and we looked up at the glow-in-the-dark stars attached to the pillars. For his love of the galaxy, Ravi would have loved this place.

By now, Moon Glow had become something else entirely. I felt like I was in a painting of a painting. Like how in *The Night Watch*, August Jernberg painted people at a museum looking at the original Rembrandt. The audience looking at the painting becomes the very art piece itself. Here at the fashion-show rave, we the audience were the art. Delilah's face, I noticed, had gone paper white, reminding me of Stick Boi. She opened her mouth to tell me something, but like me, the E had stolen her voice.

"Hey," I said, the word drowsily coming out of my mouth. It felt good to say it. *Hey* could be like real hay, the straw one you could fill scarecrows with, something that sat close to earth. "Hay," I said again. "Hey."

"Hey, hey, hey," Eva added, nodding. It was a simple word but could convey so much. We both tilted our heads toward each other trying out the word.

It dawned on me that perhaps Del didn't like Eva and I getting close. Del and Eva should become friends, I decided. Jimmy was just a guy. How could any woman fall in love with such a boring specimen?

"Baby," Del said in a small voice.

"Del," I repeated. Her voice sounded like salted caramel in my mouth. Perhaps more like a saltwater taffy. *Del. Del. Del.* Her name became the techno beats slithering over us. The pit of my stomach felt ticklish and warm. I was mesmerized by the walls covered in psychedelic images coming through a projector. Every muscle and bone in my body felt relaxed, like it was dipped and coated in Tiger Balm. I pushed my hands forward to feel the air in front of me, to see if I could feel the very stars. *Del. Del. Del.*

It was then I realized Del wasn't okay. She fell to the floor. But she didn't pass out. Del was kicking and screaming fanatically. She looked like a hamster running sideways on a wheel.

Eva gasped. There was a small crowd gathering around her. Jimmy was staving people off. He squatted next to Del.

"Get up," he was saying anxiously. "Snap out of it."

Even though Jimmy was talking to Del, I straightened myself instinctively. I looked at the water reflection shadows bouncing off the walls as projected videos played close-ups of swimming pools. I told myself that this was all very serious, and I should act in the right way.

Jimmy was still talking. "If ya don't fuckin' get it together, someone's gonna call the ambulance. Is that what'chu want?"

Yes, I thought. *Yes! We want help!* But it must not have been what she wanted because Jimmy was able to carry Del out the front doors. Like he was Kevin Costner, and she was Whitney fuckin' Houston in *The Bodyguard*. I heard the hit song from that movie in my head and everything. I had the good sense to grab our things from the heap on the floor. Del hated using the coat check, run by a group of kids that rotated all the main parties; they were always high as fuck, and she said her coat was safer on the floor than it was with them. Del's coffee-coloured coat looked like a dead animal in my arms.

"Don't forget ma' silver *top*, bitches!" the queen with the sky-blue hair was shouting at us as we rushed out. As if we weren't in the middle of an emergency. As if she was quite used to seeing people casually almost overdose in front of her.

Wait. Back the fuck up. Was Del overdosing? Did people overdose while they punched and yelled? I swallowed hard. I wanted to feel alarmed, but my body was still singing inside. Was I even a good friend if I wasn't feeling the right things? *Panic. No, don't panic. Panic. No. Don't.*

"Terrorist," a dirty jungle track by Renegade that made me feel alive with drum and bass mixed with sugary sweet vocals, came storming after us. Eva had told me the track info, bobbing her head despite the chaos. We were inside Del's Civic now, me in the front passenger seat and Eva, Jimmy, and Del crammed into the back. No one was in the driver's seat. How long could we stay here? We had the night's protection for a few more hours. And then what? Would the police come up and ask us why were in a parked car? Del was nodding in and out. And then she started wailing. Oh my god, did people shriek when they were overdosing?

"She's just having a bad trip," Jimmy offered.

"Why?" I asked.

Del yelped again then and rubbed her fists into her eyes. "Mom!" she yelled. "Mom!" It was like she was sleepwalking. She couldn't see any of us.

"I accidentally gave her PCP," Jimmy said. How does one accidentally give someone PCP? Wasn't that horse tranquilizer? "I was testing out some PCP." Jimmy apparently was still talking. "Someone gave me a sample, and I threw it in with the rest of my caps. Thought it'd be more fun to try it out that way."

"More fun?" Eva said, tilting her head like an owl.

"Maybe this PCP's too strong. Maybe Special K is a better party drug." He shrugged disarmingly.

Party drug. Something you took to have a better time. The adult version of a surprise bag. Instead of whistles and balloons you got ketamine and angel dust. What the fuck was wrong with this Jimmy dude, for real, talking like he was a legit gangster and not some skinny white dude who owned a T-shirt store?

"What do we do?" I said, trying not to panic. *Wadaweedoo, Wadaweedoo!* My heartbeat was quickening.

"We drive back to my house. I'll try an' calm her down. She needs somewhere without stimulation. I'll make her tea," Jimmy said, as if tea would fix it all. I got a picture of doilies and a little pink tea pot in my head.

"Oh," said Eva, sinking back in her chair.

"Can you drive, Baby?"

"I don't, like, have a licence?" But seeing as Jimmy was supervising Del and how shaken Eva was, I knew I was the only sane choice.

Del started up again.

I bit my lip.

"Look, I'll take her fer a walk around the sea," Jimmy said. Like he was Papa Bear. All calm and in charge. "By then, you can sober up and drive us, right Baby?"

"Right," I answered. Sure. Didn't matter that I was the youngest person in this group or that I was as high as a kite.

The moonlight shimmering on the Pacific Ocean looked like candles flickering on a bathtub. Snow edged the rims of the park, making everything look like a postcard you sent someone at Christmas time. Merry fuckin' Christmas, Baby. Anyway, winter break was over, and classes had started and shit, right? Not like my family celebrated the birth of Jesus Christ. In Ravi's time, there had been pictures with Santa and a six-foot plastic tree. But now we marked things like the one-year anniversary of my mother's death with a *shraadh* and told grandkids to get the fuck out of houses. I blinked rapidly, taking shots of the scenery with my eyes.

Jimmy slammed the door as they left. I moved to the driver's seat, readying myself for my new role. Eva crawled into the front passenger seat. I scrounged around for a tape to throw into the deck. I found one labelled *DJ MouseCat*. We became enchanted with the music, threading our hands with one another in a kind of syncopated, seated rave dance. I pushed Del away from the small nagging territory of my brain where I worried. Everything in the car seemed to be made of light. Sparkling. Eva and I touched the various surfaces: the hard plastic of the glove compartment, the smooth velvet seatbelts, the satin steering wheel. We marvelled at how comforting it was to sit in a parked car. Our own private oxygen-filled fortress where we could drive, sleep, or eat. A safety vessel, we decided. It wouldn't be so hard, making a car your home.

But then Jimmy and Del came back. They burst into our tranquil bubble, and I had to start the car.

I wasn't sure how I would drive from Vancouver to New Westminster when lights swam in front of me like I was in a morphine dream. And yet, I had never felt safer. As I drove I felt like I was in a capsule from the Jetsons, with a predestined, automatic route home programmed in, and I had no danger of being in an accident because of this. Everything seemed easy, as if we were passengers in a car commercial. Eva was humming and tracing pictures into the steamed glass like a five-year-old. Jimmy was giving me patient, even-toned directions as he held on to Del in the backseat. We were a family. Almost like that song by Sister Sledge. I felt like I was floating. The seatbelt held me down so I wouldn't slip out of the car like a helium balloon let out of a window.

SEVENTEEN

I parked safely at the curb. We were listening to Todd Edwards' "Dancing for Heaven," a bouncy garage track with a beat you could get lost in. Del rejected help from me to get out of the car but accepted Jimmy carrying her into a shabby building like she was a new bride. He ran like there was rain pounding down, but the sky was cold, clear, dry. Eva and I lingered on the front stoop, not wanting the night to end like this. First, we reassured each other that Delilah was fine, then I told her how to plot stars in the sky. She wanted to see the Big Dipper.

"That's a good one," I told her. "My brother, Ravi was the one to show me stars. The Big Dipper's the one that can be seen all year round, but it rotates. In the spring, it's upside down, like it's spilling its contents into the sky. You know, the stars change every season? Well, they don't change, but how we see them best does. The Big Dipper is so easy to find that slaves who travelled the Underground Railroad used it to help orient themselves and map out the northern states to escape to freedom. They even had songs about it, like 'Follow the Drinking Gourd.'"

The stars were scattered studs in the sky, like silver bedazzles punched into a purse. Ravi and I used to wait for nights like these to star gaze. At first, I couldn't orient myself with all the buildings around. But after a while, I saw the Big Dipper as I always did, standing in the middle of an empty street. We were not worried at all we'd be hit by a car. I showed Eva how to plot the North Star from the Big Dipper, and she freaked right the fuck out.

Then we laughed and she said, "You know, this apartment glitters in the daylight."

"Huh?" I looked at the drab, grey building.

"It's a bottle-dash apartment. Instead of the stucco being made from only rock, sparkle stucco has broken bits of glass thrown in. You know, like, brassy beer bottles, long-necked emerald pop bottles, and those old-timey Milk of Magnesia bottles that came in this fantastic purple-blue colour? Sometimes, even white quartz aggregate was added. In the thirties to seventies, the Lower Mainland used to be known as Sparkle Town. Gosh, when the sun hits it, it's really something, you know. Shame you can't see it shine now, Baby."

Eva, who soaked in weird bits of data, always knew how to add magic into the ordinary.

Clasping hands, we covered every topic we could think of. We eventually walked up the stairs of the squat building to the third floor. In Jimmy's place, we sat by the radiator, and I told her about Ravi and all the things we did together. Blue Boy's "Remember Me" was playing. Marlena Shaw's haunting, funky-jazz vocals shot off the thin walls, followed by a repeated scat of *ging, gi-gi-gi-gi-ging*, a kick-ass hip hop baseline, and jumpy house beats. The song referred to the white children that African American women used to raise for little to no pay.

Eva didn't seem bothered that Jimmy had accidentally given Delilah PCP or that now he was taking care of Del in what seemed to be quite an intimate way. Eva was one of those girls who didn't have a jealous bone in her body, either because she was completely self-confident or completely stupid. She told me she used to compete in beauty pageants when she was younger and that she missed the weight of crowns and big tulle dresses. Said it made her feel "so fucking special," like that Radiohead song. But then she became agitated with all the pressure of winning, so she quit. After saying this, Eva ran into Jimmy's room and came out with a seventies denim pantsuit that matched the citrus-green one she had on.

"Vintage fashion is so much more authentic than the ballroom gowns the judges grade you on. Let's be twins today." She said this without irony, because of course she had no idea I was a twin.

I put the jumpsuit on in the bathroom, trying to ignore the mildew on the tiles, the dirty, rusted toilet, and the foggy mirrors. Jimmy lived like a junkie. But even in the clouded mirror, I could see I was transformed.

When I came out, I discovered that Jimmy had the most outrageous collection of vinyl records. Eva said he had way more at his T-shirt shop. Eva and I danced to James Brown and suddenly we weren't in Jimmy's apartment at all, we were in a proper discotheque. Funk was the best music in the world! Jimmy was with Del in his room, which had no windows or furniture. The bed was just a mattress on the floor. But nothing else mattered at that very moment except Eva and me. She asked me if I would live with her and never go away. And I said yes because I could not imagine taking a breath without her from that moment on. We tried to figure out a plan in a frenzy: maybe she would live with me half the time and we'd stay at Jimmy's the rest. I tried to imagine my dad's reaction to me bringing home white-haired Eva to live with us. When she went pee, I went with her. It seemed so natural it was hard to picture that I had done these things alone. All that was important was making sure we could get this amazingly high again. What could matter more than this feeling?

"I should give you one of my crowns, Baby."

"Those pageant things are for white girls."

"You could be white. Why not?" Only on E would something like that be simply words of love.

"But I'm not."

"But we're, like, the same person. Can't I be what you are then?"

Jimmy came out just as Eva was trying to convince me to do more E. When Eva got near the end of a high, she seemed to tack on another train carriage and keep on going, and after that she got stuck on saying one word forever and expected me to understand.

The fucked-up thing was, judging from the last time we'd hung out, I usually still could.

"Del's gone into a bit of a zombie state," he said directly to me, sitting on the worn, brown corduroy couch. A giant cardboard cutout of Ewan McGregor from that *Trainspotting* movie sat in front of the fireplace. It hadn't come out yet, but Jimmy had stolen the prop from the movie theatre. Christmas lights decorating the edge of his paper body, it managed to be strangely festive.

"She's okay, though?"

He plucked a cigarette with his mouth out of a pack, and it hung Popeye-style from his lips. "She's saying weird things, like voices are separating from bodies, and she can hear people talking but can't see 'em. Keeps saying her mother's shouting that she don't believe her. She's experiencing auditory hallucinations," Jimmy added. "But mostly she's okay."

Mostly.

He lit his cigarette and declined the caps Eva was doling out like PEZ candies. He seemed like such an adult right then. Like someone's cool uncle. I also refused. For the time being, my concern about Del outweighed my need to get higher.

"Del's an E girl through and through. She likes her drugs Ibiza grade. But she'll be fuckin' fine. Might even benefit her personality some, being shaken up, right?"

Right.

"But she'll be normal soon?"

Jimmy nodded. "Whatever normal is; we all want to get there so bad." A long pause. And then he continued. "Look, the ER would have done nothing for her. I know way more about this shit than some strait-laced nurse, you hear?"

Jimmy was so reassuring, I must have fallen asleep. When I awoke, it was early morning, but the winter sun hadn't risen. The apartment still glowed from white lights pinned to the perimeter of the floor. Eva was examining them. She was super high. She was always way higher than anyone else. Groggily, my eyes landed on Delilah, who was cuddled up on Jimmy at the other end of the corduroy couch. He was stroking her back but staring at me. The couch was so small I hadn't realized my toes had been jammed under Jimmy's thighs. Del was still in her metallic crop top and white bellbottoms. I was disoriented. How had a night with Del ended up at Jimmy's?

But it would have been stranger if we hadn't ended up here. Somehow, we were always meant to end up at Jimmy's — right from the start.

EIGHTEEN

Jimmy lay Del down and motioned for me to follow him. Even though he was known for creating bright shirts, today he was wearing a very ordinary white T-shirt. It was crispy clean in contrast with the mess of everything else around him. Maybe he put more energy into laundering clothes than taking care of his place. His greaser hair still intact, Jimmy was the handsome fifties hoodlum.

I rubbed my eyes. Early Tuesday morning, the second day of school after the holidays. Not that I was going to go. I walked toward his postage-stamp sized kitchen. Everything looked filthier when he flicked on the light. A dusty coat of oily film covered all the surfaces. I sat on the breakfast stool where a cut-out window opened into the kitchen. All the furniture at Jimmy's was from the Salvation Army. Outdated. One of a kind. The green Formica coffee table in the living room looked oddly futuristic. The vivid green the exact shade of Eva's seventies pantsuit.

Clearly, Jimmy didn't give a fuck about cleaning. The beige carpets were streaked with grey, nothing like my parents' place, which my widower dad still managed to vacuum. It looked like pets lived here but as far as I could see, Eva, pawing the floor and purring, was the only cat. She was quite content exploring things on her own. I was just mildly faded. My high was a warm blanket around me. But Eva had slipped back into an unreachable state, where everything was buzzing and electrical.

"You want breakfast," Jimmy said, without any intonation at all, which was his style. Jimmy talked like he had grown up in a family of white truckers or some shit. "I make a mean scrambled egg with broccoli and cheese."

I could tell this was something he was proud of doing. I watched him pull out white bagels, cheddar cheese, broccoli, eggs. All the kinds of food that white people grew up on. I had grown up on spicy Indian eggs and *paratha*. But when my mom had stopped being a mom, I survived mostly on cereal, Pringles, and macaroni.

"Yeah," I said, finally. Carlie's family had made odd creations for me, but I couldn't think of a time I'd had a real breakfast.

Jimmy was a good ten years older than me, worlds apart from Stick Boi and Takeshi. I felt glossy around him. With his successful T-shirt business, even his unkempt apartment had an allure to it, like it was a conscientious, rebellious jab at mainstream society. *Fuck your stylized show home, bitches. It's 1996 and I fucking live how I want to live.* When I turned to look at Eva, I saw she'd passed out on the floor, fairy lights balled up like a yarn nest next to her.

"Hey, is Eva okay, dude? She did all that E and just passed the fuck out."

"She's fine," he said, patting my hand. "She'll be mad as hell tomorrow she wasted the drugs."

"She did a helluva lot more than I did."

"Girl can do three caps a night easy, trust me."

"Right, you'd know," I answered quickly.

I remembered then how frenzied Eva and I had been at the thought of us separating and going back to our lives as individuals after we bonded. Last night, I had imagined the three of us sharing the space together. Jimmy and his two wives. Eva and I wearing retro pantsuits, paired with her old pageant tiaras. The thought made me smile.

"What's funny?"

"Huh? Nothing," I swallowed my smile, watching him pivot to pull things out of the fridge. "Well ... Eva and I didn't know how we were gonna live apart from each other last night. We connected on another level."

"Ah, well, you can stay here anytime. You're a Sugar Kid now. Got full-time access to ecstasy without having to pay for it, right? And you dress the part. All y'all swapping clothes. Conveniently you guys are the same size. There's gotta be advantages to being Del's side project."

"Oh, hang on a sec. I'm nobody's project."

He chopped broccoli into florets and threw them into a bowl of whisked eggs. There was a craft to his cooking, the way he grated the cheese in another bowl like he was designing a pizza project for kids to make their own pies. I watched him pour olive oil from the spout of a green artisan bottle onto a pan, grind coffee beans while he waited for the pan to heat up. Still, neither Eva nor Del awoke. He put the grounds into a French press and poured hot water over them. The room suddenly smelled like an International House of Pancakes.

He handed me a cup of hot coffee and then poured the eggs into the pan. Gave me an Elvis smile of misaligned teeth. "I think you'll handle Del just fine. You just gotta be careful of her. But she picked you kinda young. How old are you?"

He said this casually, as if he wasn't the one who had straight fucked up Del last night with PCP. As if he hadn't been the one to throw a cap of PCP into a bottle of ecstasy, playing Russian roulette with drugs. I looked down at my borrowed clothes. "I'm seventeen."

"So, we let a kid drive us home last night. Don't your parents worry about you?"

"My mom's dead. My dad isn't around much."

"Oh, sorry …"

"It's whatever," I had already overshared and hated myself for it. The E made it harder to guard myself.

He set a plate of eggs in front of me. "Here ya go, kid," he said with a flourish.

"Thanks." I sank my teeth into the crispy bagel and suddenly remembered England. The bread felt like something I had once eaten before I tossed it to the pigeons in Trafalgar Square.

Just before Ravi had died, he had gone through a stage where he was obsessed with England and toyed around with an accent. He had even told our parents we should visit Buckingham Palace. He'd probably become interested because we had just watched a special on television about royal weddings, binging on reruns of Lady Diana marrying Prince Charles in 1981 and Sarah Ferguson's wedding to Prince Andrew in 1986. In December of 1994, literally right before my mom died, my parents and I went to England to honour his memory even though we never admitted that was why we were going. It was something they had saved for years to do.

On that trip, my mother had looked paler than the white London sky. It was a mild winter, all the locals had said. There was no snow on the ground, and yet I could feel a cold in my bones I'd never felt before. I could see that the grey, purple, and green of the pigeons matched the bags under her eyes. I saw myself squatting down, squealing as the birds leaped around me. It was the E taking me through a tunnel of real memories instead of just remembering myself captured in pictures. Now I could run my fingers over the sharp, nubby fabric on my brown corduroy overalls. My mother had wanted me to wear something more feminine, and we'd fought about it. The lights of Piccadilly Circus advertisements flashed down on my face like they were bits of the rainbow taken from the sky. The colours had spread over my parent's cheekbones and foreheads too — commercials running over their faces in neon patterns.

At the Tower of London, my parents started arguing loudly in Gujarati. My dad wanted to eat Pakistani food, but mom was saying everything was too expensive. She was punishing herself because Ravi was not there. We all knew it. We went to a chip truck instead, swallowing down salty potato chunks that came in newspaper cones. They cost so many pounds that we should have just eaten the Pakistani food to begin with. Ravi would have wanted us to.

I wasn't sitting on Jimmy's stool anymore.

I was looking at the salt shards that glimmered on my fingers like diamonds. Hearing the sharp London accents ringing in my ears, interrupting the silence our family had fallen into. After Dad had shouted about the Pakistani food, his voice had run dry, and Mom took pills and more pills and then she was too sedated to leave the hotel room. My dad decided to storm off and leave my mom to lie like stone. And so, I too left the room to roam the city, a sixteen-year-old alone in a foreign country.

I took the red double decker through the city. Saw a play in a small theatre. Ate a plastic-wrapped strawberry cheesecake for dinner from Waitrose. I kept thinking I would run into my father in the city, that we would speak. Connect. He would buy me an ice cream cone, and we'd link arms and walk through the city. But of course, we never saw each other. Without Ravi, my father and I had no relationship; after all, Ravi had been the one who had fought for me to be included in sports. Girls were supposed to stay inside and colour and play with dolls. Stay quiet. Learn how to cook and clean.

At night, when I returned, Mom was groggy but awake. Dad ordered food from Lahore Treats: *aloo matar ki sabzi, aloo baingan, aloo gobi*. All variations of potato dishes; one with peas, the next with eggplants, and the last with cauliflower. We all ate it like we'd never seen a meal before, with white *naan* that looked like moons with deep black crater burns from the *tandoori* oven, followed by some pink dessert that tasted like rose pudding with cashews and pistachios. That meal had made London worth going to.

I nodded slowly at Jimmy's offer to sprinkle Tabasco on my eggs. The sensation of my legs dangling off the stool made them feel weightless. It felt pleasurable, like when you get on a ride in an amusement park and know for the next while the only important thing is for you to enjoy life, and you know exactly what your reactions are supposed to be.

Worry crept in again. Soon, I wouldn't be high anymore. Soon, I would become a less shiny version of myself. I would lose my perspective on London and of Ravi. I would go back to being a high school student writing immature poetry. Maybe I should have agreed to move in with Eva and keep doing drugs and stay high for as long as I possibly could. Maybe Eva was the half I was missing.

"Earth to Baby, you really zoned out in your food, huh? Must be starved. So, hey, do you got any siblings?"

"I have a twin brother." Shit. I'd told Eva I had a brother, too. Del didn't know about Ravi. No one at school even knew I had a twin brother, and they sure as fuck didn't know his ghost paid me visits. I had only ever told my school councillor that I had visions of Ravi. Ravi, who did not die at ten, but was an ordinary seventeen-year-old, just like me, but with a Camden Town accent and a funny little jean jacket he never took off.

He nodded. "It been hard and shit without your mum?"

"Look, I'm not some fucking orphan in a Brontë novel." The fuck this guy think he was? But then I checked myself. "What I mean is, I manage. Life happens."

Jimmy took in another forkful of eggs, not weirded out at all that I'd dropped a Brontë reference casually while wilding out on his ass.

I remembered studying his book collection earlier, when Eva and I were dancing on E. He had two sideway-stacked, yellow milk crates filled with novels by Vonnegut, Hinton, Bukowski, Hemingway. All typical for a trendy white guy, and all male authors, except the one, who'd acted as if she was a man anyway. I was trembling slightly now, thinking of school and falling behind on every class. Well, except for English, because I had already done all the pre-req readings for that class. At this rate, I wasn't going to graduate on time.

"Should I be worried, kid?" he said. "I just gave you Class A drugs tonight, and seeing you in the day, youse getting younger by the minute. Yer hands ..."

I looked down to see my hands shaking erratically. Fuck, fuck, *fuck*. "Dude, I have low blood sugar is all. I'll be good once I eat. Don't forget," I said evenly, "I was the one who drove you guys here."

"Right. So, hey, your bro a young raver, too? We should all kick it sometime."

"He lives in London."

"No shit."

"Yeah. He made us all go there on a trip a little more than a year ago? Just before my mom died." I didn't add how the vacation had been a valve for her to release Ravi and give up on life herself. "Then he ended up staying behind with relatives and applying to do some courses for — for school. He freaking loves it there; even has an accent now."

Once I started saying all this, it felt like the truth. It was good to talk about Ravi and present him to Jimmy as I experienced him. My hands even stilled some. I just had to make sure Jimmy never met my skater friends. That would be an easy thing to do, I reassured myself, taking a sip of coffee. To my teenage tastebuds it tasted like bitter adulthood. I'd just keep my worlds separate.

"Pretty cool raves in England I bet."

"They have better drum and bass down there," I offered, remembering myself in that time when my mother was still alive, wandering all over London unescorted, hearing the lyrics "this is the sound of London" beat-mixed with every genre of electronica imaginable, filtering through all the outdoor markets. Those alarming, rhythmic, fast-paced drumbeats had awakened something in me that I was only now beginning to explore. All the hard-faced punks with their spiked mohawks that had ruled the eighties, just like Red from the first Gastown rave I'd been to, hawking merchandise to the new generation of pink-haired techno-heads. Mesh camo dresses for sale hanging off a line like fish on strings.

A year ago, I wouldn't have thought of myself as the type of person to give in to face glitter. I had thought I was more like my mother, unwilling to enjoy life because of what happened to Ravi, content to skate nights away, head down under my low-crown hat. But I enjoyed feeling like I was a part of a movement. I wished I would have seen London's underground rave scene. Ravi and I could have disappeared for good.

"Bristol's the birthplace of trip hop," he said. "Fucking love Portishead, Tricky, and Massive Attack. I got somma their records."

"Fatboy Slim's from England, too, right? I heard his song 'Santa Cruz' tonight and straight lost my mind."

"Yeah," he nodded. "Propellerheads also. They're from Bath, and the track that blew me away tonight was 'Take California.' That was a demo vinyl, too. But hey," he fixed me with an empathetic look, "must be tough losing yer mum, though, huh."

"What? Look, I don't, like, obsess every minute over her death."

"It's just that I can sort of relate, you know?" Jimmy's eyebrows were knitted together. "Baby, if you ever knew what happened to me ..."

"I like being part of this whole scene, you know?" I said quickly before he could share his sob story with me. I wasn't going to go deeper just because we had done some E.

"PLUR sounded corny to me when I first heard it," he reminisced. "Peace, love, unity, respect. But now I've seen abandoned warehouses turn into parties literally outta nowhere. One guy calls another, we steal electricity, someone has decks, some buddy of theirs has speakers, and bam!" He slammed the counter with his hand. "We got a house party going on. If you're at the right place at the right time, you can see one of the best DJs in the world for free and someone will gift you a cap of E just because. For me, it's that first feeling when you hear deep bass, you know? No matter you've heard that track a thousand times. That's the magic that keeps me goin'." He paused, taking a sip of his coffee. "It's really why I opt for the smaller parties, nowadays. One time, there was this badass party near my shop, so I ducked out to grab somma my primo merchandise and handed it out to the diehards still left there, you know? So we could all remember that night and shit."

I grabbed my coffee mug with both hands so I could feel the warmth. "I get it. You feel like there's this thing you're contributing to."

"Totally." He fiddled with a remote control and aimed it at a CD player sitting next to his record player. "Missing" by Everything but the Girl came on. The undertone of drum and bass in the song filled the dank apartment. It was hard not to think about Ravi when I heard the familiar opening lyrics about the singer stepping off a train, looking for someone who didn't live at the address anymore.

I couldn't help but gain some respect for Jimmy that night. He was the only adult in my world who treated me like an equal.

PART 2

SPRING 1996

NINETEEN

For much of January, February, and even March, Del had taken over my world to the point that I didn't even have time to write in my journal. The months flew by, and raving became my new normal. I was fully swept into the underground scene of the club nights Del had told me about in Subway that first night we met. It was spring now. In the day, Ravi and I would walk under the white, pink, and peach cherry blossoms that had bloomed into little frosted cakes. In the night, Del and I would rave. Doing E seemed as regular as drinking morning tea. I still had to go to school to hand things in. I didn't play up my mom's death, after all it had happened over a year ago, but I accepted when teachers empathized and pardoned me for missing classes.

Del had bought me these caffeine pills called Wake-Ups. The bottle came embellished with a rooster logo. If we had partied all night, sometimes I'd pop a few and go straight to school. Other times, I didn't even bother pretending I'd go — we'd sleep until three or four in the afternoon, hiding from her roommates. Those days, I'd wake up feeling dry, not really wanting to do anything more than lounge around eating Count Chocula cereal while Del had non-fat yogurt and fruit. Those days, I felt most rotten about everything.

Del was a mystery I was slowly unwrapping. She lived in an apartment near Commercial Drive with two men: Kwasi and Raz. Kwasi was from Ghana; he was studying to be a doctor and cooked things for us like okra stew and boiled yams. He had black horn-rimmed glasses, always wore docker pants with shirts tucked in properly, and sported a neatly arranged head of short dread twists. Raz, a white guy with ginger-coloured long dreads, was a new-age rapper of sorts. Kwasi, Del, and Raz worked at a smoothie bar on Commercial, where they'd all met. It was like living in a much cooler rendition of the television show *Friends,* but instead of a group of friends who had preppy lifestyles that revolved around a coffeeshop, Raz and Kwasi were leftist socialists who smoked pot and listened to revolutionary music.

As a result of them all working in the same smoothie cooperative, there was always an abundance of pineapples, watermelons, and mangoes in the house. The vibe was completed with colourful art and tropical wallpaper, making it believable that a parrot might fly out of a closet at any time. Kwasi liked living things. Clusters of violet-blue hydrangea flowers sat on the table. Bananas hung from wooden holders. Nectarines and plums were stacked on three-level glass platters. And avocados hung high in the air, placed in wired, black baskets that extended from the ceiling. Kwasi also tended to large potted plants. There were zebra plants, Areca palms with big heads of purple leaves that looked like cheerleading pompoms, fiddle-leaf figs, and snake plants.

In the backyard of their rented space, Kwasi was experimenting with growing banana plants and sugar cane. Raz had given up telling him the Vancouver climate wasn't right for it. There were two bedrooms in the first-floor apartment, and Raz, not surprisingly, was the one who ended up with the couch as his bedroom. He was a regular fixture there, laid out, bobbing his head to Kwasi's Bob Marley album. He always had a joint between his lips, and I was now familiar with his signature stoner greeting, "Heyyyyy guys, whaaaass happening?"

It was April and we were eating papaya that Kwasi had diced into pink cubes, which thoroughly matched the salmon sunset we were watching, when Kwasi pointed out that America combining religion into politics during the McCarthy era was the best move ever for them to become a superpower.

"Making communism godless," Kwasi said, pinching the communal doobie between his fingers, "was a smart play. God wants capitalism. Pitch the idea that people should live in hierarchical stratification because the big guy in the sky wants it. Make communism evil so that people divorce the idea it stands for equality." Kwasi had the habit of speaking like he was performing slam poetry. His voice was deep but had a bit of a kick to it, like it was laced with caffeine.

"But don't communists want to abolish churches? That sounds pretty godless to me," Del said.

"I mean, come on Del, churches are where bad ideas grow and then a whole community of people follow those horrible ideas," Raz answered in his raspy stoner voice. "Haven't you ever read *The Crucible*?"

"Best play in the handbook is when Eisenhower put 'In God We Trust' on dollar bills, man. Make money itself hold religious value. Make the money sacred but also individualistic. Make people worship the money. Make it feel right for people to justify that those who have more money earned it the right way, and those who have less are just lazy-ass mothafuckers," Kwasi followed up in his Ghanaian accent.

"Kwasi, dude man, you're beginning to sound like Malcolm X, but like a spoken word version. You need a sick beat to accompany you, man," said Raz, eyes bloodshot, looking dazed. "Lemme hook you up, bro. Come to the café and preach that shit …"

We were listening to D'Angelo's *Brown Sugar,* because even though we listened to other stuff (Aaliyah, Erykah Badu, Sade), this was the album Raz always came back to.

"I might be high as fuck," I said, "but don't you guys think the World Cup is a metaphor for the free market? Teams play each other and then act like its sheer talent that makes them win. When you think about it, participating just legitimizes years of colonial theft by making it seem like everyone really is on an equal playing field. Cheering for a team distracts people from realizing that while we are struggling to pay rent, rich people are buying and hoarding property, like the world is one big, fat Monopoly board."

"Far out, man. World Cup — a metaphor for capitalism, complete with commercial breaks," Raz said. "They play along because people have fucking egos, that's why. People like to think they deserve what they earn, man, when no one really does. They don't look at the circumstances of how people end up where they do," Raz added. "Schools will educate you by brushing over the history of colonialism and then blast you right after with the national anthem. We say we are sorry for what we did, but then it's still all 'Oh Canada, our home and native land.'"

"But people support nationalism because of the dream, you see," Kwasi said.

"What fucking dream, Kwasi?" Del interrupted.

Kwasi paused, calmly handing me a new bowl of cut pears. The fork in the bowl, nicked from Earls restaurant, had an "e" inscribed on the handle. Kwasi didn't know this, but Del and some of the other Sugar Kids had begun pocketing cutlery after brunching, declaring the "e" an homage to ecstasy.

"The dream takes different shapes. It can be dreaming of being the next rap star. Dreaming of owning a mansion and ten cars. Even dreaming of winning the lottery. This will be enough for people to vote for a political party that doesn't represent their class every single time — that's the power of having the chance to belong to something you aren't part of. Even in Ghana, everybody loves the 'rags to riches' tale, man. What nobody thinks of is the people stuck in rags while you make it to riches. Love your country, your country will love you, and help you achieve the dream. What lies."

"This guy needs to come to Urban Slam Jam," Raz said, mystified.

"Oh, gimme a break, Raz," Del erupted, finally fed up. "You really think Kwasi is some kind of performance art messiah? He's gonna be a fucking doctor. He's gonna be living 'the dream' when he finishes medical school. He's gonna be sworn in as a Canadian. See if you wanna be a goddamn socialist when you're making more than the rest of us, 'kay Kwasi? Let us know who you vote for then, mm'kay? Oh, and hey," she added, standing up and pointing a finger at them, "I'll be watching you two fools like hawks around World Cup, because no doubt Kwasi will be cheering on Ghana."

"Actually, Del, Ghana hasn't participated in the World Cup, but you never know for the future," Raz said, deadpan.

"Whatever, I'll bet you anything he has a Ghana shirt in his closet," she said, crossing her arms over her chest as she left.

I looked over at Kwasi for a reaction. I expected Kwasi to be offended but he shrugged and handed Del's pears to Raz, who shrugged back and dumped her portion into his. I, finding myself also shrugging, stood up with my bowl, following Del into her room. Raz turned up D'Angelo's *Brown Sugar* as we left, and I wondered how he couldn't get tired of the same album. I also wondered how he couldn't be sick of Del.

I was starting to fit better into her life than she did.

TWENTY

"Raz is fucking white anyway," Del said, once we were in her room.

Picturing his cinnamon-coloured dreads, I couldn't help snickering. Raz's "Blackcent" was always an easy thing to laugh at once you started. Raz had none of Stick Boi's punk gumption to make it sound legit.

"Those guys are so annoying. I'm gonna have to move out," she said.

For all Del's complaining about her roommates, she was the one who had landed the master bedroom. Del's room reminded me of a pint-sized vintage shop. Coloured wigs sat delicately perched on foam heads with fully made-up faces she'd painted and glued lashes to. Bright clothing from all eras hung on a metal garment rack. Lemon-yellow bellbottoms, pea-green sixties shifts. With turntables and a crate full of wicked house records, Del both knew her music and dabbled in DJing. When Carlie's parents ran dry it had been best to come back when the well was filled again, but Del didn't have parents; I never had to leave.

She put on Moby's "God Moving Over the Face of the Waters" from his *Everything Is Wrong* album. The emotional, cinematic composition washed over the room.

Nobody had asked me, but it was tempting for me to drop out of school, sling smoothies, and move in permanently. Maybe I'd regret that. I had a feeling Del hated that Kwasi was making something of himself when she was just a smoothie slinger. Raz, however, considered himself an inner-city poet. He performed while people ate Jamaican patties and drank black coffee at Café Deux Soleils on Commercial. He'd stay for the all-night reggae parties, one of the only accepted white guys in a crowd of Black people. Sometimes, if we were bored, we'd join him there at 3:00 a.m. I had learned some Jamaican dancehall moves that were pretty bad ass. As much as Del couldn't stand Raz, she still liked partying with him.

I walked over to her cardigans and ran one hand over a crocheted grandma-looking yellow sweater with tiny pearl buttons, still clutching my fruit bowl in the other. On Del, the sweater looked smoking hot, like she was one of Jack Tripper's girlfriends from *Three's Company*. I walked by to examine her sparkly platform shoes placed on bookshelves.

"D'ya think," she said, unwrapping a red lollipop, "if you made a pass for Jimmy, he'd go for it?" She stuck out her tongue ring at me and ran the tip of it around the red ball.

I tried to look impassive. With Delilah it was important not to betray emotion. Once, when we were high, she had tried to set me up with a DJ whose mother was in the fashion industry, claiming I'd get Chanel clothing handed down to me, even though Chanel was not practical rave wear. Del seemed to think we could rock couture pink sweaters bordered in black knit at parties and turn it into a trend. If I opposed her plans, she'd ditch me for hours.

Del didn't know that when I was wandering through the soggy plains in Chilliwack, or Abbotsford, or Mission, I finally felt free. Now that it was spring, we had been venturing into the territory of outdoor raving. I would roam behind the tents where all the equipment and trucks were and walk into the dressing rooms in the trailers. I felt like a kid left free to explore the back end of a carnival where you get to see how they make all the magic happen by looking at the power cords and tools. Once, as I was rifling through a famous DJ's makeup box left inside a trailer, a girl came on board to tell me someone had found a dead body in the fields; an older man had overdosed and was lying in the long grass, his corpse blue. Another time, alone in an RV filled with thousands of dollars of unsupervised DJ equipment, I got to witness a spectacular car fire that looked like brilliant fireworks from a distance. A part of me always hoped I'd run into Ravi hanging out back there, as a carnie loading equipment. Ravi, as a supernatural being, could live in London and still show up in random places at random times. But Ravi never showed up at raves. He had been straightforward with me about the drugs affecting his ability to visit me, and yet, I never stopped looking.

Del was a person so intense with her needs you needed a break sometimes, and E made her worse. But today, we'd only had some of Kwasi's ganja. She was mellow, looking like a nymph on her bed, pigtails of long, honey-coloured hair hanging in front of her rainbow tube dress.

"I dunno," I said. Some of my jade pear slices were upended so their flesh was showing, and it struck me that the Asian pears looked like they could almost have the same texture as human skin. I was also busy pretending I had never thought of Jimmy, even for a second, in such a way.

"You think if he went for it," she popped the lolly in her mouth, pushing it against one side of her inner cheek so it formed a pornographic lump, "that it'd be enough to break Eva and him up? She's such a space cadet, Baby. Come to think of it, you and Eva, y'all kinda remind me of each other. You're also pretty out of it sometimes. Not saying that's a bad thing," she twirled the stick in her mouth, adjusting her words to the scrunching of my facial expressions. "I mean, Jimmy might find you attractive in the way he finds her attractive. I betcha Eva wouldn't even care."

"What d'ya mean I'm out of it?"

"Like, you zone out. Sometimes I see you mumbling to no one, and you shake."

"She might care," I ventured, skipping over her insult. I didn't want to talk about my visions of Ravi or my involuntary shaking. I sank onto a white shag chair, pear bowl in hand. "Why don't you make a move for him seeing as you miss him so much?"

"No," she moaned, falling to her belly and kicking her legs up behind her. We could have been two girls from the fifties at a sleepover talking about our crushes — if not for the bottle of ecstasy I knew was in Del's underwear drawer. "I feel like if I make the first move, he won't appreciate me."

I glanced at the psychedelic poster on her wall, entirely black save for the multicoloured wires running every which way. Delilah and I had done a lot of experimenting as of late; we'd tried hippie flipping — eating mushrooms after the E was wearing down. Del and I both had watched as the outdoor spring rave we were at had turned into a different country in the new dawn of light, hallucinating people in ponchos handing kids bananas out of trucks as tumbleweeds rolled by. Del hit another car in the parking lot that day. Both her and the other driver jumped out and, seeing there was no damage, they hugged and wished each other the best day in the world. The grounds we had danced on the night before, now, in the sunlight, were stamped with flyers for upcoming raves. Girls with animal-ear hats holding lunch boxes still moved in the fields, and even though their glow sticks didn't work anymore, everything seemed like it still shone. Sometimes I found myself wondering where all those raver girls went afterward. But when we drove off from a night of partying, I always felt like every single fucking thing was perfect. That Del was perfect, too.

"Do you really want me to try?" I asked carefully, remembering how she'd discovered me in Burger King at my lowest. Del was so seductive when she wanted to be. Seeing if Jimmy would try to make a pass at me was much more attractive than dating some raver so Del could score free Elizabeth Arden cosmetics.

"I don't fucking know." Her lips were bright red, like the mouth from *The Rocky Horror Picture Show*. "Look, Baby, sometimes I want him back all to myself, and other times I'm thankful I got away. That's what it's like with Jimmy."

I closed my eyes and settled into the soft fur of the chair, trying to imagine what I'd never experienced.

TWENTY-ONE

It was with the excuse of wanting to help Del that a few days later, when the cherry blossoms had floated off the trees and turned into scattered wedding confetti, I found myself taking the bus to Jimmy's store. A well-known spot, it was off Main and Broadway. Halfway there, I convinced myself that maybe I wanted a new T-shirt, something not snagged from a thrift shop.

Jimmy's shop was a seventies surf boutique. A tiki bar in someone's old rec room. Wooden rafters crossed the high ceiling, supporting one surfboard hitched up in the centre. A few retired, very used boards were propped on the floor. Folded shirts were featured on tables skirted in Hawaiian cloth and racks of shirts hung on wooden hangers, like leftover wetsuits. There were a few potted tropical plants, well-placed surf stickers scattered on yellow walls, and an inflatable life-saving ring planted behind the register. The store smelled of incense — a lot of stores did — but nothing like my mom's Indian sticks. This was white people's incense, a less religiously stifling scent, something that smelled of fresh rain, coconuts, pineapples, and a Sarah McLachlan song, all at the same time.

Jimmy was the only one there. He was putting on a vinyl. Prince's "When Doves Cry" started playing.

"Hey Baby," he said, motioning me over. He was standing next to some colourful pictures of people surfing in Tofino in the seventies. The waves were more fantastic than I had ever seen them in real life. Slate blue triangles with tips of icy white, about to spill over into foaming crests. An oyster glaze seemed to coat photographs from that period. The pictures were snapped to capture motion, and I half expected them to come alive if I shook them from side to side. There were golden boys riding boards, but the only way to distinguish one from the other was the shorts they were wearing, yellow as bananas or pink as milkshakes. White boys with white friends.

"This here's my dad," Jimmy explained in his sandpaper voice, nodding his dimpled chin at the photo. Seeing as I didn't know which guy he was referring to, he clarified by pointing to a boy with orange shorts as bright as the innards of an exotic fruit. "Used to be a pro surfer. Had a house in Tofino too, once upon a fuckin' time. Dad used to travel the world. Eventually settled in LA and ended up with some model named Stephania. He left Mom and me the Tofino house."

"No kidding." Lately, I never felt Indian. I was simply a skater girl who raved. But Jimmy's shop was clearly full of someone else's past and culture, not mine. My father's beach experience would have had nothing to do with surfers back then and would only be complete with masala chai in his hand and perhaps an ornate kite to fly against a tie-dye sky, sponged pink, green, blue, and yellow.

"Sounds like the dude did well for himself but he died bankrupt," Jimmy continued, shrugging. "Actually, my mom's new husband bought me this shop. Believe it or not."

"Interesting," I said, which sounded like the wrong choice of word. But what else could I have said? *That sounds tragic? What a twist of fate?* I hadn't asked for any of this information but here it was and so much of it. I needed something to do with my hands, especially in case I started shaking, so I put down my skateboard and reached to tug at my hair. It had grown out. The blue in my hair looked like the shade of worn denim, and I had black roots now. In front of Jimmy, I felt inexperienced. Without Del instructing me on how to act, I was left fumbling.

"What brings ya here, kid?" I didn't have a chance to answer because he kept going. "The model my dad married got him into drugs and disco." He shook cigarettes out from his pack, pulling the tallest one out with his mouth, like he was an actor in a black-and-white film. "Stephania," he spat out, like her name was a poisonous plant, "and my dad both overdosed on a bad batch of smack."

"What? Oh my god. I'm so sorry."

Jimmy ignored this. "Want one?" He pointed to his mouth. He was wearing a leather bomber jacket indoors. On a warm April day. But still he looked fresh and clean, like an airplane pilot from an American war film or some shit.

"No. Thanks."

He used a lighter painted with dice and flames. "Right. So, my dad. World class surfer. Got some of his boards in here. Ones that won him things and shit."

"Cool. You surf, too?"

"Nah." He took a puff and blew smoke at the ceiling. "I sell fucking T-shirts is what I do. Say, I'm 'bout to close up shop."

"Oh. I just stopped to say hi." I grabbed my board. "I'll be on my way."

"Nah, why? Wanna go grab some grub? There's a decent diner on Granville. The Templeton? What d'ya think?"

We took a bus to get to the diner. The place, with walls painted retro orange and pastel yellow, had a checkerboard floor made of black and white squares. There was a small jukebox on every table and the brown, retro leatherette booths were all wedged to one side of the narrow diner, like they had spilled over and gotten stuck there. Jimmy ordered two vanilla shakes and two all-day breakfast specials with hash browns, which came diced and home cooked with rosemary. It smelled like someone's childhood — just not mine. It was nice being ordered for without having to think. He stretched his legs out under the table, and I enjoyed knowing he was comfortable taking my area up. I was grateful to eat something filling for once.

With Jimmy it was like I was a kid and a grown up at the same time, a woman on a date and a child getting a pony ride. It was such a mix of feelings I couldn't separate the two. I was in my school clothes. No frills, gimmicks, or fake lashes — just me and my shoplifted anime

T-shirt with five-dollar jeans. "Mary Jane's Last Dance" by Tom Petty was playing. All harmonicas and white folk music. All Jimmy.

Jimmy took out another cigarette and tapped it on the table. "How's your brother and stuff?"

"Fine," I said, not betraying emotion at his referring to my twin brother as someone alive and not a ghost that visited me. The song ended. He dropped a quarter in the jukebox and selected Elvis's "Blue Christmas" even though it was spring.

He nodded. "I used to have a brother. Jeffrey. He was younger 'en me by ten years." He fished out his flame lighter and set it on the table.

"Used to?"

"Yeah," he nodded. "When my dad left my mom for Stephania, he asked if Jeffrey could come see him. Just for a 'wee visit.' That's what Dad told Mom. 'I'll have him back before Christmas.' I was fifteen and didn't wanna leave my friends to go visit my dipshit dad. My dad was a big shot by then. Surfing champion and all. But I could see right through his bullshit. The fucker flew out here to pick Jeffrey up so he wouldn't have to fly alone. You wanna pie or somethin'?"

"No," I said, a little worried about what everything cost. "I'm good."

"Stephania and him partied a lot. They had a big place with a pool. You know, the kinda set up with a living room that has a sliding door opening onto a deck with a pool? Just like in *Casino* ... ever see that movie?"

I shook my head.

"Jeffrey was unsupervised a lot. He was, what, five years old? Anyway, he drowned in the pool at two in the afternoon. Stephania and Dad were in their rooms, wasted on smack. It was very Hollywood of them. No one could revive either of 'em, so I dunno if they overdosed before my brother died or after. Who knows?"

"Oh my god!" I had to stop my hand from flying to cover my open mouth.

"Yeah," he said. "Your reaction 'bout sums it up." He took a sip of his shake. "Dad had so many debts, and us selling his fucking seventies Barbie-and-Ken dream home didn't begin to even cover it."

"Your poor mom."

"She never recovered."

"What's she like?" I asked, thinking of my own mother.

"I dunno." Jimmy laughed awkwardly. "She smells like White Diamonds perfume and Tanqueray gin first thing in the morning." He gave me a sad smile. "Like some lyrics out of a fucking song. She married some rando stockbroker dude who made me learn about business and shit. When my dad overdosed, my stepdad really picked up the pieces. Went to Cali even, figured out all the legal stuff so my mom and I wouldn't have to."

"That's unbelievable."

"Still hate the guy. For no other reason except I never wanted him to be in my life. My mom on the other hand," he continued smoothly, "is a functional drunk who plays bingo every Saturday night. She's a disaster at Christmas. Tries to make weird foods she swears were Jeffrey's favourites, like macaroni pot pie."

"That reminds me of my friend Carlie's mom. She makes wild food when she gets wasted too, but everything tastes good."

"Yeah, none of my mom's food is edible." Jimmy pulled his legs back closer to his side and was now tapping his foot on the chessboard floor outside our booth. He had on alligator-green Vans. The suede looked like damp moss. "She's stuck in the last decade. Kinda got frozen in a 'Time After Time' way after Jeffrey died, you know? Loves Cyndi Lauper. Makes Jell-O desserts that look like they came out of a Dr. Seuss book. Still has this hair ..." he gestured with his hands. "She's a total rock chick. Diehard Whitesnake and Def Leppard groupie. And god, she likes to make eggs in a pie."

"Eggs in pie?"

"Quiche," he clarified. "She thinks making quiche somehow makes her a classy person."

"Yo, my friend Carlie's mom likes that kind of stuff too. One time, she made soup and stuck it into a carved-out loaf of boule bread and said people ate this kind of food in sophisticated joints. And the two words don't even go together, right?"

We were both laughing pretty hard now. "Does your friend's mom have the hair, too?"

"Yes," I said, realizing for the first time it was true. "It's crunchy in the front like potato chips. But the back is all soft and wavy."

"Hard and soft. Yeah, people can get really stuck in the past."

"True." I didn't mention that he seemed this way too, with his eclectic taste in vintage clothing and music.

"You're a lotta fun, ya know that? Hey, ya wanna take a ride picking out somethin' on the jukebox? See what kind of stuff they have in this 'sophisticated joint'?"

"I should go," I said.

"Listen, Baby, don't tell anyone about Jeffrey. Del and Eva, they don't know. I guess, listening to this old Elvis song, everythin' just came spilling out."

"Sure," I said. I got that more than he knew. "Del must be special to you. Like Eva?"

"Special? Me and Delilah?" He laughed and then seeing I was serious, shook his head. "No. That's over. Del's got a whole lotta issues she hasn't worked out yet."

"Issues?"

"Some fucked-up things happened to her when she was a kid, and it's made her a very hard person to be with. I don't know much, but Del thinks that once people get what they want from her, they'll disappear. That's why it was so important for me to stay friends with her after we broke up. Del plays a lotta fucking head games. I ain't got time for that shit, know what I mean?"

I nodded. "Look, if I had to choose, I'd pick George Michael's 'Faith.'" I pointed at the jukebox.

"That's a solid choice."

"Yeah, my brother and I loved that song when we were kids." I realized how stupid that sounded because he still thought of me as a kid. "We used to charge our parents for tickets to come watch us butcher Boyz-n-the-Hood by Eazy-E, singing along while we skipped rope. Ten cents cover price. We won all the school talent shows, though. Even sold homemade lottery tickets at school with a tab of paper covering the winnings and kids had to peel them back to see how much they won; everyone was obsessed with them."

"Y'all were really running things. Alls I did as a kid was play with Matchbox cars. Hey," he said, when he saw me rummaging through my backpack, "I got the bill."

My hand glided over my yellow leather journal tucked at the bottom. Fishing into the pages, I thumbed over the locket Takeshi had given me, the one Del had made me take off at that fancy fashion-show rave we'd gone to. I pushed them both back down.

"You sure?"

"'Course."

"Thanks," I said as lightheartedly and casually as I could so things couldn't mean more than they should.

"No problem, kid."

I saw him flick through the selections on the jukebox and drop another quarter in for "Speak Low" by Billie Holiday. The song gave me tingles. He gave me a half smile so I could just make out some of his mismatched teeth. None of the boys at my school even knew who Billie Holiday was.

He stayed behind to light his smoke. I felt heavier when the diner doors closed behind me. Go digging places, you might find things you shouldn't. And I had stumbled upon five-year-old Jeffrey. Now I had the weight of Jimmy's secrets to carry along with my own.

TWENTY-TWO

I stored Jimmy's secrets in my journal like coins in a swear jar. Del and I were going out all the time, hitting up raves that were held in military bases, sugar refineries, old factories, airport hangars, abandoned-but-once-very-fancy department stores, mills, and beer distilleries. Heritage buildings forgotten in modern times, revered only by ravers. The only reason Del and I had found ourselves smoking crystal meth from a lightbulb at a house party was because we'd finally run out of places to go. And ecstasy.

Three weeks back, she'd taken me to restock her drugs. It all started at 4:00 a.m., when rifling through her underwear drawer, she'd discovered that we'd taken the last of the E. After a 7-Eleven run, where she got us a couple of sad salads instead of the Coke Slurpee and Cheezies that I really wanted, we drove down the dark Vancouver streets in our pajamas. Apparently, the guy that had the E stash lived in a house with a southern porch off some street in East Van.

From the outside, the E house seemed placidly suburban — there was even a garden with fairies. And someone was growing things; I could smell something pungent and earthy, maybe root vegetables and cabbage. There were old strawberry vines, and a homemade hothouse. But then you got inside, and the place was two white guys sitting around a table piled with a huge mountain of white powder, as if someone had poured a ten-pound bag of flour. One of the guys asked me if I knew the address of the house, and I said, "No," and he said, "Good, you'll be a dead girl if you say shit," and they all went back to bobbing their heads to the music.

I had never seen either of the guys at raves before. One had hair so yellow it could light up a room, and the other one had a Goan-style shirt and greasy hair. They looked like they would listen to trance music or Gregorian chants, but Mark Farina's *Mushroom Jazz* was playing in the background. A jazzy vocalist peppered the beats. Trumpet. Smooth house beat. Like this was an upscale bar and not at all some shady-ass drug den.

Del and I had gone to see Mark Farina play recently. I'd worn a long-sleeved, silver-sequined romper and the pink wig we'd stolen the first night we met, and Del had worn a gold flapper dress beaded in geometric patterns with her Dolly Parton hair. Like we were jazz singers. No one carded us when we walked into the bar, and we danced with people who had real jobs and things to worry about like mortgages, investments, and cars. We drank dry Prosecco and ten-dollar dirty martinis the whole night. It was the cleanest high I'd ever had, even though we'd only split a cap of E. Maybe it was the sophistication of the crowd. Us acting like adults had made us feel like we were the type of people to care about wine and cheese pairings, and the act permeated our skin and gave us a killer buzz. That night, I felt like we could have gone off and married stockbrokers and started new lives.

But at the trap house, chilling out to the same dope music, the two men told Del to go up to a room and get the drugs they'd already capped and counted. They barely looked at us. I wondered if they had guns. We wound our way up an oak staircase. It began to look evident that someone's grandmother had indeed lived here at some time, judging from the framed watercolour art and crochet handiwork.

In the corner bedroom was an air mattress on the floor. Cigarette butts were scrunched in empty water glasses. An antique vanity dresser was lined with variously coloured perfumes with squeeze bulb bottles. Next to them, on the stained dresser, a pile of naked pills. Del didn't count, she just slid the pills into an empty makeup bag with the side of her bare palm. We left as quickly as we had come. Even if I wanted to, I'd never remember the street the house was on. I only could tell you it was somewhere in East Vancouver that had a pavilion to raise cherry tomatoes and a hobbit's garden. With a collection of vintage perfume bottles.

And then the drugs we had scored that night were gone. And those guys were apparently in India now. Not that I'd ever want to go back to that sketchy house. This is how we ended up saying yes to smoking crystal from a tampered lightbulb at a suburban house party in the middle of Maple Ridge. It was a city far enough from Vancouver that it made you feel like you were in another world; the houses were all super douchey, huge double-garage-type affairs with steeped roofs mimicking the design of Swiss Alps ski resorts. Maple Ridge allowed people who couldn't afford housing in Vancouver to buy big-ass cookie-cutter places with wall-to-wall carpeting and feel like they still made it and shit.

The crystal hadn't done much for me. I could tell right away it wasn't my drug of choice. But it was fun for talking at length about things if you had someone to chat with. The kids hosting the party had rich parents away on vacation, the classic eighties movie trope, and Del and I decided they were try-hard posers that would never understand us. We both had dressed like sixties go-go girls in knee-high boots (hers, white vinyl and mine, silver glittery). These kids from Maple Ridge, however, wore shopping mall clothes from stores that tried to be alternative but were really all copycats of one another. They were rich enough to have hobbies like pointe ballet or ice hockey instead of having to learn how to skateboard on their own because their parents had forgotten they existed. The higher they got, the more they represented things I had outgrown — grunge, plaid shirts, beer. They reminded me of Carlie and her brother, except with college funds.

One of the guys claimed to know Bryce, the bouncer I'd met with Del. He was trying so hard to be cool with Del that he found her a hook-up for meth and paid for the whole thing himself. But my hopes that the party would be filled with Bryce-types who listened to underground hip hop had been dashed when I quickly realized the edgiest music played was Beastie Boys. A bunch of white boys lip-synched to it all night like we were in a Korean karaoke bar. Sure, Takeshi and Stick Boi and I had our fun with Beastie Boys, but these people made every song sound like a nursery rhyme.

Del had brought a CD with her, *The Score* by Fugees. Del always had a mini party in her fun-fur bag: makeup, music, and usually drugs. After we locked ourselves up in one of the bedrooms, Del popped it into the CD player of the guy she was now calling Douche One. Everyone else at the party had subsequent numbers: Douche Two, Three, and so forth. Douche Seven was outside on the lawn setting up mini golf in the dark, and you could hear hoarse laughter coming in through the windows mixed with "No Sleep Till Brooklyn." But inside, we had created the atmosphere we had at Raz and Kwasi's, except with Lauryn Hill, Pras, and Wyclef Jean.

"How's school and all that?" Del asked, falling onto Douche One's bed as if she lived here. Sports trophies lined the shelves. Earlier, she'd put a few of the gymnastics medals around her neck.

"It's fine, I guess," I said from the carpeted floor. Takeshi and Stick Boi had been avoiding me. They felt scorned, and I wasn't sure how I felt about babysitting them on E all night. Carlie had made friends with a peppier bunch of girls; they were forever talking about lightening hair, gossiping about crushes, and listening to Britpop bands. There was a head girl, someone with a name starting with an M. They all had frosty hair and frosty lips. The Frosty Five, I liked to think of them.

I missed watching *The Breakfast Club* and *Pretty in Pink* with Carlie, believing we were above the mainstream of high school, but I also realized I had given her no choice but to join this group. She — with her hair dyed a rich shade of grape-flavoured cough syrup, her hooped nose ring, and her men's plaid shirts from Army & Navy — looked out of place with these honey-haired skinnies she had befriended. I had known enough not to interrupt her while she was in the process of being initiated. She still wore her Radiohead shirt though, and I admired that she had kept something of what we had liked together.

"High school for me was awful," Del was saying when I tuned back in. "I wanted to be a nurse. Did I tell you that before?" She moved the frosted lightbulb and hollowed-out pen tube away from herself on the bed.

"No," I said, grinding my teeth. I thought this was strictly an E habit, but it was turning out to be a crystal one, too. Lately I always clenched my mouth. Even in my sleep.

"I was in all the honours classes and stuff. Now I work in a fucking smoothie bar with a bunch of potheads and immigrants. Sorry, that made me sound racist. I'm not. I'm half Chinese."

I often forgot she was; I had to strain to see it. I think she forgot too, and that's why she was saying it now. It was her forever excuse to be a dick and get away with it. She flicked back her long light-brown hair and looked at me.

"Right," I said, knowing very well she thought immigrants were untrustworthy leeches. One time, she had accused Kwasi of shorting on the rent, and I had watched red-faced as he patiently explained she'd forgotten he paid ahead in three-month instalments.

"My Chinese mom wanted me to be a doctor. Like Kwasi." She rolled her eyes as if Kwasi was the stupidest person she had ever met.

"And your dad?"

"He is, like, really old. Fifteen years older than my mom. Doesn't give a shit about anything except smoking his cigarettes and watching *Family Feud* or *Wheel of Fortune*."

"Oh," I said trying to imagine these people as parents to Del.

"My mom got me a tutor. But I convinced the tutor to play hooky and we'd watch *Sailor Moon* together," Del said, reminding me of Flavor Flav with all the medals around her neck. She heaved a sigh and sank into the blue tartan pillows.

"Do you still talk to your parents?"

"Nah. My mom had a way with criticism, you know? 'Derirah, your arm getting fat. Derirah, stop-a-eating so much, aya,'" Del said in a Chinese accent. "Stuff like that."

"Hmm."

"That's all you have to say?"

"What d'ya mean?" I said, even though I was thinking it couldn't be that bad having a parent invested in you because they wanted you to make something of yourself.

"I mean, I tell you stuff, and you're all 'hmm.' Yet you seem to have a lot to say to Jimmy and Eva."

"What d'ya mean?" I said again. *What d'ya mean? What d'ya mean?* The crystal meth had stamped those words into my brain. Not in a fun way like when I did E, but like a repetitive, relentless hammer. I wanted the words to stop blowing around like loose bingo balls in my head.

"You were pouring your heart out to them over breakfast that night I was on PCP."

"I was only talking to Jimmy. Eva was out cold. I was really worried about you that night," I added. "Honest."

Del didn't contradict me. She and I both knew that Eva and I were inseparable that night. I stretched my legs out on the floor and pulled at Del's sparkly boots. They were a little too tight for me on my calves. On account that I skated a lot. On account they weren't mine.

"You know what PCP felt like?" She seemed pacified with my response. "Like I was locked out of my body, and I was trying to get back in. Like my life was a snuff movie and that was my last scene. My eyes were the camera, and my ears were the sound system. My eyes were flickering, everything was cutting in and out, and I kept willing my ears to turn up the volume, but the sound was fading, and it was out of my control. I kept," her voice hitched, "I kept reliving what used to happen to me. And I kept telling my mom, but she wouldn't believe me."

"Wait. What didn't your mom believe you about?"

Del looked like a small child on the bed, drowning in a sea of blue tartan. Uncharacteristically vulnerable. But right now, she was all doe-eyed, the crystal meth finally lowering the fences she built up around herself.

"It was my brother's friend." Her voice was raw. Stripped.

"What d'ya mean?"

"My dad's son, you know, my half brother? He came to spend a summer with us. I was, like, nine, maybe ten? The guys he made friends with were just the local losers that hung around the corner mart where my mom got milk. Simon's new friend would come into my room, see if I wanted to play video games in the living room. I'd always say no because I knew Simon would be pissed. His name was Lars, and he had this real thin moustache, tight jeans, and he smelled like mousse. I thought his name was cool. And I had all these Barbies, and no friends. He would act out Ken's role. But then …"

"But then?"

"He started touching me."

I stared at her.

"I don't remember how far it went. Sometimes when I think of it, I can only remember bits, like him sitting closer and then lifting up my clothes and asking me if I looked the same under the clothes as the dolls did. And asking me if I wondered if he did, too."

I closed my eyes.

"Anyway," she said, reaching behind herself for a spare pillow, then hugging it close to her chest. "Simon had to go back to his mom's place, and Lars never came to see me again. I started having bad dreams about the whole thing. I felt guilty. I didn't even know how women got pregnant, so I decided to tell my mom. She didn't let me get past the first sentence before saying I was making things up."

"She didn't believe you?"

Del shrugged. "Hey, maybe what I said was cryptic. But she did say I was too young to know about pregnancy because I didn't have my period yet. So that was a relief, you know?"

"Gosh, that's terrible."

"I really liked that Lars guy. I was madder that he disappeared, you know? And get this. I found excuses to go get milk for my mom so I could see him at the corner shop. And he was, like, never there again. So, I used to binge Kit Kat bars and Coffee Crisp … I lost complete control."

"You can't blame yourself. He was the pervert."

"Don't go liking him," she said, switching tracks so fast I jerked. Her light-brown eyes looked like they were on fire. "Jimmy. You never met his first girlfriend, Hanna. They were together for ten years. She was a nag, and I made a move, so he went for me. And the only reason he's with Eva is because I broke up with him. Hanna, like, never fully went away, you know. Even when we dated, she showed up at Jimmy's because he still owes her money."

Crystal made it easy for her to switch conversation topics without any transitions. No "by the way" or "hey, let's talk about this now." And yet, I was able to follow it all, even though she was talking so fast it was like she was conversing in Mandarin.

"Jimmy is like a golden retriever — happy to be adopted by anyone who thinks he's the shit," she continued.

"Does she rave?"

"Who, Hanna? No. She's from the real world. Has a desk job and stuff. But what kind of ex holds a grudge over such petty loans anyway? That shit's weird. Anyway, now Eva gets to have a decade. Unless someone else wants his sorry ass."

"I don't want to adopt Jimmy. Ew. Gross. You think Eva really wants ten years of Jimmy?" I asked.

She screwed up her face. "I don't fucking know. But I know this stuff is way beyond you."

"That's not true. Look, my dad is never around; I don't have much of a family." It was my genuine attempt at opening up. Depending on where it went, maybe I'd tell her about Ravi.

"Well, lucky you to have no one looking over your goddamn shoulder."

"That isn't how it is."

She sat up. Pushed back her purple headwrap band. Her pupils were huge and black. Edged by a light-brown rim, they looked like beautiful planets. She was one of those rare people whose hair colour was the same shade as her eyes. She looked magnificent, like Lady Miss Kier from Deee-lite.

She changed her voice to something almost sexy. "You know, I'd be careful with showing your legs, Baby."

"What? Why?"

"You have a lot of cellulite on the back of your thighs. Maybe phat pants are more your thing. Just sayin'."

I got up and walked toward the mirror behind the door. Upon closer inspection, my skater-girl legs were not the muscular specimens I had imagined them to be.

She went to take the CD out of Douche One's player and sighed. The blue Scottish-print pillow in her lap fell to the floor in her wake. Lauryn Hill stopped singing. "Killing Me Softly with His Song" hung in the air, unfinished.

"Let's go back to my place. We're gonna be up for hours so we might as well be somewhere with food. Kwasi probably made one of his weird-ass African dishes. People do crystal to stay skinny and look at me, all 'let's eat, guys!' Oh well," Del said dejectedly.

"He's not my type."

"Huh?" she said, absentmindedly.

"Jimmy. And you're, well, my best friend."

When I first met Takeshi, he had been the one to occupy my mind for months. Tall, with great hair and a sinewy frame, he had been my so-called "type." But I didn't want Takeshi's name imprinted in Del's brain.

My words had touched Del. She walked over and hugged me. Hard. Genuinely. "Are you keeping your hair like this?"

The ends of my hair were practically white. The middle, a faded blue. My roots, black. "The guy who did it for me ... I don't see him much anymore."

"Well, let me fix it," she said, like she was my lover.

I fingered loops of her raspberry scented hair around my fingers. "Why d'ya keep hanging out with him if it destroys you? Jimmy, I mean."

"You do know Jimmy is my dealer, right?"

"What? But he has a T-shirt shop." As if this explained it all.

"You think that surf shop or whatever the fuck his stepdad bought him breaks out even on its own? God, Baby, he's given us both drugs from his own pocket."

"I guess I never thought about it that deeply. And we went to that house in the middle of nowhere to get your stuff —"

"Ha!" she stretched her arms. The medals tinkled against her breasts. "That's because Jimmy and Eva keep doing their own product and leaving me with nothing. Jimmy and Eva are straight up turning into junkies. Did you see the dump they live in? Jesus. Like, handle yourselves already. Now he keeps making *me* pick it up because he's too busy getting super high on even more hardcore shit."

"You think that's safe?"

"Don't matter none. Who knows when those greasy fuckheads will be back from India? Li'l Miss Thang has a better contact. Freddie Star. He lives in Victoria. He's in a motorcycle gang. Way more professional. Screw Jimmy and his unreliable contacts," she said, shoving our drug paraphernalia into her fluffy purse.

Douche One's medals would end up coming home with us that night. Del didn't even bother to hang them up on the jewellery tree that held her necklaces before she fell asleep on her bed, fully clothed. *Nicholas Keats,* one of the medallions read, dangling from her neck off a purple ribbon, *Trampoline and Tumbling, Silver.* Matching her purple sixties minidress perfectly, Del had made that medal more hers than the guy who earned it.

TWENTY-THREE

It was early May, so close to the end of high school, and I was in the school councillor's office. It was a cool, grey afternoon, and the room was dark. Reminiscent of a botanical garden, a miniature terrarium waterfall gurgled on the desk. Leafy greens filled every corner. There was even a living green wall set up, sprouting plants of every shade. I stilled the pen in my hand, resolving not to tell Colleen about deconstructing pens to smoke crystal.

"Are you taking recreational drugs?"

Recreational drugs. What a funny set of words. Casual but with an air of danger, like a gangster recreational jogger set. I focused my eyes on the lightbulb in her unlit desk lamp, mesmerized by the dull sheen.

"Baby, I'm not here to judge you," she said.

"Isn't judging me the literal thing your job is based on?"

"Since we are talking about what our jobs are, how's your whole gig as a student going, then?"

I didn't talk to anyone at school anymore. I played the same tape over in my Walkman. *Warehouse Grooves Volume 3.* "Everybody Be Somebody" by Ruffneck featuring Yavahn was my favourite. It made me feel like I was forever at a rave surrounded by kids like me, all in phat pants and colourful, repurposed seventies jackets, a vibe altogether different from the clueless teens at school. Now I was recognizing all the music they played at events by well-known DJs all around me, like a language I could finally understand. Grooverider. Paul Oakenfold. Sasha & John Digweed. Donald Glaude. Laurent Garnier. Marques Wyatt. Andy Bollocks' killer jungle tunes. The warm weather meant outdoor parties, in Squamish, Chilliwack, Mission. Most of the party kids would get tickets at Odyssey Imports on Seymour, Bassix on Hastings, or Beat Street Records — local shops that served as much as hangouts as they did a place for budding West Coast DJs to get gear and vinyl. Sacred Heart Tattoo on West 10th and Alma was where all the ravers were getting their pixie and butterfly tattoos. There were clubs all over Vancouver hosting underground nights now, like The Starfish Room or Luv-A-Fair. Graceland kept bringing out big-ass international DJs to come out and play on Sol nights. Parties were taking place in empty warehouses in Burnaby right around the corner from my house, but the best raves were happening on mass pieces of farmland ordinarily reserved for growing corn. Full moon parties were popping up in public spaces like Spanish Banks and English Bay, all the kids doing that signature rave dance where it looked like you were miming going down a staircase or bicycling in slow-motion standing up. Feet kicking complex patterns that the music guided. Partying all night until the sun came up and turned into another day, a new party starting where the old one had left off. Birthed by British acid jazz about a decade earlier, raving was a movement, a counterculture, and it was spreading. Still, I felt like I belonged to a secret society.

But I now saw the scene as Colleen might. Everything about our generation seemed tacky in the morning light — a bunch of misfits creating a distraction for ourselves without any focused imprint. We were not wildly artistic in the way that Gertrude Stein's posse of writers and artists living in 1920s Paris were. They were rebellious in a revolutionary way, but we were the stuffed animal versions. Just kids in bunny ears and Value Village tracksuits. Our art meant leaving garbage behind wherever we went. Our revolution had no tag phrase except to party.

"How's your writing going?" Colleen tried again, her voice cutting through my thoughts.

I stared at the yellow Walkman on my lap, my portal to my other world. "I still write."

"That's good."

"Just say what you want to say. I should find wholesome friends like you have."

"Funny you think that, because I'm the wacky plant lady. The staff whisper things about me. Because I guess I basically told them I like books better than people."

"We aren't going through the same thing."

"Gosh, I think I'm supposed to feel offended now," she held her hand to her heart in mock sorrow. "Why do teenagers always think they are the first ones to experience anything?"

"Books *are* better than people."

"Damn straight," she said.

I touched my ballpoint pen to my lips, "If I write, don't write, come to school, don't, what difference does it make?"

"Ooh, teenage existentialism, how I missed thee. I'm definitely not saying any of *this* matters. I'm just trying to give you the safest options to becoming a functional adult. Writing is a good outlet for your feelings. And I bet you're gathering up a bunch of stories along the way. Is raving a transitory phase for you?"

"Like raving is a pit stop and I plan to be a regular member of society one day?"

"That is what adults do, Baby." She ran her finger over the velveteen leaves of one of her plants. "They pick hobbies and support themselves. For instance, me and my husband go to ska shows."

"Ska shows, really?"

"Look, I'm just trying to give you some useful tips so being an adult won't be as much of a degrading transition as you think it will be. Have you had any shaking episodes?" Colleen fiddled with the buttons of her bright blue cardigan. She was dressed like a kindergarten teacher, all primary colours. I tried to imagine her at a ska punk show, in tight, ripped black jeans and a coat of black cherry lipstick. But I came up short.

"I had a fit at Burger King when I first met Del, and another one after a night out with Jimmy, Del, and Eva. But that was months ago. I have mostly been able to keep it in check since then."

She nodded. "And Ravi? Does he still visit you?"

"Sure. But never at raves."

"Do you think he is trying to tell you something with that?"

Somehow, Ravi being a presence in my life even though he was dead never bothered Colleen as much as I thought it should have.

"Don't know."

"You must have some idea."

I shrugged. "Last time I saw him, I read *Wuthering Heights* while he chilled on my bed. People my age don't talk about gothic fiction. Oh, and he discussed Otto Rank and Carl Jung."

"The works of Rank and Jung will help you make sense of your own psychological delusions. It's not a coincidence you chose them."

"But I didn't choose them. Ravi did. He's the one who told me about John A. Macdonald, Canada's first prime minister, being a murderer who purposefully starved out Indigenous people, including children —"

"Information filters through without you knowing," she cut in, as if I hadn't just dropped a bomb about genocide. "History 12 has to have covered these things in passing."

"You mean covered the white-washed version."

To be fair I had always told her Ravi was an illusion, and I had never expected to convert her into a ghost believer. I knew Colleen was a critical thinker, but she probably sang the national anthem like everyone else without thinking too deeply about things. I thought about Kwasi and Raz, suddenly wishing I was in their apartment eating guavas. Was this image a contradiction because we were eating imported fruits, a byproduct of capitalism? Never mind. You couldn't be pure; you could only do the best you could do.

"Look, Baby, I think doing all these drugs is helping you feel a little more normal about having your visions of Ravi," Colleen said.

"No," I said. I focused my eyes on a plant with giant leaves that were rolled up so tight they looked like dollar bills you snorted drugs with.

"Look, this is a safe space, okay?"

The fuck it was. She was petting the petals on her African violet the same way I used to pet my poppies on Remembrance Day. Before I questioned what it meant to be blindly patriotic. Before I was a complete poser like Colleen.

"I don't want to hang out with Carlie's friends and talk about grad like it's going to be some amazing milestone, okay? Have posters of Oasis on the inside of my locker even though they have no idea I exist. I can learn from people like Frantz Fanon. What am I going to learn from these chicks? How to write fan mail to Liam Gallagher?"

"You still have your skateboarding squad, right?"

I winced when she said "squad." It just sounded so embarrassing. I hadn't mentioned them because for the most part, I'd stopped hanging out with them.

I watched her pour some of her own bottled water into her African violet, the way some people did for pets at a sidewalk café. Then, she took a sip of the same water. I had seen her carry some of her plants out to sit in the sun in front of the school building on her lunch break. Like she was walking a chihuahua or something. No wonder the staff avoided her.

"Those friends of yours should count for something. You might need them again one day," she said plainly.

I didn't bother to explain to her that lately, I felt higher when I was straight. And straighter when I was high. Last night when I had hung out with Delilah, I had locked myself in the bathroom because I felt like I was having a bad trip, even though we had decided to chill and do it completely straight. Kwasi had made avocado dip with lemon, garlic, and cilantro and served it with these big blue chips. Raz was roasting potatoes and serving them with tzatziki, mini spinach pies, and grilled, salted tofu coated with sesame oil and Sriracha sauce. Del and I were supposed to make dessert. They were vegetarians like me, except Del who ate meat, mostly outside of her commune. The pineapple dessert was her mother's recipe. To make it, she lined a pie dish with graham cracker crusts and melted butter. We mixed Philadelphia cream cheese, whipped cream, sugar, and drained pineapples from a can together, placing the composition into the pie dish. But we had forgotten the dish was supposed to set in the refrigerator, and we wouldn't be able to eat it for at least four hours. It had all felt quasi normal, just two girls cooking some dessert. But out of the blue, anxiety crept up on me like it did when I did a hit: stomach queasiness, apprehension, anxiety. But I hadn't taken anything. So, I had locked myself in the bathroom and waited out the sweating. And when Del finally got past Kwasi and had me open the door, she thought us splitting an actual cap would help. She sat on the floor, speaking to me in soothing tones, emptying half the cap into a powdered pyramid on my tongue. And then I felt okay. So perhaps doing drugs did make me feel like I was not completely batshit fucking crazy.

"I have to go." I stood up and looked around her shadowed office, memorizing it. I did this every time I saw her, so I could picture the oasis when I was somewhere else. I had a feeling that one day soon, Colleen would leave my life just like everyone else.

"You don't have anything else to talk about?"

I did.

If I could really talk to Colleen like a friend, I'd tell her that lately I'd been pushing the limits hard. What had started with smoking crystal had led to seeing Jimmy and Eva at a dirty warehouse party next to the Value Village on East Hastings Street the very next night. There was a DJ spinning records on a turntable on some tiny balcony that you could only access with a ladder, and there was no ladder in sight. It was a random Sunday night, not usually a big night for partying, but this place was packed. Jimmy gave Del a couple caps of what he said was premium E. We were too high at the time, so we saved them. It was an amazing party, which is what I said about all of them, people hugging and smiling and belonging. The next night at another party on Station Street and Prior, not far from Pacific Central Station, Del and I decided to down the caps Jimmy had given us. It was so hot the walls were sweating. This rave was filled with Calvin Klein–model types that looked like waifs — a contrast to the dingy, baggy-clothed crowd from the first warehouse party. Here, everyone was trying to act like they were someone famous with their hipster jeans and platinum hair. Like we were in a New York club and not some illegal spot that someone had either scoped out as abandoned or rented out from some warehouse slumlord. The drugs hit hard. It wasn't a bad high, just one that put us in a zombie state. It felt like we were wrapped in layers of gauze; as if someone had taken a key and locked our jaws so we could no longer speak. We were frozen, petrified like specimens in amber. Maybe other people would love the feeling of falling into an underwater grotto and swimming their way around paradise, but I only felt the weight of the water pressing down on me. It was the opposite when we did pure MDMA, because then I would wiggle my jaw so much the muscles would hurt the next day. Del said later she was sure Jimmy had given us H. We ended up paralyzed against a wall for hours. Glued there by some bewitching substance. When you've done enough E, you know when you've done another drug masquerading as MDMA.

And then Del had finally cracked and said that Jimmy and Eva were doing heroin and he'd given us some by accident. This was now the second time Jimmy had accidentally given someone the wrong drug. But after knowing what I did about Jimmy's dad and his model girlfriend Stephania doing hardcore drugs, I didn't think Jimmy would follow down the same path. I never considered that Jimmy dealing E was even close to smack. But I couldn't share any of these thoughts with Delilah, so I sat heavy-lidded, waiting for the high to go away. I stayed quiet and accepted the fact that I'd just accidentally done heroin at seventeen years old.

But I couldn't tell Colleen any of this.

"Bye," I said to her, and opened my jaw wide enough to hear a popping in my ear. Just to make sure it wasn't sealed shut like it had been the night on H.

Just to make sure I wasn't stuck in place.

TWENTY-FOUR

"No one is noticing, just chill out, yo."

"Ravi, someone'll see you and shit."

"You're just scared they'll see you talkin' to yourself, mate."

"I only ever walk through these halls alone, Ravs. Not like anyone pays me any mind."

"Just like your heroine Jane Eyre, travelling on her own journeys. Except instead of the wild country, the school hallways are your terrain. Hey, maybe you will stumble upon your own long-lost cousins in the middle of nowhere just like Jane Eyre and find yourself a new Indian family, innit? You could really use that 'bout now."

"That was such a dumb coincidence in the book. Like, how can that even happen?"

"Well, I mean mad shit happens. I'm here talking to you now, ain't I, sis? By the way, still haven't talked to Granny?"

"Not even to Dad."

"Is Jimmy your dazzling paramour, Mr. Rochester, in this *Jane Eyre* analogy?"

"Hardly."

"Since you don't have the Christian piety part to lead you through your adventure … wanna sub in some swamis?"

"Shut up, Ravi. Since when the fuck do you visit me in broad daylight in school? And can we drop the whole analogy charade? It's getting tired."

When I left Colleen's office, I tried to forget about what we talked about and put my headphones on. But Ravi was waiting for me by the only payphone in our school. I was almost tempted to run back to Colleen and introduce her to Ravi. But I waved him off at the exit and starting sailing home on my skateboard. Fuck Ravi and fuck going back to class.

Recently, city officials had built a fence along the highway because too many kids were playing chicken and one had gotten hit. But everyone knew there was a flasher in the tunnel; besides, going that roundabout way home would take ages. What are fences for, if not to climb over? Dropping my board down, I raced down the side of the highway, staying on my side of the white line. I kept my knees loose and led with my shoulders to navigate the few turns, moulding my body against the wind, hands hanging neatly by my side. I was listening to "Brighter Days" by Cajmere featuring Dajae, getting lost in hypnotic, soulful singing and layers of underground trance, when out of nowhere, I hit a patch of gravel and flew.

Everything moved in slow motion. Cars blurred past, distantly honking. My board wasn't underneath me anymore. I tumbled to the edge of the highway, just catching myself before I fell fully into traffic. A car beeped again — this time louder. My board was forging its own path, rolling straight ahead. I could have been hit. Just like Ravi had been. When everything sped up to real time, I found myself spilled over on the ground. My board must've caught a rock under the wheel. I felt pain in my right hand. Little stones were wedged into my knuckles. All the skin peeled away; blood had sprouted there like little ruby flowers. I jaunted forward to get my board before a car smashed it to pieces.

I didn't know that I was crying until I got home. I ran cold water over my fingers, trying to get the pebbles out. I would probably achieve a life-long scar from this fall, branded on my knuckles. After bandaging my fingers and throwing my torn jeans into the laundry hamper like they were a skinned deer, I found a note on the kitchen table from my dad.

To: Baby
Regarding: Current living situation.

You will be moving in to live with your grandmother. This is a home. Not a hotel. The locks to this house will be changed by May 31.

From: Dad

The letter was formal, like I was a business associate and not his daughter. Well, there was no way I was moving in with my grandmother. The words I had spoken to her echoed in my head. *Fuck all of you.* I packed up my things in the carry-on suitcase I'd used on that sad little trip to London without Ravi. Filled my backpack with schoolwork and toiletries, my journal and locket sinking to the bottom. I didn't have much; mostly I borrowed clothes from Del.

As I shut the door, I ran through other options. There was Stick Boi or Del. A small tremoring started, and I knew I was on the verge of a fit. I thought about Jimmy and Eva. Were they really doing heroin now? Hadn't one of them offered that I could stay there? My mind settled on Stick Boi. He was always the most accepting of my friends.

I managed to ride out my shaking. I found Stick Boi behind the dumpsters at the mall. It was one of the places we often went, because the guys who unpacked the trucks were ex-convicts who gave zero fucks about us being there. Sometimes they even gave Stick Boi cigarettes.

"Yo," I said, holding my bandaged hand up in greeting. I had wedged my board behind my backpack so I could walk freely with my rolling suitcase.

He was stunting, trying to get over a few boxes. He was much better than I was.

"Word." He was distant and who could blame him. I was barely around.

"Where's Jed?" I said, purposely using Takeshi's first name, though I wasn't sure why.

He shrugged. "Dunno. Maybe he's working?"

"'Kay," I said and sat down on a few flattened boxes. Stared blankly into space. The loading dock was completely in the shade, and it took a second for me to adjust to the dark. Stick Boi popped in and out of the sun depending on where his props were. A truck was parked on one side along with some giant dumpsters where the store employees threw out cardboard boxes after they finished unloading the inventory. So much waste went into malls, I reflected. How did the lingerie store keep selling pink panties week after week? How many women in Burnaby had them on?

"I'm going to a party in Victoria," I said, breaking the silence. "Wanna come?"

He slid by. Landed his mark. "Not so much. Kinda got tired of asking, na' mean? Going to a party or whatever y'all cool people call it has lost its novelty. I'm over it."

"'Kay," I said again, now picking at a butterfly sticker on my Walkman. "I mean, you could've always gone on your own, you know. There're flyers all over downtown."

"I ain't mad atcha." He clucked his tongue in his urban way. "Pish, is that you think? We all mad atcha 'cause you found shinier friends and better places to be?" He rolled away and looped back, squatting low, hand on his duckbilled hat. The sky outside was pale, one colour of white, the same colour as Stick Boi's skin. His baggy skate shirt floated around him like a parachute. It was one of Jimmy's banana shirts. Had he gone down to Jimmy's shop to buy it?

"I dunno, man. I'm not important enough to be mad at?"

"High school's almost over, na' mean?" He cruised toward me, sticking his foot out to stop his momentum. He dropped down on his board to sit on it like it was a bench. "There's, like, what, a couple months left? So, ya found new people to kick it with." He was panting a little. Kicked out one of his legs and examined a battered skate shoe. "Whatevs."

"Whatevs?" I leaned over and punched him in the shoulder.

"Come on, you're a little miffed. Just say it."

"Nah, cuz, I honest to goodness ain't. It's fucking life." He leaned back on the board, fishing out a cigarette wedged deep in his jeans and lit it. Stick Boi and his goddamn half cigarettes. Saving an inch because he was forever terrified of running out of his favourite thing. "Jed," he said, accentuating Takeshi's first name mockingly, "might be a tad more miffed than me." He took a puff like an old sailor.

"What? Why?" I waved away the smoke.

"Dunno. Prolly 'cause the dumb fuck's still in love with you or some shit."

I felt colour rise into my cheeks. "Nothing happened between us. We barely talk."

"You and Takeshi got some story 'bout each other and neither one of youse is telling me the truth. But it don' matter to me no more. Fuck it. Youse guys can keep your secrets to yourselves, man."

"Come on, dude, don't be like that." I remembered now how hard Stick Boi was to crack, how surprised I was when he finally acknowledged me, brought me into his group, allowed me to straight kick it with him. At our high school, Takeshi and Stick Boi were the undisputed kings of cool, based on the simple fact they didn't conform to fit in with anyone else. But overnight, my friendship with Del had made them look like caricatures out of *The Little Rascals*. Alfalfa and Spanky.

"You want me to be honest? Fine," he blew out fumes. Stick Boi always liked weird American cigarettes that only truckers would buy. They smelled like Nebraska. "You different now, Baby. You was, like, the smart one out of us all. Now you prolly failin' every fuckin' class. Like, no offence, my moms used to look like you when she was strung out, aiite?"

I couldn't help but laugh. "She looked like an Indian girl with blue hair? For fuck's sake, Stick Boi, I drop E once in a while at a rave. I'm not a crack addict. Why d'ya care about school, anyway? School's a joke for you."

He looked stung. "Yeah, well, I'm kinda stuck in the portables learning special math so I ain't got no choice in going places, do I? And you're going to be right there next to me by the end of the year. If you even bother to show up when that happens. 'Cause no fucking way you graduatin', son."

"C'mon. You fucking kidding me? The school councillor is less lecture-y than you. So, I rave a little. What's it to you?" Just because he'd adopted me into his misfit gang didn't mean he owned me. This was some shit. I was standing now.

He took one more drag and flicked the butt. "'Kay, well, go then. That's what you do best. Go be with your sparkly friends. What do they call y'all? Sugar Kids? Yeah, I'm no idiot, dawg. I know the cool term. And I know a crack addict when I see one, by the way. Go wig out with your new crew."

Now was the perfect time for me to say I had nowhere to go. That, really, when it came down to it, I couldn't count on my glittery friends the way I could him and Takeshi. "'Kay," I said instead, jutting out my chin, because that was easier than admitting he'd brought me to tears. I swallowed the salt rock down my throat. My fingers were wiggling. In under two minutes, he'd think I was having an epileptic seizure. I had to get away fast.

"Some of us don't have a choice, man," he called out as I rolled my suitcase away, sounding like I was at the airport. "They got fancy words for my kind of stupid. *Dyslexia. Learning disability.* I draw, 'cause that's the one thing I know I'm good at. What's someone booksmart like you gonna to do without school, bro?"

I didn't have the strength to tell his wise-ass self to fuck off. I stayed in a Denny's all night instead, my small suitcase, skateboard, and backpack sitting next to me in a corner, like the teen runaway I was. I was able to order food on account of the forty dollars I'd found in the kitchen drawer before I left my house. It was weird that I was only a few blocks from both my own house and a few more on top of that from my grandmother's. I was on the same street as the Burger

King where I'd met Delilah. Near the fucking bus loop and mall. And yet, no one would think to look for me here. No one was looking for me at all. I ordered coffee after coffee because even though I preferred tea, refills were free, and asking for hot water seemed stingy. I'd fallen asleep at some point, finding the bill folded into a tent near the sugar canisters, alongside a free slice of cherry pie. The server had given me the sympathy my own friends and family begrudged me.

At 7:00 a.m., violent tremors finally overtook me. I ducked into the Denny's bathroom stall, shaking so much that when I closed the latch on the grey doors, I had to try three times before I succeeded. I waited, hands on my skate hat, my elbows hitting the door every so often. A few minutes later, when the convulsions minimized to a hiccup that punctuated the stillness, I came out. I had come here many times with Carlie in the more regular hours of the day, ordering grilled cheeses with spicy fries, dipping them into hot mustard. But now, everything seemed much more adult and foreign. Seniors had shown up before sunrise to order Grand Slam breakfasts. Some of them were pulling out decks of cards now and winking at the waitresses. Smoke rose above their heads and seeped into the already yellow wallpaper, which absorbed it. I never noticed all the knickknacks on the shelves before, roosters and sugar canisters with painted horses. It felt like I was in the Wild West. Stuck in the world of adults with responsibilities.

At a quarter to eight, I took the bus to school and parked my luggage at the back of English class. Not one person asked me why I was carting around a suitcase. As if it was very regular to come to school with roll-on baggage. The teacher was talking, but I had already read all the books on her list. Fuck you, Stick Boi. I didn't need a school to educate me. I was doing it myself.

Indignation kept me mad enough that I didn't try to find Stick Boi. Instead, in the second period, I made my way down to the library. I found a cubicle in the back, put my head down, and fell properly asleep, without the fear of a server catching me. My mouth tasted like Denny's coffee.

TWENTY-FIVE

I showed up to Jimmy's shop that afternoon.

It was raining hard but warm. I was listening to "Spin Spin Sugar" by Sneaker Pimps (the Armand Van Helden Dark Garage mix). It reminded me of Thursday nights at Graceland. Me and Del slipping through the alleyway entrance. Both of us dressed in her PVC pants and platform sneakers, our pearlescent tops tied up in the back only with strings. Bryce giving us hugs and slipping us through. Free passes got us in, little cards with a blue sky and a sun, which we reused until they were worn — it was a sign you were a full-fledged Sugar Kid if you never paid cover to get into Graceland. The bartender and visual lights guy nodding to us as we made our way to the glass DJ booth located at the top of the stage. DJ Markem, the Thursday night resident legend, always had his favourite group of people congregating there with him, candles burning, everyone straight vibing off each other. Not too long ago, he had been roommates in LA with another DJ cult hero, Doc Martin. "Hey Baby," DJ Markem would say, always elated. "Let me buy y'all a round of drinks." We'd go back onto the dance floor, cocktails in hand. All the lights spinning over top of us as we paced out our dancing, waiting for the bass to drop so we could properly go off. Feeling fancy and light and beautiful. Those nights I wasn't seventeen. I was someone important enough to belong to a scene. Our bodies, now screen-printed in pink and purple tiger patterns from the club lights, moving to DJ Markem's set, unrestricted.

By contrast, in Jimmy's shop, The Beach Boys were playing. He had implied he hated his dad, but his shop was a museum of his father's surf glory days. I wondered why there were no pictures of Jeffrey. Today, Jimmy had on one of his newspaper-boy caps, ironic because it was made from actual newspaper print fabric. He was shuffling through a box of records.

"Hey," I said, parking my luggage.

"Hey, Baby," he looked like he had been expecting me. He came over and gave me a hug that was a few beats too long.

"Came down for another round of all-day breakfast?"

"Nah, I'm good," I said, a little embarrassed that he'd paid for me last time.

He went back to his crate and pulled a record sleeve. Cuffs folded up, he was wearing a slate sweater over a dress shirt, tweed dress pants, and very black shoes. I liked the mix of all the fabrics. This man knew how to raid vintage shops.

"What's the problem, kid?"

"Problem?" I shifted my eyes from him to the surfing photos on the wall. "Why d'ya think there's a problem?"

"It's written on your face."

I grimaced. There was a whole lot I could tell him. I could expand on my mother dying. My father kicking me out to live at my grandmother's. I could straight up tell him about Ravi's death. And add that Ravi visited me all the time. But there was something stopping me from telling this to anyone except Colleen. Maybe I was hanging on to it like a secret rainy-day fund. Something I'd need to share if things got really fucking tough.

"Carl Cox is playing next weekend," I said instead. "You going?"

"Nah. Big parties wear me out. Eva likes 'em but I prefer underground ones. More my scene as of late."

I nodded, remembering how he had told me this before. I never paid because there was always some friend of a friend Del knew. She had so many connections but no close friends. Were Raz and Kwasi her true friends? Lately, I acted like a bridge that extended out to them when Del's angry moods escalated. Last night she had even declared that she was going to stop smoking weed with them on account of their "ridiculous anarchist views" and because "not one fuckin' person wants to get high and listen to Janet Jackson like that freak Raz."

I was getting lost now, thinking of the intricacies of relationships. I was becoming the airhead Del claimed I was, especially since I was doing so much E. Hearing some rustling in the back room, I snapped to attention. "Is someone here?"

"Jie. She's staying here right now."

"Jie?" I said, trying to sound casual.

"Yeah, she needs a place to crash, and I got the back room."

"Oh." I was failing at looking impartial that a girl was living here.

"Hey, look at your face. You got it all wrong. Jie likes girls. She had a girlfriend when I met her. Eva wouldn't care even if she knew."

"Of course." Jimmy's secrets were piling up on me now.

"Anyway," he was frowning now, once again sorting through his records, perhaps unsatisfied with the one he had chosen. Happy Californian beach music was still flooding the shop. "I like Canadian girls. Eva knows that."

"Like girls born here?"

He shrugged dismissively. "You know, like European girls."

European girls, was that code for white? And what about the photo album of girls belonging to different nationalities that Del had found in his apartment? Did he just pose with beautiful women with multiple ethnic backgrounds for street cred? How the fuck could I even begin to bring that up? "And Del?" I challenged him instead.

"What about Del?"

I was going to say, "Isn't Del half Chinese?" But then I decided all this talk wasn't going where I needed it to. For some reason, I was embarrassed that I wasn't European, and that he was clearly telling me I wasn't his type. Maybe his comment was meant to reassure me he wasn't some pervert who stored girls in his back room or took teens for breakfast with ulterior motives. And still, my face went all hot. Not my business what race he liked to date. All these thoughts set my teeth on edge. For now, I had to find out if Jimmy could help me. *Think!* I told my brain. *Stop fading off!*

I didn't have a chance to answer because Jie came out then. She was, as her name suggested, Chinese. Short with round cheeks. She had lime-green hair that reminded me of a tall glass of Kool-Aid, black cat-eye glasses, small lips, and a teacup chin. Two stubby pigtails that looked like green popsicles poked out from the sides of her head. I couldn't take my eyes off her; she was like an anime character come to real life. It was weird, but she was probably the most interesting person I had ever seen.

"Jimmy, I opened the box of new inventory," she was saying. "I'm gonna go put everything on hangers."

I studied her, trying to figure out why she looked familiar. And then it hit me. I had seen her at my first rave, kissing a girl endlessly against a wall. Jie had been able to kiss that girl like it was a hobby, an art form. I flushed at the memory.

Jie grabbed a sheet of paper that was sitting near Jimmy to check something off. Her arms had bruises. I wasn't sure from what. Del kept saying that Jimmy and Eva were H heads. Maybe Jie was part of this elusive heroin scene. Jimmy nodded at her, and after reciprocating, she went back to the back room to finish her task.

"So, Jie straight up lives here?" I said measuredly, addressing Jimmy.

"Guess so. There's a cot and bathroom in the back. No kitchen or nothin'. This store used to be a residential home. The previous owner ripped out the front to build a store."

"Neat," I said.

"Yeah." Jimmy was proud. "The bathroom is the only real original feature left in here. It's, like, full on retro fifties! Has a spring green–coloured bathtub, matching toilet, and everything. And get this, vintage flooring. Yellow tiles with little green diamonds."

It sounded like the Templeton where Jimmy and I had breakfast. How very Jimmy.

Without his tattoos, Jimmy would have belonged on a Hollywood movie set fifty years ago. I was looking at him differently. He was white now, and not just Jimmy. Suddenly I was Brown, Jie was Asian, and no one was as they were the first time I went to a rave. And to think, lately when Ravi saw me, he asked me why I was so interested in reading about white people's lives in books like *Jane Eyre* when in that novel, I would be just a goddamn Hindustani. India was painted in such books as a mystical place with exoticized people who stayed unrefined and uncivilized. It was only a place good for stealing spices, textiles, and tea and even back then, adventuring. Indians wouldn't be people you'd mix with English blood. And what had changed in nearly two hundred years? Not a lot for some people, apparently. Not for Jimmy. What had I said to Ravi? "I grew up here. I'm allowed to like what I fucking like." Was I though? Wasn't there already enough content on everything to do with the West, remade, remastered, and redone and nothing out there about someone like me? Did the poetry I wrote show in any way I was Indian? Or on paper did I just sound like another hormonal teenaged white girl?

"This shop is so fucking you, Jimmy," I said.

"Yeah, pretty much." He grinned.

I hated then that I liked Jimmy's jubilant personality. Jimmy the colonizer, as I imagined him in years past, would not have taken a native wife. He'd have one imported from Europe.

"Everything okay, kid?" said Jimmy, looking at me like I was spooking him out.

I nodded, coming back to the present time, "So ... she can stay here comfortably?" I fiddled with my sapphire hair. Two kiddish barrettes were fastened on each side. Del had forced me to re-coat my hair with Manic Panic dye, but I had been too lazy to bleach the top. I now had black hair that erupted into brilliant blue. *The river runs blue,* I thought, twirling a blue lock between my fingers, knowing it would rub pigment onto my hands.

"Comfortably?" he laughed. "I mean, that might be a stretch. I got a hot plate and coffee machine in the back. I've been known to make camping food and ride it out for the count. Ya know, boiling hot dogs in the coffee machine, cracking open a can of chilli, gorging out on some canned minestrone." He gave me a wink. "Don't think Jie's into that kinda food. Whenever I see her, she is eating pho or something exotic like that."

"You're so curious," said Jie, interrupting Jimmy. I had forgotten she was around. It wasn't a judgement. She had come back for some hangers and fiddled with them near the cash register.

"I need a place to crash," I addressed Jimmy, signalling to my carrier luggage as if this would explain my situation. "I can work here or something if you'd like. But, maybe there isn't enough room with Jie being here and all …"

"Oh," he rubbed the pin-up girl tattooed on his arm. "Okay," he said, now giving me a flat smile. "If that's what ya need."

"Are you sure?"

"Yeah, 'course. It's the Christian thing to do."

"I guess," I said.

While I was annoyed it took religion for him to help me, I ignored Jie's eyebrow arch. Conspiring with her was not in my interest. Why had we never talked about religion at raves? And why had I assumed only non-religious people did drugs? They would probably need religion to pull them out with the twelve-step programs later.

"Damn straight it is, Baby," he was saying. "'Give to the one who asks you, and do not turn away from the one who wants to borrow from you.' Matthew 5:42."

"Are you a communist?" I asked.

"Absolutely not. I hate that radical shit; individuals should be able to keep what they earn. I'm happy to help out a friend in need, but you give some people a handout, and they just never fucking learn to stand on their own two feet. That godless communist shit is corrupt."

"Jimmy, you would have loved McCarthy," I found myself musing out loud, thinking of Kwasi. How he talked about McCarthyism and its purpose to clean out the no-good "reds" by making sure there was no one in America who didn't believe in capitalism and God.

"Say what?"

"He was a senator. He … never mind." There was no use in explaining. Jimmy liked his morning artisan bagel from Benny's Bagels and his white women. Jimmy liked tattoos and Christian proverbs and tattoos of Christian proverbs. And yet, sickly, I was weirdly drawn to him. My mind felt like a soggy bowl of Corn Flakes.

"'Kay. But you'll have to take up your cause with Jie, though. I guess that's the catch. Because in the end, there's only one cot in the back." He patted the newspaper boy cap on his head. "Lock up behind me, will ya? I found my record, and I'm off for the day. Ya literally just caught me, kid."

"That's it?" I said, following behind him.

He shrugged, swinging open the door and tucking his record under his arm. "Jie's the boss."

"What record did you need so bad?"

"Iggy Pop," he said. "Can't get 'Lust for Life' outta my head. Did ya know David Bowie cowrote it with him?"

"No," I said, shaking my head at the enigma that was Jimmy.

He ruffled my head with his spare hand. "Go 'head and check out my records. You'll have a blast. See ya later, kid."

I locked the door. Suddenly, I heard David Bowie's "I'm Afraid of Americans" pour through the store, loud and strong, with its industrial beat. Jie was standing by the record player, album jacket in hand. I kind of just stood there, listening. When the line "God is an American" came on, I knew she was taking a jab at Jimmy. She got my McCarthy comment. She also knew who Jimmy really was.

And she wanted me to know it.

TWENTY-SIX

I found Jie hanging T-shirts on a metal rolling rack in the back room.
"Hey. I'm going out to get something to eat. Will you let me in when I come back?"

She shrugged, neither confirming nor denying. I mirrored the shrug. I went out the back door, which spilled into the alleyway. Here were a few tall green dumpsters, tidbits of trash accumulated in corners, and cars parked in a tow-away zone. I was hit immediately by the smell of immigrant foods. Dumplings in clear broth. Spring onions on *okonomiyaki*. *Malai kofta* balls in creamy, spicy sauce. I rounded the corner, wondering if I could still catch Jimmy if I ran. But what did I want from him? I didn't even know.

I found an Indian take-away shop around the corner. I knew what dish would be the cheapest and most filling. I could only go so far on the money I'd taken from the kitchen drawer. I came back to the shop with a takeout paper bag. Inside, two Styrofoam containers were filled to tipping level with chickpea masala curry, topped with a couple of crusted pastry samosas. The smaller pockets of the takeout box had raw red onions, carrot pickle, and *raita* with cucumbers. This was the best peace offering I had.

"Food!" I knocked like a personal assistant at *Vogue* might. Jie swung open the door. I set the bag on a table and noticed a pink rice cooker. I wondered if Jie was already cooking. "Um, is Indian okay?"

"Better than okay. Hey, why do you bother liking Jimmy? He's a waste of time. Everyone knows that."

I was taken aback. And then I found I was laughing. She started to laugh as well. I smoothed a coarse paper napkin onto my lap.

"Gross. I don't."

"He's the kind of guy who is nice to us but votes for the Conservative Party every fucking time. He sides with people that don't want us in their country. You know that, right?"

"Oh, for fuck's sake, Jie. No way that guy votes."

"People like him always have a say in what happens in the world. Don't underestimate him."

I cocked a brow. "Okay, so when he isn't getting high or forgetting what day it is, he goes out and votes? Like, come on, do you even vote? No, you don't because you probably want to smash the state." I had picked up this idea from Kwasi and was glad to use it on her.

"Meh, I am less Kropotkin and more Gustav Landauer. More about occupying free places in the state rather than smashing it. Landauer is all about penetrating spaces."

"Fuck. I don't know who any of those people are," I said. Kwasi and Raz would know. They were the type of dudes to get pictures of old white guys like Kropotkin screen-printed on T-shirts. "But hey, sounds kind of like rave culture to me. The occupying free spaces bit, I mean."

"Rave culture is overrated. Now all anyone wants to do is get high. It's lost its meaning."

She may have had a point there. I changed my approach. "It's not Jimmy I give a fuck about. It's the finding somewhere to crash bit."

Cracking open my box, I took in a plastic spoonful of the chickpeas, tasting the tomato base of the curry enriched with onions, ginger, chilli, and garam masala. I hadn't realized how much I missed Indian food. Now that my mother had died, I would probably never learn to cook it. I wondered if Jie knew how to cook her own cultural food. Not knowing made me feel more orphaned.

"Ah, so this is your sales pitch." Jie picked up a pair of chopsticks to eat her samosa. I marvelled at the way her fingers pinched the sticks and attacked a corner of the deep-fried exterior. Turmeric potatoes, cumin seeds, and peas poured out. Never in my entire life had I seen a person eat a samosa with chopsticks. It looked so functional I couldn't even fault her.

"I could help around the shop."

"I've been handling everything fine myself, okay?"

"Okay. I'll find somewhere else," I said levelly. I knew I was already behaving creepily showing up at Jimmy's shop when he was Del's ex. But I didn't have a lot of options. I couldn't imagine living with my grandmother. A sense of panic rose in my throat.

"Oh my god, you're trembling."

"No, I'm fine."

"Look, you can stay. For a short while. Don't make me feel bad. I don't need that kind of drama."

"Don't you mean karma?"

She shrugged. "Maybe I don't need that, either."

"Thank you, Jie," I said, trying to gain control of my hands.

She stood up, bringing the pink rice cooker to the table. It was covered with a Hello Kitty emblem. Jie didn't seem so tough anymore. "You want me to add some rice to your box? Make the food go longer?"

It was then I realized she was fighting to survive as much as I was.

TWENTY-SEVEN

Jimmy had been leaving Jie and I in charge of the shop for pretty much the whole month of May. After we closed, Jie and I would take money from petty cash to eat at DV8 Lounge. There, listening to hard house under purple lighting, we'd wait for the bass to drop, watching the blackened windows of the street nearly rattle. We would dip too-sweet yam fries into too-garlicky sauce and tell each other our life stories. The fries were never enough because we'd only paid to be somewhere cool that had ketchup in baby bottles. So Jie and I started bussing it all the way to Kingsway to eat pho at a place that sounded like profanities in English.

We shared the small cot. Because of all the concrete and lack of insulation (as no one was supposed to live in a storage room), it was cold at night, even for spring. All we had was a lousy space heater and on account of the weird smell of singed wires when we turned it on, we rarely used it. In the mornings, Jie would make pancakes on a griddle. I was grateful that Jimmy's asparagus-green bathtub had been spared when renovations had been done, so we could bathe and behave like we weren't couch surfing. Jie let me use her shower products. They smelled of cucumber, melon, and green tea. Jie also washed all my clothes by hand in a bucket and hung them all on lines she strung up. They dried into crispy crackers, which she would later iron out on the floor using a three-dollar gadget that looked like it was from 1934, scored from the local Salvation Army. She carefully put my things in one of Jimmy's cardboard boxes which now, in her delicate penmanship, read *Baby's things*. Jie was a combination of hard and soft. It was a funny thing, for example, to discover that underneath her painter jeans, anime shirts, and eighties Adidas tracksuit jackets, Jie had a thing for saucy lingerie. She was all about lilac and periwinkle undergarments made from scanty lace and satin. It seemed so unlike her and totally like her at the same time.

Everything I wore took on the smell of Jimmy's incense. This week it was something that smelled of cardamom, cloves, and coconut. Like these cookies my mom once made another lifetime ago. But still, I decided there was no reason that I should tell Del about my living conditions. Jie and I were close enough now that she'd say whatever I needed her to say. As time went on, I invented new ways of redefining my situation. Perhaps it was Jie, not Jimmy, who had invited me to stay in the back room. It could be true.

Del had scored tickets to a rave happening in Victoria, and when I told Jie she said, "Partying isn't my scene anymore." Lately, Punjabi gangsters were showing up to settle their vendettas at raves held in Indian wedding halls. The last one happened at Riverside Banquet Hall, and the kids were more pissed about the cops shutting the place down than they were worried about being shot. No one got refunds if a rave got busted. As a result, there was a hall full of drugged out kids with nowhere to go. Now a lot of raves were taking place on Indigenous reserves where people said the cops couldn't set foot on the premises uninvited.

The day I was going to catch the ferry to the Victoria rave with Del, Jie was sitting on the shop floor cross-legged, glasses sliding down her nose like a scholarly owl, filling out some applications to get into Langara College. There was an hour left before we had to open. Pieces of hair that didn't reach her light-green bun spilled out, like a Las Vegas hotel waterfall.

"I don't care if you go," she told me, not looking up.

"Are you absolutely sure?"

"One of us has to open the shop. So, you might as well enjoy yourself," Jie said.

"Right."

When I hung out with Jie, I was always calmer. I wrote poetry in my journal again. One time, Ravi came right into the shop. Brushing shoulders with Jie, he rifled through a few T-shirts and left. I didn't go to the smoothie shop as often to bait Raz and Kwasi for mango shakes or to talk about Marxism or rappers anymore. Instead, I stayed at The Grape Monkeys. I talked to surfers, skaters, ravers, and gangsters both pretend and real. In the daytime, we played the best of nineties hip hop: The Roots, Gang Starr, Brand Nubian, and Wu-Tang. We'd crank up Ol' Dirty Bastard's "Shimmy Shimmy Ya" and dance theatrically, battling each other as we rhymed along with the raunchy lyrics. At night, we played deep house classics like Round One's "I'm Your Brother" (the club version mix) and Round Two's "New Day" (the club vocal mix). These were the type of songs I imagined would end up aging like good wine, with their smooth, simple, no-fuckery sounds.

"Jimmy came here when you were at school," Jie said. "Lift the cash tray in the register."

I opened the till. Under the tray used for dividing monies were two envelopes. I pinched the rectangular paper with my name on it between my fingers. Inside, there were a bunch of twenties. Now, we didn't need to steal change from the register. Now, Jimmy needed us more than we needed him.

"Hey, I'll be back before you know it," I said, more for me than her.

TWENTY-EIGHT

On the last Saturday of May, the ferry on the way to the Victoria rave was stuffed with kids wearing colourful earmuffs and lifesaver bright jackets, all holding eighties lunch boxes. Del and I had come in Marvin's car. Marvin, a Filipino club promoter, infused the classic "rave" style with a gangster vibe. Today, he was wearing an eighties royal-blue track suit, a thick gold chain, and orange-tinted lenses. On the ferry deck, Marvin held up a big sign promoting a new club night, as if crocheting grandmothers were his target demographic. Del stood next to him handing out flyers to random passengers. I wondered if any one of them would end up at a rave.

Also with us was The-Chris (named this in case there was any confusion as to which Chris). He was known for his startling eye makeup, four-inch platform shoes, and capes. Scrubbed of all makeup, however, he was a beautiful boy with high cheekbones, and short, mussed, silver hair. We held hands on the ferry, and he shared his ice cream with me. When a couple stared, he kissed me full on the mouth. I wondered if Stick Boi and Takeshi would buy our charade.

JoAnne, known to everyone else simply by her DJ name, Li'l Miss Thang, was our final companion. She was half Black and nearly six feet tall, looking equally splashing when she made an entrance with The-Chris. She strode onto the ferry wearing a forties-style white satin slip dress and a shocking pink faux fur over her shoulders, à la Marilyn Monroe. Unsure if she was famous, passengers snapped photos of her, many pretending they were catching something else on the ferry that interested them. She had short, magenta hair styled in finger waves with lips painted to match, eyebrows so thin and sculpted they reminded me of a silent movie star from the twenties.

Her mixing style was to blend old classic jazz singers into progressive house music, so it wouldn't be unusual to hear Billie Holiday singing clean and clear straight through a heavy bass line. Louis Armstrong's punchy trumpet was sprinkled into many of her tracks. JoAnne said only white people called Louis Armstrong by his name. To her, he was Pops, what Billie Holiday had called him in "My Sweet Hunk O' Trash." She'd burned two albums, *Speakeasy House* and *Prohibition Techno,* onto CDs that she hawked out of her purse.

When I climbed up the ferry stairs leading to the top deck, I found JoAnne smoking a cigarette in a holder straight out of *Breakfast at Tiffany's.*

"Baby Doll, what's wrong? No outfit for tonight?"

Her arm was draped elegantly over the rail. The sky and the waves were steel grey. The spring wind whipped over everything. She should have been living in LA doing screen work, not amongst us mere mortals on the ferry.

"I can wear this," I said offhandedly, pointing at Jie's Sailor Moon shirt.

"Nonsense! I'll find you something."

I smiled and pushed my body against the rail looking out at the horizon, enjoying the ocean breeze lapping over me. Ravi had told me about negative ions being released in the air when you were near waterfalls. Oxygen atoms picked up an extra electron, hence creating the negative charge. A similar feeling to E-induced peace. Suddenly, before I could stop myself I said, "Hey, JoAnne, ever talk to a dead person before?"

If it was an odd question, her femme-fatale face did not betray emotion. I pictured her in her apartment with a Ouija board summoning the spirits. If you could call it an apartment. She and The-Chris were leasing an unfurnished commercial studio space in Gastown that was largely concrete. Dead centre in this colossal warehouse was a carpet, two sofas, and a lamp. There were no doors or rooms or connecting walls, and instead JoAnne's and The-Chris's beds were set up to the respective right and left of the cold dungeon. Tons of beautiful windows bordered the building, where you could sit upon a ledge and take in Vancouver like you were watching a movie.

Li'l Miss Thang and The-Chris recouped their ridiculously high rent with secret gatherings, charging cover to everyone but us. The parties drew Vancouver's artsy crowd: tattoo artists, fancy hair stylists, body piercers, and Red Seal chefs with knives inked on their forearms, probably all of whom were gentrifying what was left of the downtown slums to build suave barbershops and organic food restaurants. At every party, the Aveda hairdressers offered to cut my bangs for free, and the body piercers invited me to their lairs for complimentary piercings.

"Yes, I've talked to the dead," she answered, fiddling with a large emerald cocktail ring, which she had once told me belonged to Priscilla Presley. "Once, I was as high as kite and had a full conversation with Marlon Brando, Baby Doll. I have a framed poster of him sitting against one of the studio walls. He climbed right out of it and decided to have a chat."

"Once?"

"Why, I tried other times, honey. But Mr. Mumbles hasn't come out to play again."

"Mr. Mumbles?"

"Sinatra gave him that name," she looked down at her bright red nails. They should have clashed with all the colours she had going on, but somehow tied her look in even more.

"What'chu talk about?" I pushed.

She pressed the metal edge of her cigarette holder against the dip of her bottom lip. "He said, 'You're not some carefree flapper girl from another time. This is Vancouver and it's 1996 and you're living in a fucking cement palace with no central heating. Can't go living like this forever, sweets.' But fuck him. I plan to be famous. I have a five-dollar cuppa coffee every day for breakfast. With a shot of Baileys thrown in. Heck, I hand the mickey right over to my favourite barista."

I nodded. This untouchable, magnificent woman also questioned the sustainability of her current living situation. Not surprisingly, JoAnne had a famous ghost chastise her for her bad behaviour.

I cleared my throat. "Do you, uh, think it's a sign you need to stop doing what you're doing?"

She faced me head on. Standing together on the top deck of the ferry made me feel we were in a movie of some kind. I was immersed in that British Columbian blend of sparkling waters, landmasses lined with skinny trees, and the navy and steel blue profile of mountains.

"Do I need to stop because I'm having a conversation with a phantom when I'm faded as fuck? I mean, if that's not happening then what good are the drugs I'm doing?"

"I guess ..."

"I'm going to end up at Ibiza one day. You know? I'm not just going to be some homegrown DJ spinning at the local café forevah. I'm going to be a goddamn megastar, girl. Raving is about balance, that's all."

"Balancing doing drugs, you mean."

"Exactly. You gotta keep track of what's what. Your escape cannot be your permanent home. That's the trick."

"What if I don't know where my permanent home is?"

She pulled her pink faux fur shawl over her shoulders. Inhaled from her silver wand and tapped into the ocean. "Aren't you in school, Baby Doll?"

"Yeah, but I don't relate to the people there. Plus ..." I gathered myself, "I don't even think I'm gonna graduate on time." Talking to her was far better than Colleen.

"What do you see yourself doing?"

"With my life? I guess writing."

"Then use that to ground you. Everyone has to have one thing."

"What's yours?"

"Me? Being a fucking artist, that's fucking what." She set off looking into the sea again, just her and her cigarette.

"Yeah," I said. Satisfied, I climbed back down the narrow steps. I passed a display of brochures on things to do in Victoria: whale watching, kayaking, visiting the wax museum, seeing a flower garden. All things that very regular people did in very regular times. A world I never had after Ravi died.

Who wants to bird watch anyway?

I pulled a battered copy of *The Great Gatsby* out of my bowling bag and sank into a bucket seat. I looked out of the big, rectangular window at the sea, thinking of the rambunctious, rioting parties at Gatsby's and how everything could be fabulous if I just stopped overthinking it all.

TWENTY-NINE

After we docked, we piled into Marvin's car, joining the lineup of other cars. Our windows rolled down, music poured out. It was En Vogue's "Free Your Mind," mixed into house. The crescendo was building. CeCe Peniston found her way in with "Finally" when the beat kicked in. Robin S. came in then, fragments of "Show Me Love," all mixed in and perfectly beat matched. People stared at us as we rolled out from the belly of the ferry onto the road, watching a bunch of kids throw their hands up to mainstream songs that had enough fire to be turned into garage remixes.

As we drove further into Victoria, we listened to Sven Väth. DJ Keoki. Roger Sanchez. Dirty Beatniks. Basement Jaxx. Underworld. Even mainstream stuff like Chemical Brothers and that iconic dream trance song "Children" by Robert Miles. We liked our local DJs too; they were the ones who kept our scene alive. It seemed like everyone was named after juices or vitamins, like Vitamin E and Minute Maid. There was also Czech, Isis, Little T, Tripswitch, Rob Shea, Noah, Quik Fix, T-Bone, Dickey Doo, Ali, Mike Shea, Lace, Quest, Flyte, Pascal, Slim, James Brown, Grooverobber, and countless others who made up the West Coast rave culture. Marvin was driving. JoAnne sat beside him, her short fuchsia hair flying freely. I was wedged in the back between The-Chris and Del, who were both gyrating maniacally. *Bam!* The beat dropped again and again.

We drove to the Victoria, BC, sign. Marvin pulled over. We got out and laid on the letters with our bodies to change the spelling to Rave, BC. In our brightly coloured clothing, we must have looked a bit like a travelling troupe of Teletubbies. A couple of preschoolers smiled and waved at us. Marvin, feeling inspired by this, dropped to the floor and began breakdancing. JoAnne pretended to spin invisible records and The-Chris made a pretty good beatbox with his mouth. People crowded around us, like we were buskers on Robson Street. Del and I snapped pictures that would probably end up in all our photo albums, forever stacked and buried under other memories. Fresh plants bloomed everywhere in purples, pinks, and yellows.

Once we had piled back in the car, Marvin put on Jamiroquai, The Orb, and Orbital, things we usually played the morning after a rave, to mellow out. We went through a drive-thru because Marvin said he needed a coffee, or he wasn't going to make it. Like he was a tired dad who needed a boost. I didn't even like the stuff much.

We went to Freddie Star's house, JoAnne's friend. He was the guy Del wanted to start getting her drug supply from. Freddie Star was in his fifties. He owned a big house with a boat sitting on wheels on his front driveway. The house hadn't been renovated since the seventies. Inside, everything was covered in wood panelling. Glittering stones surrounded his fireplace. The carpet was orange with blue designs, and mini floating staircases led to weird half floors without any clear sense of purpose, like a creepy doll house. Del had told me Freddie Star was a white biker who ran the Victoria drug scene. I wondered if he would like an Indian girl at his house. But when I thought of it, all four of us were dodgy occupants: Marvin was Filipino, Del was half Chinese, JoAnne was half Black, and The-Chris was gay.

None of this mattered because I had a strong feeling that I wasn't going to be meeting Freddie Star. In a bedroom with a seventies clock that had a thousand spikey arms and smelled of stale, decade-old cigarettes, JoAnne tossed me a vintage white-and-orange flowered pantsuit.

"Go 'head Baby Doll, you can have this."

"You sure?"

"It's too small for me."

I changed while JoAnne rummaged through a crate of records that Freddie Star had left behind for her. JoAnne put on Billie Holiday's "Lover Man." Billie's voice sounded like good merlot. JoAnne opened something that looked like a gun case and set to work transforming her face.

A couple of hours later, we all dropped E at the same time. Del, Marvin, and I were ready to go, but Li'l Miss Thang and The-Chris needed time to present themselves like the glittery showstoppers they were. JoAnne was playing a surprise set at 2:00 a.m. so we left her and The-Chris behind to meet us at the rave. It was assumed that Freddie Star would appear out of thin air and drop off Li'l Miss Thang and The-Chris.

Del had negotiated getting free tickets to the rave by volunteering to dance behind shadow screens set up next to the turntables. That night, we danced like go-go dancers from the sixties, our bodies enlarged and projected to the audience in surreal proportions. After a while, it seemed like everyone wanted a turn to be an eight-foot sex goddess, so we gladly retired.

The rave was held in a local ice-skating arena. There were some good DJ headliners. As usual, Loopy had set up the smoke machines and pink and blue lights to complement the visuals, cut-outs of short films and videos that played on large screens. The music itself seemed out of this world; it echoed through the building and shook the foundations. Concession was off to the side, put on by Swing Kids. You could feel vibrations in your throat. Del and I were vibing. But when a Josh Wink track came on, I had to walk away because the build-up in "Higher State of Consciousness" was making me dizzy — I felt like there were fifty football coaches all blowing whistles at the same time. It made sense that the style was called tweakin' acid; the Jib Kids always went nuts for the trippy song.

I walked alongside the rounded edges of the dry rink where groups of ravers were huddled up. Everything was too bright. Too pulsating. I saw a guy that looked identical to Stick Boi. He grinned at me, nicotine teeth like Stick Boi, and I was shocked when I saw he was Asian. A guy with a giant camera on his shoulder bumped into me. He was taking video footage of the rave. "Hey," he said, swinging the lens at me. "Having fun? Want to say anything to your future self?"

"No," I said, sidestepping away just as two girls with pixie cuts and svelte bodies caught his attention. They looked like they should have been foraging golden leaves from some mystical forest. I moved to give them camera time. They gave a beautiful and articulate interview, their faces washed in glitter, their smiles true and deep. "Music is medicine," the one with the turquoise hair said to the camera. "People just don't understand how therapeutic and transformative a place like this can be," the one with the forest-green hair added.

When I walked away from the camera, I started to think of Takeshi. The locket. How he had given it to me. How wearing it had become a part of me and then I just took it off when Del had told me to. But what had happened between us? Had anything? Did we mean something to one another?

At 2:00 a.m., I dropped a quarter into a payphone located by the benches where you changed your skates. When the line picked up, I heard that sound when the quarter meets the bed of other quarters. I was near the room where all the skates were stored, but the music still found a way to vibrate the walls. It smelled like caramel popcorn, hot chocolate, and cotton candy — all the things they sold at the ice-skating arena. Everything smelled wholesome. Regular. Just like it had before Ravi died.

Jed Takeshi spoke as if he knew it was me. "Hello?"

I couldn't talk; my mouth was dry. It was the middle of the fucking night, I realized now. Had I woken up Takeshi's entire household? I was so high. I wished Takeshi was here. I could ask him if he had really liked me, and if so, why hadn't he said more? I pressed my ear into the black phone receiver until it hurt, my hand holding the thick, metal cord.

"Hello?" his voice demanded again.

There was so much to say, but my mouth wouldn't cooperate. I didn't know much about Takeshi's home life. But I knew both his parents and an older sister lived with him. Maybe she was in college, I wasn't entirely sure. They probably came to skating rinks like the one I was in now all the time. Who was I to invade his perfect life?

In the background, I could hear the DJ playing Goldie. Deliciously layered drum and bass. Melodic vocals. Maybe it was the real Goldie himself. One time downtown, I'd met someone who claimed Goldie was her foster brother, and we became what felt like instant friends. She was older than me, a white hippie lady, cool as fuck. Regular celebrities meant nothing to party kids unless they were the type of people to drop E, listen to Morcheeba, and just chill.

My mind was trying to hang on to thoughts, but they disappeared as fast as they came. Wasn't JoAnne supposed to be playing her jazz mixed into progressive house now? Why wasn't she on?

"Anyone there?" the voice implored.

I had noticed Takeshi before he noticed me, with his sculpted blue hair and Hawaiian shirts that fanned out around his lean frame when he skated. But it wasn't until fall of last year that we first spoke. A few months before my mom died. The air had a bite to it, and everything around us was rusting over. The tree at the back of the school was banana yellow, leaves falling like pieces of fire onto the cement. I was standing by the chain-link fence at the side of the school admiring the skaters, a daring move since they owned that turf. I was wearing a dress my mom had picked, paisley and edged with frills.

If Takeshi thought my dress was awful, he never said anything. Out of nowhere, he just started talking to me about how he collected Japanese manga. The conversation was nothing deep. I remember him sort of looping his fingers in through the fence unnecessarily close to mine. He asked me what I did for fun, and I said I read a lot, and he asked me what. "Two things," I had said. "Stodgy old English writers and works by psychoanalysts." He seemed interested in the latter, so

I told him a bit about Lacan, and how Lacan said desiring something went away as soon as you had it. Takeshi said he desired skateboarding but that he didn't stop desiring it just because he boarded.

"But even if you landed all your tricks, tomorrow you'd want to land new ones and maintain what you had. Desires never truly get fulfilled," I explained.

"Come on, Baby. Then what's the point of anything."

"There isn't any point. I think that's the point."

I told him then that *Jane Eyre* was my favourite novel. I said I wondered why Jane had gone for Mr. Rochester when I might have chosen the pragmatic St. John in the novel, who was as steady and reliable as a good fire in a farmhouse in winter. It was something like a confession, telling Takeshi something private like this about myself. Talking to him like I was legit from another century. He told me he'd read the book so he could tell me what he thought of it. I smiled at him in that polite way you do when you know the person will never read the book you recommend.

After that, we always made it a point to catch up at the fence after school, like it was our thing. I knew a lot of girls liked him. He would come around to the other side and chat with me inside the courtyard. His nonchalance was attractive. He didn't belong to any of the other typical groups in high school: the preps who wore cologne samples from the mall, the grunge kids who lazed around like lumberjacks, the homies with their flat-capped basketball hats that still had the shimmering silver retail stickers they came with. Takeshi was forever wandering off to skate alone and smoke cigarettes. A single amidst clustered pods.

"Isn't it funny," he once said to me, "that my parents wanted to give me the coolest Western name they could think of, Jed, so people wouldn't see me as Japanese. But people still fucking call me Takeshi anyway?"

I had laughed at this. He was telling me so many things with this sentence: while he knew he'd been accepted by the white population at our school, they still kept his Japanese signifier there. Maybe I got him because I knew what it meant to carry the burden of having a culture that everyone else viewed as foreign and ethnic.

"I met this dope Indian girl," he said. "And she likes Victorian novels and psychoanalysts."

"Would you rather I was into saris and Bollywood movies or some shit? 'Cause you're gonna be disappointed as fuck if you do."

"Nah. I was thinking maybe something more mainstream. Like TLC. Wait, are you telling me you don't follow Indian movies at all? 'Cause even I know that song '*Ek Do Teen*.' Sounded mad cool until I found out Madhuri Dixit was just singing the goddamn numbers. Stick Boi'd have a field day with that one. Hey Coconut," he teased, "you do know who Madhuri Dixit is, right?"

"Obviously," I snapped. "Not that anyone here would give a shit. And hey, I get your name issue. I wasn't named Baby. I have a brother and when he was two, he pointed at me and said 'Baby.' And it stuck. We don't get to choose how people see us. Somehow, other people think they see you best. Their version becomes reality."

"Ain't that the truth. Does your brother go to this school?"

I looked at him then, really taking him in. His skin was lighter than mine, flawless yet made up of hard features, with a square jaw. Angular.

"He's older," I said vaguely. Ravi had been older than me by minutes, which was the punchline of the story about when he'd declared me the "baby." But I didn't feel like sharing anymore. No one at school needed to know I was born a twin.

"Hey, I got something for ya."

"Oh yeah?"

"It's a necklace."

"It's really cool," I said, taking the oval pewter locket from him and inspecting it in the light. I ran my thumb over the embossed, raised pattern of swirls and flowers intertwined.

"It's vintage. I, uh, got it at an auction place. Dunno, it made me think of you for some reason."

"Thanks."

I thought he'd maybe kiss me or some shit, but this was real life, not some after-school special. I opened the locket and inside, I found a picture of a young Asian woman washed in pinky, brown tones. Stumbling upon her gave me the same feeling I had when I saw Ravi, that the woman was from a different place and time, and I was meeting her under magical conditions.

After Christmas holidays last year, I dared to enter the area on the other side of the fence, going past the inner courtyard and exiting to the place where the skater boys did their tricks. There was a cement runway here, next to the vast green football field layered in a crunchy coat of dew. My mother's death had made me bold enough to come to school in thrifted skater pants, which I then wore all year, and which eventually made my grandmother kick me out. If Takeshi remembered me in frocks with satin sashes around the waist, looking like a Prairie woman or Mormon, he said nothing. Just waved me over.

Takeshi and Stick Boi eventually lent me their boards while they huffed on cigarettes during breaks. I wasn't a threat. Just someone they were indulging. I was officially initiated when, one day after school, Stick Boi had given an acknowledging fist bump before he left to buy a pack of smokes. By then, I could actually do some things on a board, and what I couldn't do I made up for by not worrying I'd get hurt. I was willing to try anything. That was when Stick Boi and Takeshi ended up putting together a board for me. A present of sorts, because I had no money to go into a skate shop and pick out a real one. When I tried to thank them, they waved me off, saying they were so over phat boards, and that I should know the wheels they gave me were squeaky as fuck.

Now, somewhere in Victoria, Takeshi felt like home. He stayed silent on the line while I got lost in all my jumbled thoughts, feeling like he could hear them. I missed when he and Stick Boi used to hound me for not landing a trick. I missed leaving them to go watch cartoons with Carlie when smoking doobies and getting baked on the couch had seemed like the most badass thing to do. I was wistful remembering high school and how it would have been had raving not taken over my world. Freddie Star's ecstasy was the purest I'd ever done. I felt everything clearly. But my jaws were wiggling so much I couldn't get them to cooperate.

I tightened my grip on the phone receiver. Suddenly, it hit me hard. That necklace Takeshi had given me was not from an auction place. It was his grandmother's. I had seen the same picture that was in the locket when we'd done a project at school about our ancestry. I remembered admiring his grandmother's face in the photo, in that same sepia hue, her hair in a peekaboo hairstyle, soft waves cascading over one eye — unsmiling, head tilted at a glamorous angle. This picture had been pinned on a poster board explaining where his family had come from. Why had he lied to me about the locket?

"I'm going to hang up now," the voice said threateningly. But he sounded like he was faking it.

I should have stayed a girl in a dress from another time. I should have never stored Ravi inside me like a ship in a bottle.

I knew Takeshi would never hang up. So, I did first.

THIRTY

When we got back to Freddie Star's in the morning, we found The-Chris sleeping on JoAnne's lap.

"You never came," Delilah realized, kicking off her platform sneakers.

We all had that muted morning high, like you're wearing sunglasses and your perceptions are dimmed. Everything glowing shades of brassy brandy and rose pink. A champagne dream. Del glided on socked feet to put on Frankie Knuckles, *Live at Ministry of Sound, 1991*.

"No," confirmed JoAnne. Beats pulsated through the house, changing the energy. Del was already spinning around to the music with Marvin, two kids on a playground.

Something seemed off. JoAnne's and The-Chris's faces were fully made up as if they had been preparing for a high-fashion magazine shoot. But they were rooted in place on the psychedelic patterned carpet. JoAnne's pink shrug was crumpled on the floor like a freshly skinned bright pink rabbit. She was wearing a long, baby-blue dress made of sporty material, with dark blue straps. But only one art deco emerald earring hung off her earlobe. "When y'all left," she said dryly, "The-Chris's face went blue, and I couldn't wake him up."

Del and Marvin froze. The happiness they felt from the MDMA started glitching on their face as they were forced to rearrange their facial muscles. "Oh my god," said Marvin, succeeding first at finding an expression of concern. He let go of Del and hugged himself. "Is he fucking okay?"

"He is now," said JoAnne. "But he wasn't breathing. I slapped him. Freddie Star splashed his face with water, and then The-Chris came back. Freddie Star said we shouldn't call anyone." From JoAnne's face I could tell she hadn't agreed.

The-Chris looked so small in his soft pink My Little Pony T-shirt, even though he was six feet tall. Legs folded underneath him, his eye lids were a cool blue. Whatever he had planned to wear tonight hadn't made its debut, but he had dusted silver glitter on his cheeks.

I crouched next to JoAnne. Losing my brother and mother had made me older than Marvin and Del, who were like antsy grasshoppers, not knowing what to do or say. "Did he throw up?" I asked.

"No," said JoAnne. "That's why Freddie Star thinks it's not an overdose. He doesn't need his stomach pumped. Freddie thinks The-Chris just had a reaction."

"Like the kind Selina has?" Selina Wong was notorious in the scene for ending up in the ER because the combination of E and strobe lights gave her seizures. She'd even fallen off a stage once, but it had never stopped her from dropping a cap.

"Not like Selina. The-Chris went cold and dead."

"God. Does he seem better?"

"Yes," JoAnne bit her lip. "I think he's just really tired now."

Marvin and Delilah were now clutching each other like lost children in the woods, saucer-eyed and not much help. I ushered them away. As Del left, she trailed her hand along the parquetry, feeling the grooves between the connected pine boards.

"JoAnne, why don't we have someone look at him once we're home? If we still need to?"

"But what if I called a doctor now, Baby Doll? What'd happen then, huh?"

What'd happen then, huh? What'd happen then? I assumed a face of authority. "If they admit him now, they'd probably just try and calm him. We can do a better job than the nurses. Don'tcha think?

Freddie Star has tea and a warm bed." Hadn't Jimmy once uttered these words? Hadn't they made me feel better?

Del and Marv had put on some come-down music. It was a smuggled copy of that Sarah McLachlan "Vox" song (the extended remix version).

"You're right," she said.

I'm right, I repeated to myself in my head. We were all safe. There was no need to worry anymore. No one was going to fucking die tonight.

THIRTY-ONE

The ferry trip home on Sunday was far less jubilant. I had been thumbing through *King Lear*, but so far nothing was sinking in. Shakespeare just sounded like words baked in words, iced with more words.

JoAnne approached me. In overalls and a trucker hat, she still looked like she was someone important. I was seated next to a picture window that sealed me in and gave me a new artistically rendered view of the sea every second. A chlorophyll sky complemented sea foam crests tinged with algae, slapping gently against the sides of the ferry. Ravi was seated next to me, his shaggy hair a mess. Earlier, he'd been reading lines from my book in mocking tones: "Many a true word hath been spoken in jest, who is it that can tell me who I am?" Now he was doing air drums and looking for pretty girls. When he saw JoAnne coming toward me, he stretched and went for a walk. JoAnne sank into his spot.

"I thought he was going to die," she said, addressing the smudged, thick glass of the ferry. Headphones sat on her head. I could hear the faint buzz of music. She examined the three pink roses inked on her wrist.

"I know," I closed my book. "But he's fine. Really."

She shrugged as if this was besides the point. "It was so stupid to drop E at a dealer's house. Those assholes will never call for help if someone takes too much. And it has happened before."

"It happened before?"

"Yeah," she bit the drumstick part of her hand before continuing. "His heart just stopped at one of our house parties. I had my hand over his chest. But then he came to. Maybe we just oughtta fucking stop." She kept her eyes on the water, watching the twigs gather at the top of the waves. The small refuge refused to disperse into the vast green liquid meadow, remaining fastened to the surface of the water like they were held together by magnets.

The space under JoAnne's eyes looked hollow. "Maybe everything I told you about being able to stay ahead of this lifestyle is a lie. Everything is so very grandly fucked up, Baby Doll." She plucked the headphones from her head and let them drop on her lap. Lou Reed's "Perfect Day" spilled out. She leaned her head against my shoulder. Which was awkward, her being so much taller than me.

"It kinda fucking is," I agreed.

"I don't know what to do, Baby Doll. The-Chris won't quit me, and I don't want to stop partying. What's raving without the drugs?"

"You could try it?"

"I did a few times, and it's like living life without having your five senses. You can't tap into other people's vibes. There's this force field, and you're on the outside." She paused. Gulped air. "He coulda died yesterday."

"He needs to quit, JoAnne."

"I know," she said numbly. But we both knew that The-Chris and JoAnne were as inseparable as an old married couple. "Who was that guy that was sitting next to you just now?"

"What guy?"

"The Brown guy in the denim jacket and Metallica shirt," she said. "He had the same face as you."

Never before had anyone seen Ravi. I should have been alarmed at JoAnne's declaration, but her comment felt very normal. Colleen was the only one who had even heard of him visiting me as a ghost, or as she liked to think of it, my own subconscious appearing to me as a hallucination. "I didn't notice anyone," I lied. And then, for good measure, I added, "All Brown people aren't related, you know."

She chuckled at this. Del would have been offended if had I said that to her, because she mostly forgot about her Chinese side. But JoAnne embraced her Blackness.

"I haven't slept in years," JoAnne said, yawning. "Let's run away to Ibiza together. Just you and me."

"But I'm in school. And, you have The-Chris," I pointed out. As if this was the biggest obstacle preventing her far-fetched idea from being carried out. But in a way it was, wasn't it? She wanted a replacement for her friend who couldn't handle getting high with her. I waited for her response. But she was fast asleep on my shoulder, her neck stretched at an awkward angle. I tried to sit up tall so I could support her. A few ravers travelling back on the same ferry stared. To see L'il Miss Thang, the legend herself, asleep on me.

THIRTY-TWO

It was surreal to walk right back into my normal life with Jie. On Tuesday night, take-out Chinese sat on the floor next to us on a tatami mat. Vegetable chow mein for me, lemon chicken for her, and spring rolls for both of us. We didn't have to raid the spare twenties Jimmy left under the cash register tray anymore, but we did have to order cautiously. Often, Jie cooked for us, a simple stir fry or *yaki udon* or whatever the hot plate allowed. But today she was nostalgic for a Canadianized version of childhood food.

She got up to make us tea from stuff she'd bought in Chinatown, putting clumps of what looked like plucked meadow grass into a strainer balanced atop a tea kettle with a fifty-cent sticker on the bottom. I watched as she poured hot water over it.

I wondered, not for the first time, how I would survive life without Jie. Even without the means to a real kitchen she'd created a makeshift one, with her pink rice cooker, mismatched vintage glassware, and hotplate. Stacks of instant noodles sat on one shelf along with other nonperishables, wrapped in brilliant red and green plastic packaging. Some foods I'd eat, like nori or mandarins. Others I'd avoid, like shrimp chips or fragrant barbecue fish strips. She had a glass bowl filled with Chinese candies called White Rabbit. I thought Del would get a kick out of them. If only I could tell her about Jie.

She handed me a small ceramic cup with Hello Kitty on it. Loyal to Japanese pop culture even though she was born in China. "Jimmy's hanging around the H kids now." She blew on the matcha in her teacup, a contained sea of green. "It's not looking good, Baby. He's, like, deep in the scene now."

"Who are they?" I said, as if hearing their names would help. I unwrapped a waxy candy from the bowl and sucked on it, letting it mix with the bitter taste of Jie's matcha.

"That Scandinavian exchange student who never seems to study but parties full-time. He organizes all the Full Moon parties; he has, um, rainbow-coloured dreads and plays the drums."

"Helmut," I said. "Who else?"

"That skinny girl who looks like she never eats and has a septum piercing, you know? With eyes that look like silver dimes? She dances all night, and she's, like, really fucking good at it."

"Calista."

"Yeah, right, Calista. And that boy," she said, gesturing with her hand to indicate that the boy was tall. "He talks like a robot and wears space boots. I think he plays experimental music."

"The-Chris?" I said cautiously.

"No, no, not The-Chris," she said to my relief. "This one always dresses in boy clothes." She put her fingers to her lips. "I guess you don't know him. He has a weird name … Got it! Billy Be Good."

"So, they all hang out, just shooting up?"

"I guess."

"Oh my god," I said, suddenly feeling cold. "What about Eva?"

"Maybe Eva will outgrow it."

"You think Eva will outgrow H? That girl has never met a drug she didn't like." If Eva had been the one to do that wild-card dose of PCP at the fashion-show rave instead of Del, who knew, she might have even liked it.

"She'll be fine."

"You don't know her that well."

"Maybe you're right. Jimmy and Eva aren't fucking rock stars who have the resources to kick drugs when they're tired of 'em. Stopping heroin is not the same thing as cancelling a magazine subscription," Jie said. "Quitting is hard work."

"Are they really going that hard?"

She shrugged. "Jimmy and Eva think they're untouchable. It's no joke when you need to start switching from uppers to downers and juggling them just so your body still feels things. Eva and Jimmy are chasers," Jie went on. "They're always trying to score a better high than the last. Know how I know? I was the same damn way. I used to work at the Red Dragon massage parlour."

"Right. You said that you worked at a massage parlour before."

"Yeah, well, it wasn't just for massages."

"How d'ya end up in a massage parlour that's not just for massages?"

"You remember I told you my family came here from China when I was a kid," Jie said. "We lived in this government housing in Chinatown where the inside of every apartment looks like a hospital room, right down to the colour and type of flooring they had. Maybe the same company that makes hospitals built our building. My parents worked at a laundromat. That's how I met Raymond Shu. I ran away with him."

"No way. How old were you?"

"Sixteen." She set her tea down. "We got broke fast, and Raymond suggested I work at the Red Dragon and give out 'extras' for cash. It started off easy but then I got burned out, and I never banked any money because Raymond was managing it. One night, when I was super tired, Raymond said, 'try this, it will relax you.'"

"Try what?"

She wrinkled her nose. "Probably meth. When I smoked it, I finally had energy. I enjoyed cleaning. I couldn't fall asleep because everything was zinging around in my brain. But at least when I was high, I was so disconnected from reality that I felt like I was just doing normal chores instead of giving gross guys hand jobs. But after a while, my teeth started feeling weird. And I was wired, awake for days. Raymond looked in my mouth, and he said, 'Fuck, Jie, I can't afford you losing your fucking teeth.'"

"What the fuck is wrong with this guy?"

"It gets worse. The next night he offered me something different to smoke that would take the edge off. He called it 'black' and put it on some foil and gave me a straw. When he lit it up, I was immediately comforted. I had that same feeling you have when you're sitting over a cinnamon bagel and coffee. It was like heated caramel had replaced my blood. Smoking this stuff made me feel like I had a home I never really had, you know?"

"Okay," I said cautiously. I thought about the home I never felt I belonged in after Ravi left.

"It was heroin," said Jie, starting to pace and officially deserting her tea. "Look, Raymond was never mean to me or anything. In the beginning, he flooded me with love and attention. But not one year after I met him, he was dating this skinny little Vietnamese thing named Cynthia. They were literally fucking in our place while I was out turning tricks. She had fake blonde hair and blue contacts, all trying to be a white girl. By then, I was legit shooting heroin. Whatever money I gave Raymond appeared on Cynthia as new foil highlights in her hair or spiky stilettos. He was grooming her — is that what they call it? If I needed the promise of a home, she needed the promise that she was going to be famous."

"This sounds unbelievable."

She didn't acknowledge this. "Raymond kicked me out. Said he needed the apartment to shoot videos to help promote Cynthia. Sometimes, in the middle of my nod-out sessions, I would imagine that Raymond would find me on the streets and bring me back. I had the same guy rescuing me in my fantasies as the one who had put me in the bad situation to begin with."

"Dude, wow."

"Then, one day, walking on the Chinatown fringe, I saw a girl with orange, stringy hair. As strung out as me. She was standing in front of a convenience store holding one of those crispy burritos they keep on a warmer. 'Jie!' she shouted, waving at me like we were best friends. She had snags in her fishnet dress. Cynthia. She gave me her burrito because that's how junkies are with each other. Raymond had thrown her out too. And then for some reason all I wanted was to save Cynthia the way I had wished Raymond would have saved me."

I rolled the candy wrapper into a tiny ball and looked around Jimmy's back room, now a little worried that Cynthia might leap out from behind the closed bathroom door.

"Cynthia was so small," said Jie, interrupting my thoughts, "I probably fell in love with her right then."

I nodded, getting what she meant even though most people wouldn't.

"Cynthia and I lived on the streets together and both had the same love for H."

"How d'ya end up here?"

"Well … one time, we heard this house music. It sounded ethereal. And this guy Bryce? He let us into this rave for free."

"I know Bryce."

"Everyone knows Bryce, dude," she said. "Anyway, Bryce spotted me some cash and I rented us this ten-dollar-a-night hostel on Main Street. We shacked up there for a while. I went to a street clinic that gave me methadone to help me wean off, but Cynthia was still doing everything she could get her hands on. Heroin. And E, too. I'd be the one to make sure she remembered to eat. She hadn't lived with parents who worked in a laundromat. She'd been sexually abused by her uncle for years, and she always thought people were following us or spying on us in the hostel."

"She had paranoia?"

Jie considered this. "Yes, but there was this one guy at the hostel who really did watch Cynthia like a hawk. God, sometimes, she'd get so high she'd shit in the hostel shower, and I'd have to wipe all the waste off her body, like, everything, dude. She was so skinny she stopped getting her period. One less thing to clean. I wanted her to quit the shit."

"How the hell does Jimmy come into all this?"

"I knew Jimmy from raving. We were at a party not so long ago, and I told him my story, and he offered me a place to stay. I thought for sure he wasn't serious. But he brought me here. Put his key in the lock and showed me around the shop and everything. Trusted me, this fucking ex-junkie! Said something about wishing someone got his dad out. But honestly, now I think Jimmy was shopping around for a nanny for this store."

"Hey, I saw you at a warehouse rave in December." I left out the kissing part.

"Yeah, man," she said quietly. "Cynthia and I used to, like, do everything together."

"What finally happened? To Cynthia?"

"I came back to the hostel to say: 'I got us a place, it's safe.' Only no matter how many times I checked the streets, the hostel, I couldn't find her. And then, I saw her picture in the paper: 'Young Female Identified as Chao Nyugen Found Dead in Warehouse.' They used a raver picture of her of all things, in a foil jumpsuit. I wondered how they got it. They blamed the Vietnamese gangs for her murder, but I think it was that white guy that used to smile at her at the hostel. I keep seeing his face in my head. He had a beard and a weird grin. Looked like that guy from that TV show, *Home Improvement*."

"Al?"

"Yeah, Al. Can't stand that guy's face now. But I'll never know for sure how she ended up there, alone in a warehouse. Dead."

"I'm so sorry."

"She sang, you know. She was real fucking good. Did this killer version of 'These Boots Are Made for Walkin'.' Sounded just like Nancy Sinatra. She didn't need Raymond for that shit. She didn't even like dudes after what her uncle did." She took a long pause. "You know, the weird thing is I'm not even tempted to get high now, dude."

"Really?"

"No. That's why I got these watercolour tattoos. They look like heroin bruises, but I keep them there to remind myself of who I never want to be again."

I looked down at green, yellow, and purple swirls inked masterfully into the crooks of both her arms. "I really did think they were bruises when I first met you."

"I can cover them whenever I want with new tattoos. Turn them into another kind of art. I signed up for school, Baby. One day, I'm going to be someone."

Cynthia had been engraved in Jie's heart. I now knew the feeling of Jie's pain when she ate pho without Cynthia or saw knee-high boots Cynthia would have liked in a shop window. It made sense now why, one time when we were hanging out, Jie had run after a petite blonde Asian woman for two blocks. But in that back room filled with fortune cookies, factory T-shirts, and broken girls, I could only think of how I lost Ravi.

"I didn't even know her real name until I read it in the paper," Jie muttered. "I didn't even know her real fucking name."

THIRTY-THREE

Jie and I had turned Jimmy's shop into our own underground blues bar, no joke. It had all started one night, when I played Nina Simone's "Blues for Mama" on the old record player. On Thursday the moon was in the waxing gibbous phase; the illuminated portion slowly gaining brightness. I'd been wanting to dive into Jimmy's blues collection for ages because Li'l Miss Thang was always playing such dope stuff. Jie had been changing into pajamas. Her current underwear was nothing but lavender strings. I wondered how in the world she could be comfortable in something like that. The back room lights were on, casting a golden glow on the otherwise dark store front. That song immediately transformed the place into a bourbon-soaked dance floor with a whiskey bar.

"Madam, this music calls for alcohol," I called out, making for Jimmy's collection to pour us shots.

"Jesus Christ, Baby, let me at least make us a cocktail."

"Well, what do you know how to make, huh?"

"I make a damn good whiskey sour. The Red Dragon did give me some kind of education, you know. I have stolen sugar packets from the café down the street, a lemon, and one egg left. You just wait and see what I can do with that shit."

After that, we got proper hooked on blues. Jie got stuck playing Etta James's "Stormy Weather" for one entire rainy Sunday. Etta James, it was turning out, was Jie's soul twin. We pillaged through Jimmy's records and lip-synched along theatrically until we got to know the collection a whole lot better than Jimmy ever did. Every night after we closed, rich voices filled every corner of Jimmy's surfer's paradise. The harmonica, slide guitar, and guttural sound of the deep south were somehow relatable to us.

We wore out an album labelled *Mississippi Blues,* which featured a young Black boy in a cap on the cover. We loved its sister album, *Louisiana Blues*. That cover displayed a photograph of an old man washed in blue tones. Jie liked to stomp and clap hard to Sister Rosetta Tharp or sway to Lightnin' Hopkins. I liked the scrappy, thread plucking guitar version of "Nobody Knows You When You're Down and Out" by Scrapper Blackwell.

One night, when we were dancing to "I Just Want to Make Love to You" by Etta James, I saw Ravi walk by the store. Jie knew every break in the song, and my arms were on her waist. For the last few days of May and a big portion of June, Jie and I had gotten lost in moments just like these. Illuminated rain ran down the street windows, pouring out of a crow-black sky. Ravi was moving fast, head dipped low, the late spring downfall pounding down hard on his denim jacket.

I wanted him to come inside. I wanted him to meet Jie.

But just that afternoon, I'd seen Del at the smoothie shop after school and agreed to go to an outdoor rave with her. Ravi didn't like me going to raves with Del or doing so many drugs. Almost as soon as I thought of going to one, he'd skip visiting me altogether.

The whiskey tasted like metal and fire in my mouth. Ravi was giving up on me. Eventually everyone did.

Jie was so lost in the song she was unaware of any of my thoughts. She couldn't fill my every need. Because she hated partying, I still needed Del. When Del and I were high, we almost had as much fun as Jie and I did when we weren't. I was living for the moment, not planning like Jie was, with her college applications and organization skills. The nights were growing warmer; summer was around the corner. I was drawn to techno and bass. To cooling down in air-conditioned dark clubs, doused in turquoise and fuchsia lighting. To dancing in fields of corn. I wanted to borrow Del's outfits and make an artistic statement. I wanted to get into places for free, never pay for drugs, and be recognized everywhere I went.

    I wanted to be a Sugar Kid.

PART 3

SUMMER 1996

THIRTY-FOUR

The outdoor rave Del took me to was not the infamous Summer Love, but something close. It was in Whistler. June had five fantastic Saturdays in it, and this was the fourth one. Rappers and rockers were going to perform on one of the multiple stages. DJs were going to play progressive house and jungle. Del had gotten us special passes to wear around our necks so we could get backstage and into the VIP area.

I drove us up in Del's car. It was becoming silly of me not to just get my driver's licence. I could parallel park, drive comfortably in the left lane on highways, and back into stalls better than Del herself. One time, Del was so high that I got us home from the club, crashed at her place, and then drove myself to school the next day in her car. I had come into the parking lot blasting an underground drum and bass tape by Doc Scott while all the other kids came in playing Korn and Limp Bizkit. I had kept Del's car for two whole days before she bothered to page me and ask for it back.

Other ravers travelled there in big herds, like they were kindergarteners on a field trip, waiting for a shuttle bus that would take them to the secret location. If you wanted to drive yourself, there were numbers you could call that led to other numbers, which finally led to the destination. Del would never travel in a shuttle bus with "the peasants." But today, she was confused with the directions she'd cajoled out of one of the promoters.

"These directions don't make any fucking sense," she muttered.

"Do you want to pull over and call the hotline number?"

"Fuck that. Hang on a sec. Baby, look, there's a shuttle bus. Follow it!"

"What if it's a decoy bus? Or a Korean tourist bus?"

She shrugged. "Then we'll go see some sights?"

Not ten minutes later, the bus pulled into a parking lot filled with ravers.

"See, it always works out," Del said, as she fanned her eyelashes to help the glue to dry faster. Tori Amos's "Professional Widow" (the Armand van Helden's Star Trunk Funkin' mix) was playing. A bootlegged version, because it wasn't even on the streets yet.

Tracking down the location of the Whistler rave reminded me of this game that Ravi and I used to play when we were five. We both had the same dream of finding a majestic carnival in the jungle where animals talked, and there were rides, popcorn, and shows. We conjured up the fantasy that only little children could find this fantastical place using the directions given to them in their dreams. We told our dad, and he played along with us. He and my mom took us on a car ride, and from the backseat Ravi and I would shout random directions to him. He would take every turn we narrated. Somehow we never argued over which direction was correct, in the hopes we would eventually stumble upon this vision. Twelve years later, following that shuttle bus, I finally did.

I hopped out. I had dressed in a tight blue satin top made of baseball jersey, cropped high enough to show several inches of my abdomen, low-rise jeans, and my pink wig with a beanie. The T-shirt was an upgrade from the worn-out cotton blue Yankees shirt I had worn back in December that caused my grandmother to blow a gasket. Del was wearing her blonde wig and a dress made from the same material as my top. We matched as a fashion statement: she was supposed to be the feminized version, and me, the masculine. We did variations of this look often; usually she wore the dress while I wore phat jeans, but we both put on wigs and similar, glittery makeup.

Both of our outfits for this party had supposedly belonged to the television actress Alyssa Milano. Del seemed to always have hook-ups from movie wardrobe departments.

That night we posed for a lot of pictures. I never saw any of them. We modelled on the hoods of cars sucking on purple lollipops looking like the Sugar Kids we were. The performers wanted proof that they partied in Whistler with these legit West Coast ravers. It was kind of a reverse celebrity hustle.

The indie rockers usually knew how to have a good time, having been to European raves. There was this band with mechanical, whining sounds first manufactured and heard in Europe. Carlie would've liked them. The drummer and I talked a bit, and it turned out he read the same kind of books as me. But you could always tell who the rappers were right off the bat because they were dripping in blinged-out ice, spicy-sweet cologne, and brand-name jeans. They seemed uncomfortable in a space where people danced in flared pants in the dust, high on E, handing out candy necklaces like New Orleans parade trinkets. The rappers, made up of crews of Black, Asian, and white guys, would stand off to the side, staring at the candy-sucking, pastel-outfitted elf-like girls who were only interested in each other. They couldn't catcall anyone. Even if they tried, they were silenced with face stickers and glitter. The rappers who tried ecstasy for the first time often got lost in the fields, perpetually confused in the way I worried Takeshi and Stick Boi would be if they dropped caps, and they were Del's favourite thing to babysit. She loved taking the thick-chained, bandana-clad men into corners, keeping them around her like pet tigers.

Now, my lips were dry, I felt light as a feather, and my belly was weightless. Del and I had dropped E almost as soon as we had parked the car, even though the sun hadn't gone down yet. I pulled my top lip over my bottom, reaching past it as far as I could go down, marvelling over the way the microscopic peach fuzz under my lip felt like a patch of velvet. I hadn't eaten dinner. On the drive, Del had rebuked my suggestion to stop at McDonald's, saying we'd get higher on empty stomachs. Soon, she had said, I'd forget food.

But still, my body pinged with an internal alarm system, signalling hunger without the pain. Ravers did not value food stands. In the UK, I heard they served fresh fruits at raves. I would have loved a slice of something tropical. I was thirsty for sure. But raves were charging obscene amounts of money for bottled water, reminding me of the five-dollar milkshakes in *Pulp Fiction*. If you were a rave veteran, you would look for the Jesus stall. There you could find people wearing fleece jackets who gave away free bottled water from pop-up tents decorated in signs of salvation. But they always wanted to talk about Jesus. It was always embarrassing to turn to the Jesus tent out of thirst.

I looked around, parched. I'd lost Del to the lead singer of the band. There was a faint ringing in my left ear. The sky was stained by a spilled cup of tea, Earl Grey soaking the clouds. Like a mirage, I saw Eva before me, white-blonde tufts blowing in the wind. She was wearing a white halter dress with a swing-out skirt, just like Marilyn Monroe in *The Seven Year Itch*. I felt like we were standing in the middle of a desert. In her hands was a huge bottle of water that gleamed in the setting sun like a container of liquid diamonds. Without asking, I took her bottle and drank like I was standing under a majestic waterfall.

"This is one the best nights I have ever had," I said.

I could hardly believe it. On the outskirts of the crowd, I saw stands serving buttered popcorn and caramel apple sticks. I could make out rollercoasters weaving between trees, up behind where the mountains were, tracks looping high in the sky. I could see a man giving out bags of hot, salted nuts to dancers. They said that E couldn't make you hallucinate, and yet I saw these things. My mouth felt strong and alert as if I had downed a cup of hot coffee on a lukewarm morning, and I was able to tell Eva everything. I was back in the magical carnival in the jungle that Ravi and I had imagined. Who had the dream first? Had I, after waking up, filled Ravi's head with the idea so he thought he'd had the same dream? Or had we really shared dreams?

Somehow, even through all the music, Eva nodded.

"Wow," she said, her hands in the sky. The night was like a pair of blue suede shoes now, with boysenberry clouds inked here and there. White fairy lights lined the stage and in all our talking we'd been pushed to the front. The lights made it feel like we were at some intimate event, perhaps a Parisian dinner party hosted in a courtyard.

"I had the same thing with my sister, Lila," she said. "Except our spellbinding place had horses, and we imagined they'd be decorated in glitter and have rainbow manes. We thought if we stepped on the right patch of grass in our backyard, we'd unlock a secret meadow and pink-tailed ponies would be waiting."

"Wow," I said mystified. "Do you think all kids dream this kind of escape?"

"I dunno," said Eva. "I think it's really special we both did."

"Do you see the fair I'm talking about? Out over there," I pointed behind the rave stage.

"Sure. I can even hear the coaster."

I hadn't even told her there was a coaster. I squinted at the mountains. She resumed her frantic kick-step dance, one hand on an imaginary cap, channelling a break dancer from the eighties. Several chains of candy, layered on her neck like jewels upon on an ancient queen, bounced gently against her clavicle.

"There's my enchanting meadow," she pointed to a grassy hill to the left of the stage. "Bet if we walked there now, there'd be ponies with diamond-speckled rumps. Lila won't come to these parties. She's still entering those beauty contests I quit. Guess who she wants to be?"

"Who?"

"Miss Canada."

We burst into manic laughter. Tiny sparks were coming off Eva and she was glowing, fairy dust outlining her body like she was an angel. She was goddamn otherworldly.

I saw the people around us rise and fall in dance. Happiness, I thought, was that feeling of weightlessness. It came from not worrying about tomorrow, enjoying time as a standalone unit in the now. Not worrying about dying or getting old, or if you produced the best human being you possibly could have, or overfishing, or world politics, or global hunger. I sighed and a rainbow breath came out of me. I wanted to ask her if doing heroin bubble-wrapped her and kept her safe from the world.

"I wish other people could enjoy this," I said. Stress fell away from me like trees clearcut in the Amazon.

"People are too busy taking from one another to enjoy the beauty of sharing moments," said Eva.

"All the evil in the world is built on the idea that for me to have more, you should have less."

"Imagine if we were all to just accept everyone should have the same things?" Eva added.

"But there are hierarchies, colonies, monarchies."

Sweet Drop's "Hallelujah" was playing, the remix by Doc Martin. This flute played a melodic riff and the word "deeper" kept popping out. Doc was legendary for unravelling spools of acid house into his hardcore, tribal basslines.

Eva and I were standing face to face, the crowd roaring around us like a live fire, the techno growing louder. A single tear rolled down her face, like the emotion was too much for her body to handle and it had squeezed its way out. The way Colleen's devil's ivy plants spilled water out from the tips of their leaves in her office, crying out their nutrients. I could see the whole rave in the drop-shaped diamond coursing down her face — the DJ, the screen behind him projecting the image of tropical islands, the spheres of purple lights bouncing off dancers. It would have been sensory overload if Eva wasn't holding my arms tightly, anchoring me to the floor. Like when that Josh Wink tune had sent me over the edge at the Victoria rave. I couldn't count on Del to bring me back to Earth the way I could count on Eva.

I wish Jie and I didn't have to live in Jimmy's back room, I thought. Worry leaked into me like water onto a compromised raft. But did Eva even know I lived there? Should I tell her now?

I have so many secrets, I wanted to say to Eva. *And it all begins with my twin brother ...*

"Why is everyone so greedy?" she asked, her green eyes still sparkling with wetness.

I saw humanity for all its ugliness. I saw concentration camps with rooms filled with human hair, Roman gladiators fighting each other to the death, an atomic bomb blooming like a mushroom over Hiroshima. The Spanish inquisition and the Salem witch trials, and all the missiles dropped by presidents, even the revered ones. People stolen from Africa, whipped, and shackled on boats. Sweat shops filled with children in foreign countries. Beggars maimed to make money. All the horrors I knew of filled my brain. All the way to Jie's boyfriend first offering her meth, then heroin.

Del said noticing skin colour was the problem. As if our modern society was not built upon the very stratification of colour. If people didn't notice I was Brown, why did Jimmy make it a point to tell me he only dated European girls? When I raved, admittedly, I felt like a raver and not a Brown girl anymore. Just like when I skated, I was a skater girl first. But deep down I knew I wasn't fooling anyone. Just like the way people at school called Takeshi by his surname because no one forgot he was Japanese, not ever.

Could I tell Eva about these thoughts that had started bothering me so much more lately? We hadn't dropped E at the same time, done the same batch, or even consumed the same amount. And yet, we seemed to be riding the same wave.

"Say Eva, would it bother you if Jimmy only liked white girls?"

The music was hard techno now, like a rave anthem of some sort, classic dubstep, and people were jumping, all chanting the same slogans, doing that universal dance, part of some secret society. And suddenly, I was an outsider looking in.

"Jimmy what?"

"Jimmy, you know, saying he preferred white girls. Is that weird?"

Was it fair to blame people for having certain sexual attractions? Weren't we all trapped inside skin costumes that we had no control over choosing? All these imagined categories meant things to other people. I wasn't sure I should have said anything to Eva, but it was too late to retract my words. They were ringing through the air, bouncing back and forth, an auditory boomerang.

"He dated Del though. Isn't she half Asian?"

"Yeah, but," a man shoved me while he sang along with the others. *Bring down the bass. Make it drop.* An Expo '86 visor covered his face in a menacing red shadow, and he held one hand to the tip of it, churning his body back and forth. "She passes," I said, regaining my footing.

"Passes?" The crowd was swimming against us, but we were still trying to have a conversation.

"Like Daphne in *Devil in a Blue Dress.*"

"Who?"

"Daphne is a Black character in the book, but she passes as white and thus gets all the privileges that go along with that."

"Oh," said Eva. My window into her lucidity was closing. She was looking up at the amethyst sky. Belgium praline chocolate and pink-coloured clouds raced across it. It had been a million different canvases tonight.

"Well, I never thought of people that way. As colours, I mean. I would date anyone. I always wished Bryce would kind of take notice of me. Do you know him?" Not waiting for me to answer, she continued, "As far as people go, I don't even care if they're guys. I think Li'l Miss Thang is cute as hell. She kissed me once, did ya know?"

"No." I wondered what Eva would think of Jie with her saucy attitude. To me, Jie was the most alluring person in the world. But what did I know about any of what Eva was talking about, having never kissed a boy, or girl for that matter? I didn't even really know where I fit in any of these spaces.

"I'm a person who loves all people," she said. Then she melted me in a hug. "One day, Baby, you *gotta* try hard candy with me. It's even more delightful than this. We'll lie there and not even talk, just communicate with vibes and be rolled in a sugary cloud."

This was the first time Eva had casually mentioned doing heroin. As if she was talking about drinking an artisan beer or seeing an obscure rock band that was famous in some other country.

"Gosh," I said. Suddenly I was afraid everything that was pure about rave culture would end because good people like Eva had moved on to heroin. Someone shoved me and again I lost my footing. "Things are kind of spinning," I stammered, "I didn't eat much ..." *Stay in the now! The now!*

"Okay. I got you. Think of the magical carnival in the jungle, okay?"

"Okay," I said, willing it all to come back. The man near me roared like a lion. "It's coming."

"Good," she murmured, rubbing my back. Eva would make the best mom. We swayed like that to the beat, head-to-head, our thoughts synching up once more. She saw things the same way as I did when we were high. She was my E-twin and had the key to my thoughts. While Del saw skin colour but wanted to pretend everyone was on the same playing field even though they weren't, Eva had a hard time seeing race at all. But because Eva loved people so wholeheartedly, her heart was as pure as a toddler's. I couldn't fault her for not seeing me as Brown. It made me want to protect her all the more.

THIRTY-FIVE

After raving, I felt like I had no skin. It was a Sunday night, so at least the shop was closed. It was that horrible after-E feeling, where my body felt wrecked and used, and my mind was consumed with repetitive thoughts. Nowadays, E always seemed to be cut with speed. My mind looped on a figure eight track. I felt unwashed no matter if I was freshly showered. Everything looked smudged. Maybe I'd never be pure again. Even if I was sleeping next to Jie, who made me feel like the best version of myself, I still felt like dirt.

"Do ya ever feel like if you think too hard about breathing, something that's supposed to be involuntary no longer is? Now that you have to remember to breathe, it becomes so tedious that you start hyperventilating?"

"Nope," Jie said. She was used to my weird post-E questions. She never judged me. Not even the time I called her, lost, in the middle of the night. I had gone to some afterparty that ended up at Café Deux Soleils on Commercial where Raz rapped. He'd given me the flyer for the night, a simple piece of white paper with carbon ink graffiti that I'd tucked into my journal. They were playing reggaeton, and I had ended up taking free E with a girl I'd just met. I had Del's car that night, so I had driven the girl home. But I had gotten so lost, I had to stop at some totally sketchy family restaurant on Kingsway. I called Jie from a busted-up payphone booth to talk me down and give me directions back to the shop. I knew what a stupid risk I had taken that night. I also knew very well it wasn't E I'd done that night. I'd never know what the hell I'd taken.

"Oh," I said, trying to keep my breath level.

"I do much stupider shit though," Jie said. "I pretend I'm dead in bed, okay? I keep my eyes open as long as I can and let my body go completely limp. Until I realize how exhausting being dead is."

I let out a dry laugh. "You're crazier than me."

"No shit."

"I swear I've forgotten how to breathe."

"Cynthia used to have panic attacks. You need a break. Who knows what the shit you're doing is laced with?"

"Do I remind you of Cynthia?"

"Go to sleep, Baby."

I spent the whole night panicking about having panic attacks.

THIRTY-SIX

I was calm when Colleen paged me over the school intercom the next day. I was making buns in Home Ec. I wanted to try something different after being the only girl in Carpentry 11 last year. Everything was scientific: sprinkle this much baking powder in and get results that were just like everyone else's. They were served on paper towels and eaten quickly, steam burning the roof of every mouth because the class was almost over and there were still dishes to be done. I gave my classmates an apologetic shrug and took what was left of my buns on cheap paper towel, wetting the top of my math book with their heat.

I'd come into school to hand in a whole bunch of worksheets I'd done in Jimmy's back room and to pick up my next shipment of homework. The one-year anniversary of my mother's death had fallen in December, and now school was nearly out. Grief had a time limit, and I had passed mine. But lately, I had been getting ill more often, more sore throats, more colds. These sicknesses were my new excuses for the teachers. Not one asked me if I did ecstasy.

As irritated as Jie was with me, time and again she cooked me hot pots, filled with so many vegetables I could not name them, to nurse me back to health. The tradition of the Asian hot pot, she told me, was that each visiting friend was supposed to bring a unique ingredient to change the flavour. One day, I hoped Jie would be surrounded by real neighbours so she could share in many nights of hot pot. One day, I had faith that I would not have to keep living so many separate lives, because it was hard keeping track of them all.

Initially, I thought I'd give Colleen one of my buns and confess about Eva and Jimmy doing smack, with a lot of wit and banter thrown in between. Maybe tell her where I was really living. But then I remembered she was the school guidance councillor, and she could lose her job if she didn't report me as a runaway.

By the time I walked toward her office, I lost the nerve to go in. A bunch of poems I had written were jammed inside my math book; buns balanced atop. My last had been about the world swirling around Eva and I like a hallucinogenic cocktail at the Whistler rave. These were skeletons of writing. I would lie next to Jie and absorb the thick pain of blues singers and Victorian-era novelists, then pour out my own teenage reflections in overly ornate prose. When I reread them, I grew hot in the face at the amateur handiwork.

Without thinking twice, I opened my math book to let the pages of poems slide into the waste basket outside Colleen's office. They landed with a satisfying plunk, because the buns had accidentally followed. Oops. I shrugged at my misfortune. I pictured Colleen inside her office watering her African violets, dressed in their little gowns of purple velvet blossoms. I thought of the window where her monstera plant sat, giant leaves spread out as if she had taken scissors and cut ridges and holes into them. Her bird of paradise plant strained to reach the sun, the pot it was housed in almost tipping over in its eagerness. Tropical madness. This absurd *Little Shop of Horrors* Colleen ran while she waited for me to talk, talk, talk.

I decided instead to go to the library to gather as many books as I could stuff into my backpack. The anxiety of being at school was turning out to be worse than the anxiety of worrying about not being here.

Takeshi caught me by surprise. He was standing in front of the basement library — a well-lit vault filled with trilogies, war stories, novels, and a large collection of Victorian titles — as if he always hung out there.

"Hey Baby," he ran his hand through his blue hair. I had forgotten we had the same hair. It threw me off, seeing a tall, lean version of what people must have seen me as: unapproachable and standoffish, a person part of some subculture they knew nothing about. Though I avoided socializing, the school population noticed me now, and they looked at Takeshi that same way. Like a C-list celebrity. Ravers and skaters were a rare entity in our school filled with homies and preps. He was holding his skateboard awkwardly, like it didn't belong so close to a place filled with books. We were two high school misanthropes, but while I had gained the distrust of the female population, he had gained their admiration.

"Hey," I answered, avoiding his eyes.

"Hey, so, I got a weird question," he said, casually blocking my way. "Did ya, by any chance, call me in the middle of the night?"

"What? No."

"Come on, Baby, I could hear deep bass in the background, you know." At this comment he half smiled at his own detective talents. "Like techno or some shit?"

"I meant to call someone else," I shrugged, trying to get past him. What could I have said? That I had thought of him at some illegal rave in the middle of the night? I felt like the rave scene would ruin Takeshi, and I wasn't ready to leave it yet. It had become my identity. Takeshi went home to a good dinner every night, no matter if his hair was blue or if he could skate the spine of his board down a staircase railing. He would either fall too hard for drugs or remain on the periphery rejecting it all.

I was fucked up and he wasn't. And I wasn't about to fuck him up with my bullshit ways.

He looked hurt at my obvious lie; it must have been hard for him to approach me. He might have fooled everyone else into believing he was a hardcore skateboarder, but I'd seen him dutifully attend all his classes and do far too well in the world of academia to be considered a real rebel.

He tipped his head to one side, trying to form more words. But only one shaky sound came out. "'Kay."

"'Kay," I parroted back. "See you 'round, Takeshi."

"Yeah," he was blinking hard now, unsure how to reach me. "Sure."

I walked away, giving up on withdrawing books. He stood rooted to the floor, right where I'd left him. I was mortified but couldn't stop myself from walking away. I'd find some other boy who would give me his grandmother's necklace and look at me with stupid stars in his eyes, right?

Ravi had left me with so many of his boyish attributes, I felt like I didn't know how to communicate like a girl.

THIRTY-SEVEN

I went to sit in the empty cafeteria. Sometimes, if I was by myself, Ravi might come hang out. But Stick Boi strode toward me. Eased his backpack off and plopped down across from me. All the tables had benches attached to them, mimicking outdoor picnic-style eating. His face was as white as milk; hair, a nondescript brown. Thin strands of it crept out from under his Das EFX hat. He scratched his face, and in the sunlight, skin flakes danced onto our table.

"Where ya living, Baby?"

"What?" I said, a little thrown.

"I'm axin' 'cause I went by your place the other day."

"You went by my place?"

"I wanted to see if ya wanted to grind." When I didn't reply, he added, "Maybe check out that new bowl and half-pipe they built? You know, in North Burnaby, in the rich kid area?" When I still didn't offer a response, he continued. "I was a little harsh, ya know? There ain't no need for me to police you and shit."

I cracked my neck. "Nah, you were right. I can see why you feel ditched. Funny thing is, I saw Carlie more than you and she isn't mad at all. I think I set her free."

"Who ya think me and Takeshi gonna hang out with now that youse gone and left us, huh?" He tilted his face up at me defiantly. "You think we gonna let any dope into our crew?"

"You guys didn't want me to begin with. I fucking face-plant every time I try any good trick. I'd prolly just be hanging out at the lip of the bowl anyway. I'mma sidewalk skater."

He put his hands up on the curved edges of his hat. "Nah, you right," he agreed. "You was like a dead weight holding us down. Now we can ask Rufus to kick it wit us, dawg."

"Rufus who raps, Rufus?"

"Always thought I'd look good in one of Rufus's white track suits, ya know," he made a face like he was in *The Godfather* and reached up to pop the nonexistent collar of his T-shirt. "Wit a gold chain to boot. That'd be tight."

I laughed. "Aw, hell naw. Rufus is not letting your white ass anywhere near him."

"Pish, Baby, Rufus's getting tired of the 2Pac and Biggie shit his boys've been playing. I seen him hanging 'round the fence asking Takeshi 'bout our music, no lie."

"Okay, good for you guys. You're really moving up in the high school ladder of coolness playin' 'Passin' Me By' on repeat. Baiting poor Rufus."

"Don't go fuckin' knocking The Pharcyde, Baby."

"Does this mean you're over being mad at me?"

"Mad? Fuck, no. Ain't that dramatic. Went by your place, didn't I? Know what your old man said? That you ain't living there no more. He didn't seem to care where you was. Yo, I thought that was straight fucked."

My face paled. I thought my dad would have sent off search parties by now, maybe put my face in the paper. After all, I had been missing for weeks now, off his radar since May and most of June. How did the boy abandoned by his dad and raised by a recovering addict have pity for me? Was it because Indian girls were all supposed to have live-in grandmas that made them hot curries and roti? I hardened my face. "I don't give a *fuck* about his reaction, okay? I'm staying at a friend's right now."

"Oh, okay. So, you is fine and proper then, right? That why you got that whack suitcase you rollin' around like a little ol' lady last time we talked?"

"Yeah," I said, my face growing hot with a need to prove I didn't need his concern. "You know The Grape Monkeys, right? In the West End? You know the owner of the shop? Jimmy? He lets me stay in the back room."

His face changed, and I suddenly saw how perverted this sounded. "Not alone, G. I stay with this girl, Jie. We work in the shop. Jimmy's cool. I'm really good friends with his girlfriend, Eva. We're all cool." *Stop saying cool.*

"Do you gotta freezer?"

"What?"

"A freezer." If he was impressed with my newfound connections, he wasn't showing it.

"I mean, we have a small refrigerator." Jimmy had brought in the mini pistachio-coloured piece for beer, but right now, it was a place where unused soy sauce packets and the tamarind sauce that came with samosa orders went to die.

"Ah, good. I was kinda worried the place you'd be staying at would have nothing like that. For reals."

"You think I'm squatting in some crack den? Wait. I'm not storing any hash or fuckin' drugs for you." In my mind's eye, I pictured Stick Boi wearing an apron and baking weed brownies in his crammed kitchen while his mother worked. It seemed like a Stick Boi thing to do, taking a step from his hot-knifing days to try something a little more profitable.

"What?" he said, looking so wrongly accused that it was hilarious, and we both laughed, finally releasing tension. "Naw, dawg. I got a job. At McDonald's, as, you know, a burger flipper." He lifted his chin up again as if he expected me to make fun of him.

I was in no position to make fun of anyone, so I gave him a mild nod. Satisfied, he continued. "They got pizzas and shit now; ya know that? Anyway, I stole a whole bunch for you. They all cheese and veggie and crap, don't worry." He started pulling what looked like frozen frisbees out of his backpack.

"Thanks, man," I choked out. *Why do you know I need help?*

His face said it all, though. One forgotten kid always recognizes another. I looked down at my nails, painted a shade of blue and gold mixed together like something found in the sea. Something Jie had spent ten dollars on at the Shopper's near The Grape Monkeys. I told her she was out of her mind, but then proceeded to paint every nail on my body like I was coating myself in liquid gold.

When I looked up again, Stick Boi was gone. It was not until he walked away that I realized we didn't even have an oven.

THIRTY-EIGHT

Minutes later, Colleen found me in the cafeteria. I was still fascinated with my blue-gold nails. She looked out of place in her koala-coloured cardigan, the same shade some yuppie downtown would paint their condo. But like most people her age, she didn't seem to notice she didn't belong. She threw a stack of papers down on the table. They splayed out like a dealer's deck of cards, but grease-smeared.

"Huh. What's all this?" Was all I could string together.

"It's really good," was her response. "For someone who keeps standing me up. You have to be a pretty good writer for me to admit that."

Puzzled, I saw my own handwriting looking up at me, foreign and displaced.

"I can't believe you tossed your poetry," she said, staring at me evenly.

"It's kind of terrible. My thoughts are all over the place."

"You're seventeen. You write like a seventeen-year-old." Seeing I was going to interrupt, she rushed on, "But in a good way. You have that perspective, and that's an advantage. Think of Anne Frank. She wrote like a kid, and no one else could have better captured her feelings for what she lived through."

I felt dazed.

"There's a contest and you should enter it." She gathered the papers back up.

"Isn't it illegal to retrieve my garbage from the wastebasket? Or unethical? Or something?"

"See the one on the top?" She tapped it. "That's the one I'm going to submit for you. If you let me."

I winced when I saw it. It was about a starlet with burgundy hair. She was beautiful and talented, and the society she was performing for was devouring her. Eating her alive. It was about JoAnne and her alter ego, Li'l Miss Thang. Written in a shocking style rather than the black-out, redacted poetry I sometimes favoured, here I used one word to say many things. I alternated this with a few lines of more haunting details. It was formulaic in a way that tried to be deep, but Colleen was clearly reeled in.

"I mean, go ahead. I don't care," I said, wishing I had a hat on to pull down over my eyes. Why couldn't people just leave me alone already? The only person I wanted to see today was Ravi.

"Does that mean I can submit it for you?"

I stood, shoving a frozen pizza back down in my bag. "Whatever," I mumbled, not wanting to talk about anything anymore. I definitely didn't want her to choose the one I'd written about my twin star, Ravi. That would unravel me.

> On the Big Dipper's handle, the middle star is called Mizar.
> It has a twin star, Alcor.
> Out of the famous duo, Mizar is the one that can be seen
> most clearly from Earth.
> Only some will see its fainter partner orb, Alcor,
> shimmering next to it.
> Ravi is my Alcor, shining dimly beside me and I am his Mizar.
> The one that Earth can still see.

I felt dizzy. Like I might puke or some shit. I stood up really fucking fast and got ready to break the hell out of there. I should have thanked her for believing in me. I should have said a lot of things. She smiled brightly at me, even though I was rude to her.

People were saving me in the cafeteria. Maybe their care would keep me from sinking.

THIRTY-NINE

"I found all these, like, weird, plastic-wrapped discs in the bottom of the fridge," Jie said to me that night. "They're covered in mushrooms. Must be some drug Jimmy wants to sell at parties?"

"Frozen pizzas," I declared. I left out they were from McDonald's. Thai hot and sour soup and Lebanese falafel were Jie's staples, but I'd never seen her touch a Big Mac.

Still, she wrinkled her nose, aghast. "Why?"

"Why not," I said, stretching my legs out on the cot. I was looking at my Biology 12 homework trying to figure out how to answer questions about the lab work pertaining to dissecting a frog when I hadn't been there. Not that I'd support the act regardless, even if I hadn't partied with Del and The-Chris at Mars the night before the dissection assignment. I cleared my throat and added in a lousy French accent, "Don't worry, I'll have the chef make you something else. Are you in the mood for black truffle ratatouille tian and a glass of sauvignon blanc? Let's take a swim first and then decide, okay?"

"Okay, wise guy," she said. "I guess we could use the savings," she pulled out a compressed wheel. "Where'd ya get these?"

"A friend."

"You have a friend who boosts pizzas?"

"Don't people boost anything nowadays?" We lived close enough to the Downtown Eastside that I'd seen people hawking everything from rubber boots to knock-off colognes. "We could have 'em for dinner."

"But we don't even have an oven."

"I realized that after I'd taken them." I set my frog diagram down. "But since you keep spending petty cash to buy weird appliances from Value Village, there must be something around here to defrost them."

"Not petty cash. Like, leftover coins that no one will miss. Tips, really."

"Okay, whatever," I conceded.

"Maybe Bryce'll like them," Jie said.

"Bryce?"

"Yeah," she was looking at me like I was the one who said something outlandish. "You know, 'Hip Hop Bouncer Guy'? I told him to come to our blues party tonight."

Jie and I knew our shit now. Freddy King was a fucking genius. Muddy Waters was the best music to sweep and mop the floor to. Albert King's smooth singing could put you into a trance. And then there were the women. Aretha Franklin. Bessie Smith. Ma Rainey. Big Mama Thornton. Memphis Minnie. Mamie Smith. Patti LaBelle. And jazz women who could still murder a good blues song. Dinah Washington. Diana Reeves. Sarah Vaughan. Billie Holiday's "Lady Sings the Blues" was often a starter song for our nights. Then we'd dance to B.B. King's "Every Day I Have the Blues" like we had been there with the legend himself.

"Tonight?"

"Why the hell not? He knows a lot about music."

"I guess."

There was a time I had thought Bryce was pretty darn cute but now I liked the space Jie and I had carved out for ourselves. And how would Jimmy feel about us turning his shop into a hang out? But Jimmy was coming to the shop less, leaving Jie in charge. I'd come after school and help her close. We knew how to run the whole operation without him. We expertly recorded totals, dropped money and credit card invoices into canvas bags, and safely deposited everything at the bank. Jimmy hadn't ordered new inventory lately, and some things were running out of stock. Still, the place remained a trendy hub for ravers. They loved the shirts that copied popular franchise designs — "Crave" instead of "Coke" or "Pride" instead of "Tide" or "Messed" instead of "Crest." Ravers left behind truckloads of flyers, which Jie and I would leave in tidy stacks near the cash register next to Jie's favourite incense, *nag champa,* made from sandalwood, magnolias, and frangipani. It made the whole shop smell like smoked flower petals.

Jie, however, had been feeling stressed when she did the books. More than once she'd asked me if she shouldn't go ahead and order the trendy items she'd seen at the other shops we frequented down on Granville Street. Sparkly wallets with chains like the one Del had. Handmade halter tops made in India. Raver jewellery: bright, eye catching, and shiny. But the few times we saw Jimmy we couldn't ask because he'd been too out of it. Frankly, it was getting to the point where neither of us knew when he was going to run out of money, and we'd be out on our asses.

The last time I'd seen him, Jimmy had a Chuck Berry album tucked under his arm. He was examining some of the whiskey bottles he'd stored in the back room. I was worried he was going to notice we'd been drinking them, but when he felt me staring, he turned around and flashed me a weak smile. He kept the smile pasted on his face like it was held there by cheap kindergarten glue until he reached the front door, where Jie followed to lock up behind him.

"The two of youse are lifesavers. I couldn't hold up here without ya." He seemed unsteady on his feet. Record glued to one side, his shoulders were stuck in a sheepishly high position, like a child caught misbehaving.

Jie reached for the bolt. He nodded farewell, hands buried deep in vintage denim. As if he would disintegrate into a pile of ashes if he lifted one finger to help her.

Still, it felt a bit naughty letting Bryce in later when he knocked on the back door, like we were geishas entertaining men in some dimly lit den. He set the beer down on stacked boxes. But Jie and I were whiskey drinkers through and through. In addition to the small white plastic table, we had two chairs, a functioning bathroom, a growing amount of kitchen appliances, and a heavy industrial door we'd put rave stickers on. All of which opened to an alley full of trash. Jie had stocked the shelves over the table with Japanese curry mixes and Chinese walnut cookies. Jimmy had dragged us in a case of dishes someone was giving away on the curb, surprisingly in good condition. Once, he had even pulled in a TV, and we had all screamed our heads off when we realized there was an animal living inside. In the end, it was Big Ralph from next door whom we'd begged to remove it for us since by then, of course, Jimmy had already left the shop.

We each opened up a beer with a metallic crack and fizzy hiss. Jie put the rest in the little avocado-coloured refrigerator. Jie had on jean overalls while I had a top on that I'd grabbed from Jimmy's racks an hour before Bryce had come. I tucked the rainbow iridescent tag into my journal; the reflective material looked like a mirror.

Bryce was filling the space with his man vibes, like a lion in a new den. Staking out his new environment, he wandered to the box that Jie had labelled *Baby's Things*. Victorian novels were stacked haphazardly upon clothes. Jie had suggested we get more items in the stockroom — bookshelves, lamps, plants. I told her politely that we should save this kind of thing for our own place. Even though the prospect of us getting there was unrealistic, for now we both kept saving and dreaming. Like we were Jennifer Aniston and Courtney fucking Cox.

"Wow, you read all this stuff?" Under the fluorescent lights of the back room the diamonds in Bryce's ears glinted.

"Yeah," I answered.

"Hm."

Hm? Most times, people were impressed by my taste in books, which I knew clashed with my appearance. I saw him tentatively lifting my copy of *Cranford*. Placing it back. He studied *Wives and Daughters* and then *North and South*, my favourite from my collection of Elizabeth Gaskell books. I had heard that she originally wanted to call the novel *Death and Variations*, which I much preferred as a title. Then there was *Rebecca* by Daphne Du Maurier, *The Tenant of Wildfell Hall* by Anne Brontë, and *The Woman in White* by Wilkie Collins. I smiled, enjoying the covers of my favourite books becoming unearthed. I loved falling into the strange, eerie weirdness of other times.

"It's just funny," he said, turning to me. "These are all white-people books. If you were a white girl, I'd expect it, but —"

"But?" How condescending and judgemental was this? If he was looking at my music collection and saw I liked Pearl Jam or Nirvana, would he be like, "Hey girl, where are the sitar players in your collection?"

"Girl, a bunch of ol' stuffy white people read this bullshit."

"Victorians are my kind of people. They, you know, embark upon adventures and make reflections about life —"

"I mean," he said, pretty much talking over me, "y'all invited me to listen to blues and these books are literally about a bunch of rich white colonialists living off other people's profits. Amiright?"

"How the fuck would you know if you've never even read one?"

He blinked back.

"Look," I said, trying a less emotional voice out, "Jane Eyre was thrown into a horrible institution for girls where she was starved and little ones around her died of disease."

He shrugged. "Baby, what d'ya think was happening to women in Africa and India when she was off having her 'adventures'?"

"I *like* this period in history. Am I not allowed to like it because I'm Brown? That's a pretty limiting constraint."

I thought of how Kwasi talked about capitalism and how the developed world was legalizing theft by buying commodities from other nations at rock-bottom prices rather than pillaging them. How Ravi himself had been riding me about the fact that all the books I loved seemed to be framed by colonial ideologies. Maybe reading these Victorian novels was helping me draw parallels between colonial and postcolonial times. How did Bryce know? Hadn't I been the one to tell Kwasi that at school I was learning Western Civ and English Lit, and that nothing of my people were ever mentioned?

"I mean any good book collection's gotta have *The Color Purple* and *Roots*. You're Indian, right?"

I nodded, fuming.

"Well then, stuff about your Indian culture, too. Ain't that your responsibility to your heritage?"

My Indian Culture? My responsibility to my heritage? The fuck he knew about that. Why did I have to stay in a box while everyone else got to explore the world freely?

"I've done a lot of research on my last name and I'm trying to find out where it is in Africa I came from, you know? My history is slavery, so I'm a bit touchy when it comes to people romanticizing the colonists. My surname is some fucking plantation dude owner's last name. You gotta familiarize yo'self with your own identity before you reach into other peoples'. Or else how do you know how to contextualize your experience?"

"And you think I don't know how to contextualize my own experience? All because you saw a box of books by white people in my space, you know how I think?"

Just then, the song "Strange Fruit" interrupted us. Tonight, Jie had put on Nina Simone's version instead of Billie's. It deflated us both.

Bryce looked at me. "This song gets me every time."

"Me too," I agreed, letting the poetic and sad lyrics about lynching wash over me. I didn't have the energy now to argue. "That really sucks about not knowing what your real last name is. I can't imagine that."

We dropped down to sit on the tiny cot. Jie, unaware of our recent outburst, came and flipped over a milk crate, lighting a joint. She inhaled, her legs spread like a forties gangster, pinching the tube and blowing out indigo smoke.

Once Bryce started to talk, he didn't stop. Turned out, he was from Seattle. He educated us about the Jim Crow period. Civil rights protests. Jie mumbled something about the Free Mumia Abu-Jamal posters that Bryce had shown Jimmy. Abu-Jamal, incarcerated for apparently shooting a white police officer, was a renowned Black political advocate. Even behind bars, he still managed to publish prolific material exposing the long and disturbingly intricate history of racism against African Americans. Jimmy had refused to put up the posters, claiming he "wasn't political."

He clenched the doobie Jie had passed him. "What a privilege to say you ain't political. You Canadians have quite the brutal slave history too. Ever heard of Marie Joseph Angélique?"

"No," I said.

"She was a Black slave from Montreal, and in 1734, was blamed for starting a fire in what was Old Montreal. They crushed her legs and knees with a medieval torture device and then hanged her. Did you know in Nova Scotia, in 1784 — that's an easy date for me to remember 'cause it's fifty years after Marie Joseph Angélique — white loyalists drove Blacks out of their Nova Scotia neighbourhood in Shelburne? All that seems ages ago, but today we still have racist colonial statues all over this city just sitting in their bronze glory."

"We still have Mao statues in China whether people love him or hate him," Jie chimed in.

Bryce nodded. "In the Congo, people took down statues of King Leopold, and that motherfucker cut off Congolese people's hands and feet. And here in Canada, colonizers that did their bullshit get moulded in steel, and we watch tourists take pictures of them? Shit. But why should I expect more when there's racist department store art sold at The Bay next to sixteen-piece dish sets?"

"Racist department store art?" I asked.

"Yeah man. You know, like miniature figurines of tall, skinny African women holding bundles on their head from the plantation fields they just came from. They make fine companions next to any old white lady's wine collection."

"Bryce, it's Hudson's Bay; their whole company is founded on the fur trade and exploiting Indigenous people, what do you expect?" Jie said.

"I still can't believe people buy that shit." I shook my head.

"By the way," Bryce said, "There are more Free Mumia posters in this shop. I hid them on the shelf under the cash register when Jimmy wasn't paying attention."

"Wow, look at you and your big fuck you. How did you even get back there? Well, never mind. I can do one better. Jimmy's never here. I'll go put them up."

"You can do that later," I said, not wanting to be alone with Bryce. She ignored me and padded away in her fuzzy pink Hello Kitty slippers.

I pulled off my hat and started tugging lightly on my hair, a habit I'd picked up to distract myself from shaking. I did it a lot around Del, who was supervising my food intake lately. If Kwasi served me carbs, she would cover my plate with her hands, intercepting how many fried homemade chips with chili and lime I would be allotted.

"Those plantains look like potatoes, Kwasi," Del's voice rang in my head. "I don't care if you say they're bananas, Baby and I, we aren't having any."

Looking down at the rows of coloured bracelets on my arms, I saw tracers. Neon green, electric blue. I shook them back and forth. If I smoked weed, I could sometimes tap in into the E part of my brain.

Just then, Etta James's "I Sing the Blues" started playing.

"No one has a better collection of Black music than a rich white guy who owns a T-shirt shop, I tell you what," he said. I watched as sweat trickled down his neck.

My laughter broke the strain. Once I started, I couldn't stop.

"Hey," he said. "Look, I didn't mean to come down so hard on you earlier. I was only trying to elevate you." He nodded his head toward the door. "Let's take a walk, Baby."

And because I got a flash of Bryce listening to Souls the first time I met him, I agreed.

FORTY

"This whole rave scene sucks girls like you in like a fucking Hoover," Bryce said once we were outside by the very green trash boxes. "Gets 'em hooked on that drug shit."

As we walked, I admired a buttery camel-coloured coat hanging in a shop window. It was marked up so high I could never afford it.

"Even jazz singers did drugs. I don't think it's a whole big deal like you're making it out to be."

"The fuck you think Billie Holiday died from?" He'd stopped in front of a Vietnamese restaurant with the menu taped to the outside window. It was one of Jie's favourite places to get *banh mi*. "Etta James and Dinah Washington, too. You love them, right?"

I was taken aback. I was constantly stretching my jaws and had new patches of eczema appearing on my body, my inner arms, my throat, my décolletage. I broke away from his stare to look over the variations of pho on the menu. "Maybe inner turmoil and suffering spark creativity."

"My dad was a crack addict, man. So, spare me from your naïve portrayal of narcotics. He threw his whole family away for drugs. Smart guy, too. Thought he could control himself. Lost it all. Don't know if he's dead or alive."

He took my hand in his. "My mom had to raise us on her own, man. My dad came back once and lit our whole house on fire. Not on purpose, just him being a fuck up. Anyway," he said, giving my hand a squeeze, "I don't want to repeat the cycle."

"God, I'm sorry." I looked down at my shoes, seeing the laces were unravelling. I'd need new shoes soon.

"Yeah." He had calmed down. "You know, once I read this excerpt written on skid row in the thirties by the *LA Times*? Skid row was originally where all the immigrants went back in tha day. You know what they said about Blacks back then, Baby? And I will never forget this line. Plan to use it in something one day: 'Dapper Negroes, better dressed than any other vagabonds, wander by in riotous groups.' Even when we all dressed up, we pose a goddamn threat to the system, na' mean?"

I nodded. Kicked a pebble.

"I fell for a girl, and she was a Sugar Kid like you are. I saw all the potential spill out of her." I snuck a look at him. You could see how much he cared for this girl on account of his face. "I see girls like you and Jie and I want to save y'all from yourselves. But I really can't."

I looked at the streets, seeing the world as he saw it. A skinny woman pushed her own wheelchair, the broken bone of one ankle jutting out at an ungodly angle because it had healed improperly. The silent flashes of red from an ambulance parked in the distance, because someone had overdosed on the pavement. A man in dreads, dope sick and throwing up in a potted city plant. There was a kid too, not much older than me, ranting on about the Jesus heads, the Mafia, the sun and the moon. Once, I had agreed to buying a guy food on my way back to the shop, though I barely had much money myself, and the guy ran into a 7-Eleven for a donut and a Slurpee. Crack food. And I understood what that felt like; the need to get through, just one hour at a time.

"Do you still love that girl?" I asked, my words too sharp. I wasn't even sure why that mattered.

"I mean," he said. He let go of me then. "I dunno. She's somewhere in Asia. Not sure if she's in Bali or Phuket. I keep thinking if I meet someone new, I'll move on. But then, hey, I'll get some shiny postcard from her … all green islands and blue sea. And I'll be right where I started."

I wasn't more exciting than someone who sent snapshots from exotic places. I was just a stupid high school kid with overdue biology assignments sitting in her backpack.

"What's her name?" I asked.

For a second Bryce's face looked blank. And then I saw something shine in his eyes. "Athena."

"Athena," I said, trying out the name of someone I would never be. Now I remembered Del had told me Athena had summer-blonde hair. That it was shiny and hung down to her waist. Athena was a white girl with an exotic name and sophisticated tastes. Athena wore handmade Indonesian halter tops and cut-off shorts.

"Look," I said, trying to sound impartial, "we should get back to the shop. Jie's gonna wonder where we are." My words were dry. Chapped, like they needed a coat of balm.

Even though there was a part of me that really liked Bryce, something didn't feel right about any of this. I shoved my hands into my pockets before he could take one again and claim it as his.

FORTY-ONE

I went to school the next day, now an unusual thing for me. It was an ordinary Tuesday. I desperately wanted an ordinary Tuesday. Still, I ended up ditching the last two periods to sit in an aisle in the library to read *The Celestine Prophecy*. It was the best place to read the book because of the yellow lighting, the mustard carpets, the yolk-coloured walls. There was a sense of peace that went unduplicated in any other space in the school. The librarian didn't tell on me for being there when it was clear I was skipping. Posters with has-been movie stars told you to read, and lined up next to them were solar system charts so bright and vivid you wondered if outer space could possibly be that colourful. It was not unlike the walls of what a ten-year-old boy's bedroom might look like, all rock charts and fantasy fiction forests.

When I stood to stretch my legs, I saw Takeshi sitting in the history aisle, legs sprawled out. A large, glossy book was on his lap, the page opened to a black-and-white photo. His face was in deep concentration. It felt unfair to look at him without him knowing I was.

"Hey," I said quietly. All the awkwardness of our last meeting was gone, maybe because I sought him out when he seemed vulnerable. "Whatcha looking at?"

"Internment camps."

Wordlessly, I settled down beside him. I followed his gaze back down to the picture of the Hastings racetrack converted to one of the camps for the Japanese people rounded up during World War II, their properties sold to pay for their imprisonment. Japanese people living in Vancouver, from what little I knew, were considered enemies and spies, no matter how many generations they had been in Canada.

"My grandparents were in one."

"No shit," I said, imagining how the Pacific National Exhibition fair was open in the same spot that Takeshi was looking at now. Every summer, you could wear a fancy hat and bet on horse races or walk down to the fair to buy corndogs or ride roller coasters. I remembered a picture of Ravi and I sitting on sparkly motorcycles that went around a circle, our dad in seventies aviator shades holding on to our seats, oblivious to the history of the place.

It was so quiet I could literally hear him flipping the pages over. There were photos of beds stacked next to each other. Of truckloads of Japanese families looking visibly distressed but impeccably dressed, disembarking at the Hastings racetrack. He kept turning. Horse dugouts converted to homes with curtains. Spaces made for washing clothes. A couple that looked like movie stars caught by the paparazzi. The girl had on a sundress with short hair set into beautiful rolls, and her beau, shirtless from doing manual labour, had a cowboy hat in his hand. They looked unprepared for what was going to come next. Takeshi slid his hand over the smooth paper. More photos. Flyers boasting amazing deals from Japanese businesses that had been forced to close, homes for sale at scandalously low prices that whites would profit from. Some Japanese people, it said in small print, were sent to live in log cabins in the interior. There were shots of men on the side of the road doing work. Ladies in the compound at Hastings cooking in the stables. Belongings sprawled out amongst the horse stalls. People peering at us just the way we were peering at them, except we had the protection of years gone by.

"My grandmother burned all her photos in case the soldiers would think they were conspirators. Some were of my family in kimonos doing, you know, traditional things. They left their valuables with a family they trusted before they got sent away, but they lost contact with those people. You know, my family used to run a sushi restaurant on Powell Street? That was once Japantown. Pretty sure there's a rock 'n' roll bar there now."

"Unbelievable," I said.

He gave me a dismissive shrug. "My grandparents met at a camp. Don't know if they fell in love the way we imagine it to be, but they got married. And then they had my mum."

I nodded, a little mystified. It was oddly intimate, me experiencing his life and how he came to be through the pages in the library. But I felt a little robbed, too, because I didn't know too much about my own history, and I had never felt comfortable asking my grandmother questions about the old soda factory in India.

"I don't usually talk about this. At home, there is a deep shame about it, even though my grandparents were unfairly targeted. Now, even I feel kinda embarrassed about the past. How fucked up is that? That's why I decided to talk about my Japanese heritage in that stupid fucking project where we talked about where we came from."

"In History 12 class, you mean?"

He nodded. "I have to hide in here and learn about my own history like some fucking fugitive," he said.

"Do you speak Japanese?"

"Yeah. But get this. My grandparents didn't want my mom to learn Japanese. They made her speak English at home. But my mom rebelled the other way with me and sent me to a Japanese school. She married a Japanese guy that barely spoke English too, even though she had a white boyfriend for years. And yet, it was my mom's idea to name me Jed. She thought I'd have an easier time growing up with that name. She named my sister Megan. Instead of, you know, Megumi. Which was the name she really wanted for her." He kept his eyes down. Crossed his ankles. "My dad's, like, a total off-the-boater, yo. He even eats these weird tiny fish that look like pepper flakes but when you look closer, you'll see they have eyeballs. And still, no one wants to talk about the past."

"Wait, back up a sec. Fish eyes?" I made a disgusted face.

He laughed, "Yeah, dude, I always wonder what would have happened if she married the white boyfriend."

"You wouldn't have been born."

"I always think I would be, but I'd be like half white. And our names, they'd make sense, you know?"

"That's fucked up, Takeshi. And impossible, too," I gave him a little shove.

We chuckled some more. Then he turned to me and said, "Where ya been lately, Baby?"

"Around," I said.

"You know what I mean," he rushed on. "I miss hanging out with you. You're so distant lately."

"I'm not distant right now," I said. God, that sounded like something a soap opera star might say, in a Dallas drawl. But he didn't seem thrown off. We were sitting so close you couldn't slide a ruler between us. What was so wrong with me that when I was alone with guys, they got all deep? Still, he was different from anyone in my scene. I liked all these differences, even if they made him less worldly. He wasn't a know-it-all like Bryce or a washout like Jimmy.

The book slid off his lap onto the carpet. He was inches from my face. I offered him half a smile. He ignored it. I could hear soft footsteps coming from the carpeted row in front of us. Someone selected a book, coughed, and walked off.

"You don't wear the necklace I gave you."

"I ..." The rest of my words got jammed in my throat. How could I tell him that Delilah had criticized it at the party by the ocean in Stanley Park and it had lived in the bottom of my backpack since then? How Del and I did coke that night, and then the scenes around me were ground into an espresso machine and reformulated brighter and more vivid, so that I felt more alert than when I was straight?

"I mean, I just took it off this one night, you know ..."

"At some rave or something?"

I opened my mouth and stared ahead at the neat rows of books in front of us and their call numbers. How could I tell him that at "some" rave I had connected with Eva in a way I had never with any single person in my life except Ravi? That Eva knew my every thought without me speaking, and we relived one another's childhoods? How could I begin to tell him that one time, "some" rave turned into Mexico before my eyes and I'd seen workers in colourful ponchos unload bananas, and if I crossed over, I'd surely be in another country? That The-Chris had almost died, and his face had gone blue, but he'd come back and now, once again, he was the most gorgeous character you ever saw in glittery eye makeup and capes, a goddamn icon, like Elvis or Prince? How would Takeshi feel about me if he knew I had smoked crystal meth from a lightbulb in some boy's bedroom in Maple Ridge? I couldn't say, hey, Takeshi, one night Del and I stumbled into a drug den with these guys who had a mountain of powder on the table, and it was the most scared I'd ever been. Or once, on a ferry, JoAnne, who reminded me of Billie Holiday but with pinkish-red hair, saw my dead twin sitting next to me as plain as day. Takeshi did not know one thing about the world I was in right now. Not. One. Thing.

"Not at a rave," I said, my words finally clicking and falling in place where they should. I licked my lips. "I mean, I guess it sort of was." Even though I hadn't said a word about my thoughts, I could tell they had spilled out for Takeshi to see. He was sliding away from me.

"Don't worry about the necklace. It was stupid," he said. *All of this is stupid,* I could see him thinking.

"It's not stupid," I said.

I kissed him.

It was the only thing I could think of doing to keep him with me. He tasted like those piña colada candies he was always sucking on. A touch of woody cigarette smoke. He didn't smell of expensive cologne like Bryce did. That would have made him older, part of a different subset of people that I didn't really belong to no matter how much I pretended I did.

"Hey, Baby, I uh, I don't think this should happen."

What? He had pulled away now. I felt foolish. He wasn't supposed to say that. He had sobered the moment, weighted it down with heavy words. For fuck's sake. Weren't teenagers supposed to have fun and all that? Jie's music started playing in my head. Etta James. "A Sunday Kind of Love." Pain moved into my chest. He got up in one swift movement and tucked the history book back in its place on the shelf. Sad pages of recorded time finding its place next to other accounts of wars, bombs, killings, deaths. A humanity so fucked up that we had to fill shelves with all the harm we did to one another.

"Are you leaving?" I asked dumbly.

"For now." He was standing over me, shoulders slumped. Stared down at his Etnies, scuffed from all the skateboarding he did. Gave me a crooked smile before he walked away.

Why couldn't I let him in? I was made up of different material. Impenetrable. I looked down at my nail polish. All that was left of Jie's expensive nail polish was sad chips of blueish gold. If I didn't keep picking at it, maybe I'd stay the same person that Takeshi had once liked.

FORTY-TWO

I headed to The Grape Monkeys after school. It was dark and eerie inside, like that old-time museum in Burnaby where you could see how people lived in the pioneer days; the shops all set up with only ghosts to work them. I tented my hands over my eyes like binoculars up against the window so I could see better. *There is a cash register. A folded bunch of T-shirts. Some posters. See the clothing store of the late twentieth century.* I hadn't seen Jimmy in a while, but Jie always opened the shop on time. If she popped out for a bite, she'd always leave a sign. Puzzled, I went and pounded on our back door in the alley. No answer. I went to the front again.

It was then that I saw a tweed hat. A vintage caramel leather jacket. Like the one I'd been admiring when I was window shopping with Bryce. Jimmy. He was bent over on the floor. I tapped on the window. He looked up. For a second, I was sure he was going to ignore me. But he came and unlatched the door.

"What's wrong?" I said, resting my backpack and board on the shop floor. Outside, the sky was a grey, woollen sweater, and it was sprinkling rain. *Why are you here?* I wanted to say but didn't.

"Jie isn't here."

"Okay," I said, even though I hadn't asked that.

"She took off, real angry."

His James Dean eyes looked like sunken stones. He had a coat of scruff on his face — something, no matter how strung out he'd been, I'd never seen. "Because … because I told her some shocking news."

"What?" This was beginning to feel like a choose-your-own-adventure book that I needed to play out in a certain way to get an answer.

"Eva died."

I hit my board with my foot. It rolled forward, meandering into a table topped with T-shirts. "What the fuck are you talking about?"

Now he was crying, back on the floor. "I told Jie, she just took off."

"No. I mean, what happened to Eva?"

"She overdosed, Baby. We've been doing lotsa hard candy at my place. I guess I hadn't realized how much. Eva just falls asleep, dude, even in the middle of taking a shower. If I'd known this time was any different than all the other times, I'd have called the ambulance, tried to get some Narcan into her system."

I blinked rapidly. Everything was so disjointed. Nothing he said was making sense. For some reason, I kept imagining Jie's Cynthia in the shower. "What d'ya mean she falls asleep in the water? Did she drown?"

"No. She was on the couch. We'd just gotten high. She even started making gurgling sounds, you know, like she was snoring? You know how she always falls asleep when she's high, Baby? You've seen her do that, like, a million motherfucking times! Jesus Christ, how was I to know she was overdosing? I was high, too. High as a motherfucker. But she always had to be the highest. Like it was some goddamn competition or shit." He had worked himself up.

"When did this happen?" My body was cold.

"Last night."

Jimmy had lost so much weight I might not have recognized him anywhere else but in this shop. Jimmy had a chiselled chin, this I knew; he had been built like a man from another time. But he was ordinary now; all those features that made him special were washed away. I had crouched beside him, but I couldn't bring myself to touch his bony shoulder.

"I didn't know what to do. I didn't know what to do." He sounded like he was singing the chorus in a song. "We were alone."

Not with Helmut. Calista. Billy Be Good, I thought.

"They put me in a program," he looked up, eyes wet. "No one blamed me, not even the cops. What gives Jie the right?"

"Don't worry about Jie right now," I said.

We both sat in the shadows for what felt like forever.

I imagined Eva spinning at the rave in her Marilyn Monroe dress. Eva, who would be lucid one moment and lost on some cloud in another. Eva, in her heavenly meadow with her ponies with rainbow manes. I thought about her sister the beauty queen. I shivered. Jimmy wanted some sort of redemption, and I could give him nothing. I felt numbly detached. Like the time Del and I had tried coke. Then I thought about Del and how she'd always wanted Eva to be gone for good. I was really mad at Del right then. Really good and fucking pissed at her.

"Don't go," he said to me, his voice faint. I realized that I'd been gearing up to run away from all this. Something soft was playing in the background. A singer I recognized but couldn't name. His voice slipped like silk through the air. It was raining good and proper now.

"Everything'll be okay," I said, my voice far away.

I knew he had people who had already left this world, his dad, his stepmom with the unusual name, Stephania, was it? And Jeffrey, his little kid brother. All three of those people, whom I thought about more maybe than he even did. Maybe this was the time to say that Jeffrey never died that day, that only one half of him died, and it was up to him, Jimmy, to keep the other side going. That now, he had to keep Eva alive, too. Or maybe I should have passed Jimmy off to Del, allow her to be his keeper. And then, out of nowhere, I remembered what he had said to me about white women being his "type." Suddenly, I wanted to tell him he was a cocksucker. More than anything. I wanted to spit that out at him.

But I didn't say or do any of these things.

Instead, I led him to Jie's cot and peeled off his jacket, slowly. And then I kissed him until his tongue came alive, and he could do the kissing for the both of us. I thought he'd be too stunned to act, but he was a man. He didn't taste like candies. He tasted like nicotine. Cigarette butts crushed in ashtrays. Everything in him knew how to act. Suddenly, I recognized the singer on the record. Phil Collins, "Another Day in Paradise." I froze for a second, glitching like a scratch in a record, my body realizing this was happening. I started trembling, but Jimmy ran his hands down my body and the shaking just stopped. Like he knew how I worked better than I did.

He had taken off his shirt. He kept kissing me, like if he were to stop, we'd both remember what we were doing. Phil Collins was bothering me, like a mosquito hovering near my ear. I had half expected to hear Chris Isaak's "Wicked Game," the song that reminded Del of Jimmy. I wanted to eat succulent watermelons on a dishevelled bed like she had. I wanted effortless connection. In the panel shadow box window in the top corner of the back room, I saw rain stream down. I thought of Jie and me drinking whiskey and listening to blues. But it didn't feel like our place anymore. I closed my eyes to block out the room. I saw myself skateboarding with my friends, our hats down low, zigzagging down the street.

Even though he was so skinny he was barely there, Jimmy knew exactly what to do with me. How to position my arms. How to lower himself on me. How to kiss me while he undressed me. He lifted my shirt and my bra up around my collarbone, so I was exposed. Even though I had initiated everything, I was now a passive spectator watching a play. My jeans and shoes weren't on anymore and he was on top of me, and I no longer had control over what was happening to my body.

And then suddenly it was too late.

Jimmy's stubble scratched my cheek. I didn't know how to touch him back, so I just let him do what he wanted to. His rockabilly hair, without the cap, was flat. His eyes, colourless. If fate gave me the chance to choose between them, I'd always choose Eva. But I couldn't make that selection. I tried to imagine Jimmy as he had been. Cocky smile. Superman chin. Del's Jimmy. Even though I wasn't sure

I wanted this, there was a part of me that wanted Takeshi and Bryce to see that someone knew what to do with me.

    The rain slid and slid and slid. I saw Jie's ramen boxes stacked atop one another, a rainbow of colours and flavours. Her organized fruits. Mandarins and bananas and apples. A bottle of sesame oil, chili-garlic sauce, soy sauce. When Jimmy had finally pushed through all my layers and seemed satisfied, I moaned like I was supposed to. It felt good to do what was expected of me. Maybe he'd chased out the boy inside me. Maybe I could officially be the girl who everyone always wanted me to be. Maybe Jimmy had exorcized my dead twin.

    I pulled my clothes over my breasts and tried to find the panties that had fallen under the cot by trailing my hand along the floor. In the shop window nestled in the corner ceiling of the back room, I felt someone looking in. Only someone who would go through the effort of getting on top of the dumpster could peek in. A face was framed in the box for one second, the summer rain drizzling over it. Jie. I felt like someone was squeezing my heart. And then, she was gone.

    Jimmy fell asleep on the cot. I lay on my back, panties on now. It wasn't late enough for the sun to set, but an ashen overcast consumed everything. It was almost black in the back room without the lights.

    The shop would never open. I felt a shock run through me. I had to get away. I put on my skate jeans and worn-out shoes, the soles so smooth they were like pond pebbles. God, I really needed new shoes.

    At the foot of the cot, a disco-silver sequined dress and matching bag caught my eye, like a sparkling fish in the ocean. Del had lent it to me for another upcoming fashion-show rave. She'd promised it would be filled with rich people who did cocaine. She warned me never to wear the silver top "like, ever fucking again" when she gave me the dress, because Del wasn't one to forget a mistake, even if it had happened in December. Now, I shoved the dress and purse in my backpack. I wanted something shiny to take with me. Something with promise. Something that would make me authentic. Like Bryce's Athena.

I opened the stickered door out to the alley. Rain hit me like wet insults. I walked by the green trash cans which looked greener still, in the rain. Board in hand, I looked around even though I knew Jie was long gone.

I hated myself.

FORTY-THREE

I found myself at the smoothie shop on Commercial that same evening. I'd been walking for hours. I felt dirty, used, but I had nowhere I could take a shower. All I wanted was a pineapple smoothie with kale and a shot of protein powder. That drink legit kept me full for hours, sometimes all fucking day long if I needed it to. Kwasi always made them for me when he was working, and I never had to pay. "Betcha you're happy that your friends work here and not Starbucks," he'd say, and I'd always reply, "Dunno man, I could use a grande latte right about now," and we'd snicker, like two old men telling the same joke over crazy eights. Then he'd make me listen to a sermon on something, the occupation of Palestine, the impossibility of the World Bank's debt payback program, or how we could smash the fascists. Kwasi was not a man who tolerated light topics. Propagandhi's new album would blast political punk in the background, with a sample of Noam Chomsky starting off track thirteen. And I'd drink my favourite drink in the whole world through a thick straw and feel like my eyeballs were getting hydrated. Kwasi filling me with everything drugs had taken out.

Tonight, I needed him more than anything.

But Del was behind the counter when I pushed open the door. She had a Rainbow Brite T-shirt on, two sizes too small. Two pigtails. A sparkly turquoise skirt with a scandalous slit. Socks with sneakers. And she was gorgeous. She should have been an actress, not a smoothie maker. British acid jazz percolated in the shop, throwing around mixed beans of sounds. It was that group, Red Snapper. The one Jimmy liked. *Where the fuck was Kwasi?* I had the smoothie shop's schedule memorized.

Everything was wrong about this. I swallowed.

"What the fuck do you want?"

"What?" I said, a little thrown off. "I dunno, a strawberry smoothie?" I gave her a coy smile. Strawberry was Del's personal favourite; she liked to add a splash of vanilla soy at the end. She never used protein, said it was chalky and bulked people up. It would have been a betrayal to order Kwasi's drink from her.

"Sure," she said, in a too-sugary voice. But she didn't motion to get the ingredients. The shop was empty except for me, but there was evidence that people had just been here. Raspberry-stained cups sat on the bar.

I moved to throw the empty cups out.

"Funny thing, I just saw Billy Be Good," she said.

"And?" I said cautiously.

"Eva's dead."

"I know."

Her eyes ran over me like her rag over the counter. "Shouldn't you be all broken up then? You were so into Eva."

"I'm in shock."

"I see. Did ya find out because you're living at Jimmy's shop?"

I blinked. "Yeah, I stay there sometimes. With my friend Jie."

"You mean the Asian prostitute."

"Well," I flushed at this, "she isn't a ... a sex worker anymore. She's still Asian, though." I gave Del a wane smile. Looked at the fresh fruits sitting in a pile behind the counter. So much colour and texture it hurt the eyes. Green guava, ruby pomegranate. Hairy brown coconuts.

"Isn't she a junkie? And a lesbian, too?"

"Um," I was fumbling, confused why Del had put lesbian into the sentence like it was some kind of disease. Jie tried on guys but liked girls better, but that wasn't any of Del's business. "Who cares, right? She's good people, you know? Like us."

"Like us?" she laughed derisively. "You've been secretly sleeping at my ex-boyfriend's shop for weeks with a Korean hooker. Good people, huh. Wow."

"She's Chinese," I said, the words nearly jamming up in my throat before they came out.

By now, my hands were shaking. I wished I had real epilepsy so I could carry around an EpiPen or something, but a doctor had told me ages ago it was only stress that caused it. "If you put your mind to it," he had said, "You can control the shaking."

"And hanging out with Bryce too, right?"

"Bryce?" I squawked.

"Yeah, you know, my best friend's ex?"

"Athena's your best friend?"

"Does it even matter to you if she is?"

I felt like I was emitting Jimmy's cigarette smell mixed with musky vintage clothing. I could feel his bristles on my cheek. Even though he had to be crushed over losing Eva, he had taken the time to study every inch of me. I had thought my inexperience would show. But it was all very natural. Like any woman and any man in any time.

"Billy Be Good said that Jimmy complained all the time about you girls. Bryce was apparently coming around Jimmy's shop when he wasn't there. Not yours or the Asian dyke's shop. *Jimmy's*. Bryce left his fucking revolutionary posters behind," she scoffed. "Which I can assure you, Jimmy'll throw in the dumpster. Or set on fire. He might do that, too, you know. You don't know that side of Jimmy."

"Jimmy lights shit on fire?"

"Jimmy can't fucking stand your guys' fucking ethnic politics. And guess what? Neither can I. You know, your whole lost teenager act? It's getting fucking old."

My tongue got stuck in my mouth like it was crammed with gummy bears. "I —"

"Jimmy told Billy Be Good that you and the whore drank all his good whisky. Said he's all outta his dad's vintage stuff. You know, his *dad who is dead*, dad? I guess that's his own damn fault, keeping you two sketchpads around his shop. And not having the balls to tell you not to touch his stuff."

I searched for something to say. "That's just silly."

"Oh yeah, and Jimmy told Billy Be Good that Bryce took somma his records. His Patsy Cline and Peggy Lee."

"What? No, he didn't." I almost laughed because if Bryce wanted to steal anything he'd have gone for Roy Brown or Ethel Waters.

"So why didn'tcha tell me about Bryce?"

"Bryce only came over one time." Everything was slipping out from underneath me very fast. Jie and I had practically run the shop, but it wasn't ours. Jimmy was clearly irked by us. We were squatting on his land, after all.

"I brought you into the rave scene and all you do is lie to me."

"I never lied to you on purpose. I had nowhere else to go."

"Then why didn'tcha ask me?"

"It never came up." My voice was getting smaller.

"You know what else never came up? That you turned my ex's shop into your goddamn home and entertainment centre. You don't think that's even just a bit fucked up?"

I wondered if I should tell her the truth about Ravi. It would be my get-out-of-jail card: me offering up my personal tragedy to excuse everything. Maybe I'd even tell her he visited me.

"I'm sorry, Del. Look, you can trust me."

"Trust you?"

Even before she replied, I already felt stupid for saying it. All the times I relished in shaking Del off when I'd lost her at a rave; all the times she put me down, lifted me up, showed me the way, bossed me around, acted superior, made me worship her. And in the end, I still did her worse.

"Fucking cunt." Her voice was clear. "Get the fuck outta my life."

Pure gangster. I got up slowly, like I was in a Western movie and I had just put my guns on the table. Then, just as my hand was on the door, Del said something that made my body jerk.

"I *know* you slept with Jimmy," she tossed out. "Because guess who else came here just before you, bawling his eyes out like a goddamn baby? Can you guess? Huh? Can you?"

Oh my god. No. I was shaking good and proper now.

"Yeah, you know who. You think seducing a twenty-eight-year-old heroin addict who just lost his girlfriend makes you grown up? Jimmy's freaking the fuck out because you're a minor. You're not eighteen until July, right? That's statutory rape. He's scared outta his mind that you're going to report him and shit."

"You know I'd never do that." *Just like Bryce would never steal Jimmy's records.*

"But you know what else I think? That you're a fucking lesbian. I shoulda left you in that pathetic Burger King where I found you."

What? "I didn't mean for any of this to happen —"

She blinked past me. "I was trying to save you. From all the bad things that happened to me. But guess what? You will never be me."

She didn't have to say all the ways I wouldn't. I would never look like a girl in *Party of Five*. I would never be a supermodel about to be scouted. I didn't even know how to dress like a woman, not without Del's major intervention. My jaw was locked. Like that time that we accidentally did heroin. Nailed proper shut.

You will never be me. She was right; all along I had wanted to become Del, have her connections, her roommates, her job, her style, her ability to have boyfriends like it was no big deal. It was as if she had electrically shocked me with those words. I got a hold of myself and controlled my body, just like the doctor told me I could. It wasn't so hard. I locked my arms super straight. And then my legs, neck, and back followed, until everything was rigid.

I opened the door and let myself out into the night. I could never go back to The Grape Monkeys again. I would have to ditch the stuff that was still left there. I had most of my schoolwork with me, my skateboard, hat, and of all things, Del's couture dress and matching bag in my backpack. I probably should have given them back to Del. I didn't even like dresses. But it was my last fuck you.

I walked fast through the rain. I imagined selling the dress and purse to some rich West Van housewife and renting a hostel room like Jie had. Someone had to get a kick out of custom-made movie star clothes. Imagine if Carlie knew I had Tori Spelling's dress in my bag. Carlie, my once-upon-a-time best friend who had spent her whole year planning grad of 1996. There was that store on west side of Hastings where you could consign your clothes too, wasn't there? It had those wicked turquoise platform Fluevog shoes sitting in the window. But then, for some reason, I kept imagining the creepy guy in the hostel that had taken off with Cynthia. The Hostel Ripper. As I stepped over a puddle, I saw a young man with shaggy hair in the reflection, standing under a bus shelter in a denim outfit. There were bystanders approaching the bus stop. But I didn't care. I ran and threw my arms around him.

"Ravs!" I cried out. "You showed up! I really need you today."

"What the fuck, man," said the guy. He pried my arms from his neck. My runny nose had imprinted itself on his jacket. "Do I know you?"

We stared at each other for some time. Him, disgusted. Me, confused. He had the same face as me, and that telltale Londoner accent. He looked like my dead twin brother. But ghost Ravi had never acted this way. By now, a bus had swished to a stop. A few of the strangers were peering over to see if the drama would go anywhere.

But it didn't. The guy got on the bus. Flashed a pass. He was a real person, and not the illusion only I could see. "People are fucking psychos in this city, innit," he said. I heard the bus driver grunt a response to this. Three more people followed closely behind him. I let the doors close on me and watched the bus sail on in the rain.

My shaking fits stopped after that night. Somehow, I knew I would never see Ravi again.

FORTY-FOUR

With Ravi gone, so was a whole section of my poems. Shredded edges remained where the paper had once met the binding, soft and chewed paper bits remaining, like an animal had eaten a chunk. That night, after the smoothie shop confrontation, I didn't sell any celebrity dress or go to a hostel.

I went straight to my grandmother's house. She led me to a room as if she had been expecting me all along and immediately went to a closet to bring me outfits from Sears with a seventies vibe. Marcia Brady blouses with sashes that tied at the neck. Everything was either velour, chiffon, or corduroy. Paisley, burgundy, or mustard.

At school, I clung to Takeshi and Stick Boi. If Stick Boi thought it odd that I was doing tricks in wine velvet pants and a plum-colored puffy top with a knotted bow, he said nothing. Takeshi had just started dating a blonde girl with caramel highlights — the leader from Carlie's Frosty Five. Carlie gave me waves, mild like grilled cheese made with processed Kraft squares. Carlie was done with me, and she had no regrets.

In the hallway, Colleen the councillor told me she was moving school districts. She was ecstatic to also tell me I had won the poetry contest, and she would leave the award for me in the school office. I had, of course, missed the event like I missed everything else that happened at school. I wondered what would happen to the jungle of plants in her office. She had once told me tropical plants feigned death when they were moved to different locations even within the same room.

It was amazing how someone could be such an important part of your life and then, bam. Your relationship with them just ended. Like what I had with Kwasi, Raz, Del, Jie, and so many others. How had everything changed so quickly in the span of a few days?

After school, Stick Boi insisted the two of us get pizza at some joint he knew near Commercial Skytrain station the day before grad, because "the crusts were stuffed with dope, gooey cheese." The Italian shop was all sunny murals and wrought-iron patio furniture. Stick Boi ordered for us, and we went to sit outside. Stick Boi dug out half a cigarette and lit it.

"Do you intentionally only smoke leftovers?" I asked, waving away the odour.

"They ain't leftovers, Baby. They called snipes or shorts. But I prefer the term halfsie."

"Bro, halfsie is like if you're going in on something together. Like me and you, on this pizza. You know what else they call a halfsie? A half-erect penis."

"Aw, fuck off, Baby. Halfsie is a cute name."

"As a racist endearment, maybe."

Just then Kwasi walked by. He had a canvas bag thrown over one shoulder, overflowing with a bounty of vegetables. Spokes of a pineapple and sticks of leek poked out.

I shrunk inside myself.

"Hey, Baby! I am making a peanut stew and fufu," he said in a bright baritone. "Are you coming over? Why you such a stranger now, huh? Got a boyfriend, eh?" He smiled warmly at Stick Boi.

"No, we, uh —"

"What you think I should make for dessert, huh? I was thinking homemade donuts with papaya on the side, no? But I bought so many different groceries no need to stick with this menu, nah?" Kwasi loved nothing more than to get stuck arguing with himself endlessly in singsong until someone had the nerve to cut in.

"Right. I mean, I can't come. School work and all," I justified numbly, trying to find my verbal footing. He was so cheery and bubbly. I missed hearing D'Angelo while nestling into Raz's Afghan-covered couches.

"You don't miss my pineapple smoothie?" he said, feigning heart pain. The twists on his head jumped a little as he talked. Kwasi's face looked flawless and sculpted, the picture of health next to ghostly Stick Boi. "She drinking lattes, now?" He was looking at Stick Boi but aiming his age-old joke at me. "Come on, you can tell me, man."

Stick Boi was not good at conversing in general, leave apart with strangers. He shrugged and made a muffled sound, and I could tell Kwasi was offended neither of us were playing along.

"Okay, man. Guess I'll see you around," he said, punctuating the words in a way that said he was sure this would not happen.

I nodded, watching him carry away all his goods.

"What's he, like, thirty years old?" Stick Boi said.

"Dunno. He's a medical student. Friend of a friend."

"Du-u-u-de," said Stick Boi, shaking his head as he watched Kwasi stalk off in his watermelon-coloured shirt tucked into navy pants. "He legit looks like he just stepped off *Sesame Street*. I feel like he's about to sing the alphabet song with Big Bird."

Stick Boi had known that Kwasi was someone I could no longer have in my life for reasons I wasn't telling him, and he had tried to make it better. He knew that everything I had gone through and not talked about had somehow led to me moving in with my grandmother and inheriting Brady Bunch clothes.

Grad fell on June's fifth Saturday. I couldn't believe that only a week ago, Del and I had been in a rave in Whistler. Stick Boi had worn me down to go with him and Takeshi. He framed it like "the joke'll be on everyone else," but I knew he was super pumped about going. Quite simply, I didn't want to have to wear some long, regal dress that should have appealed to my love of Victorian gothic but just felt stuffy and confining. I found Del's dress and matching purse glittering under the guest bed at my grandmother's. Seeing as one of the chicks from *90210* had worn it, I figured it would be better than okay for an event this pedestrian. I had no girlfriends now, so Stick Boi and Takeshi picked me up in Takeshi's dad's car. Apparently, the Frosty Five captain had wanted to be with her friends in a limo. It was awkward waiting on my grandmother's porch to be picked up by not one, but two dates. We took photos, them in their black tuxes holding on to me, shining like a disco ball in the centre.

The party had been awful. I had sat most of the night watching everyone else make conversation at the fancy hotel convention centre. My RSVP had been so last minute, the staff had brought me a plate made up of vegetarian sides. I fiddled for lip gloss in Del's bag, wanting to leave. My finger slipped into a side chamber and landed on something that felt like silk. What was this? I pulled out a baggie with two capsules of E.

"Okay, so the afterparty is next," Stick Boi reported, sliding beside me after some rounds taking pictures. I had refused to take any with anyone and stayed at the table. Takeshi joined us, leaving his girlfriend behind in cloud of Body Shop perfume. Dewberry. Vanilla. White musk.

"I found something," I said, looking away from Takeshi.

"The meaning of life after losing your old one?" Stick Boi grinned, elbowing Takeshi in the ribs.

"Look down."

"Nah, dawg, I can't eat more mashed potatoes."

"Not that, Stick Boi, at my hand!"

He saw my fingers clenching the Ziploc baggie. "You're focking kiddin' me. Are those disco biscuits?"

"Why do you sound Scottish all of a sudden? Yeah, it's E. Look, you and Takeshi always wanted to party with me, right? This could be, I dunno, a last hurrah? We can split these three ways." I didn't mention that this would barely be a buzz for me given what I was used to packing away.

"I dunno, mate."

"Are you planning on sounding like you're in *Braveheart* this whole night?"

Stick Boi swallowed and looked at Takeshi. "How's Takeshi supposed to ditch Michelle, yo?"

"I thought it was Mindy."

"Really, you guys? You both know who she is," Takeshi interjected. And then seeing our blank faces he added, "She's the blondest one."

Stick Boi nodded seriously. "That actually really clears things up, mate."

"Stick Boi thinks he's in Scotland, and Takeshi has a date with Christina Applegate. I'm so thrilled to be a part of grad '96. You fuckers seem like a choice group of people to drop E with," I said, and calmly put on my lip gloss.

FORTY-FIVE

The afterparty was at a club that played pop country. I'd never raved there. Tonight, it was closed to the public so a bunch of teenagers could feel like they were embarking on adulthood. Takeshi drove us from Canada Place to the Granville Strip. The three of us walked in together to hear a big beat rave song. At the DJ stand, L'il Miss Thang's signature bright hair was visible even from a distance.

"What in the world?" I said and made for the turntables. When I reached them, a man looked up, his burgundy wig flopping to the beat. He had a ginger beard and looked to be in his midforties, with several Mardi Gras necklaces dangling from his neck.

"Lemme guess, you don' like Prodigy?" he said sourly in a British accent. "For fuck's sake, don't get all bent outta shape, kid, you staring at me like you is some kinda psycho. Relax, I got Montell Jordan cued up next."

"How about Sasha & Maria, 'Be As One'? I'd love to hear something a little more off the grid."

He pushed over the mason jars filled with glow sticks. "Is you a Sugar Kid? Real and propah? Look, if I play progressive house, your classmates is gonna have me head on a plattah."

I was trying to figure out who this guy was. I grabbed one of his stacked business cards.

DJ MouseCat ᕕ^•ᴥ•^ᕗ Divorces, Lindy hops, Basement raves. Whatever you want to celebrate, I put the hip in your hop. Call 604 765 1090.

"I listened to one of your mixtapes with my friend Eva for hours in a car once," I said.

"Eva who overdosed?"

"Yeah," I said sadly.

"Jeez, kid. Sorry to hear that. She was an angel. But your school's grad committee interviewed me on my exact playlist."

"C'mon, are you worried they won't hire you again? Besides, don't you want to be a headliner at a real rave?"

"A real rave?" he laughed. "Honey, do ya know hard it is to get gigs nowadays? Everyone wants them a fucking star. The last promoter knocked me out of Seattle because he got Aphex Twin."

"That show with Sneaker Pimps in a couple months?"

"Damn rights. Know why that prick calls himself Aphex Twin? He said he had a brother who died before he was born, and that his mom was so broken up about it she gave him the same name. What a crock, right?"

"Hey," I said, deciding to not comment on this for obvious reasons, "your music is dope. I like jungle and ambient mixed together. You DJ'd at the first rave I ever went to."

"Laying it on thick, ain't you, kid? Fine. I'll go full house tonight. Maybe throw the Chicken Dance into my set." He raised a black lacquered vinyl record in the air and gave it a little shake. "For Eva."

"For Eva."

He dropped Armand Van Helden's mix of The Bucketheads song "The Bomb! (These Sounds Fall into my Mind)." Best mix of disco funk and house I could think of. I could almost see Eva and I dancing in Jimmy's living room in her seventies pantsuits.

Takeshi approached me under the purple lights. Everything looked like it was stolen from a Prince album: crushed velvet purple walls, persimmon-coloured carpets surrounding the dance floor.

"Hey," Takeshi said softly. Always unintentionally charming.

"So, you game?" I said, in a business-like tone.

"Last hurrah, right?"

"Right. I can't ruin your life in one night."

He paled at this.

"Relax," I said, laughing. "I'll give you very little. To make sure we all don't die and shit. If you want, we can split a cap three ways and if you're game after, we can split the rest. It's a good amount to start with."

Stick Boi nodded, now behind Takeshi. In their matching tuxes with silver bowties, they looked like groomsmen. We ducked into the men's room and closed a stall behind us. Carefully, I unscrewed a capsule and expertly poured powder on top of the bathroom toilet dispenser holder and separated it into three piles. I wet my finger, pointed it at them and dabbed.

"Bottoms up, boys. Take down the sugar."

"Oh my god," said Takeshi, screwing up his face after he did the same. "This fucking tastes vile."

"The viler, the better," I said, parroting Del's life mantra as I watched Stick Boi grimace.

A little while later, I sat on the eggplant-coloured sofa and waited for my senses to be heightened and for everything to grow warmer and fuzzier. Nothing happened. My dose was far too little for my body to react. But when I saw Takeshi and Stick Boi dancing up a storm to Mighty Dub Katz "It's Just Another Groove" (featuring Andrew Mac and G-Money), I knew they had gotten buzzed. This song was a staple at every rave and club I'd been to since I'd started going with Del. The disco-inspired, velvet-smooth house beat spread over me. The boys came at me, fists pumping the air, and we burst into the bathroom to do our second round. We bumped into Peter Wu and Denis Patel at the urinals. They stared at us like we were having a threesome. But I didn't give a fuck. This time it was way more fun splitting the caps. Takeshi was excited more than nervous, and Stick Boi's pupils were huge.

I sat once more on the couch letting the house music wash over me. Armand Van Helden's "The Funk Phenomena" was playing. It was like I was at Graceland or Mars with Del. And I felt it now. My hip joints loosening, waves of sensuality undulating over me. I tasted the drugs in my throat and reminded myself to tell the boys to hydrate themselves. Not too much though; there was a rumour that some girl had drowned herself by drinking too much water because she was so afraid of becoming dehydrated on E. Suddenly, Takeshi was beside me. I had to resist the urge to push back the blue sculpted waves of hair cresting over his forehead.

"I want to kiss you."

"What? No! Your girlfriend is over there."

"I don't care," he said, leaning in.

"Jesus, Takeshi. That's like Zack breaking Kelly's heart on prom night on *Saved by the Bell*."

"I didn't have the guts, you know. To go for you."

"Look," I said, not allowing the E to reel me in, "I'm a fuck up. Honest."

"I don't care," he said. "Everything is unicorns and gummy bears and that includes you."

"And what of," I hesitated, "Mandy?"

"You literally don't know her name? Look, we can't go back to normal, Baby. We're more than that."

Normal. What a fucked-up word. I thought of how I had lost everyone who had meant something to me in my quest of achieving normalcy. "Not like this," was what I said instead.

I wasn't sure he had heard me because he was buzzing with an E glow. I remembered my first time with Del being the most extraordinary time ever. A trio of girls from Carlie's crew came and pulled Takeshi up.

"C'mon Takeshi," they cajoled, a blur of satin gloves and sprayed updos. The kind of hair and makeup that said they had gone as a group and paid to get it done at a salon. They didn't acknowledge me, and I moved over so they could claim Takeshi.

"Getthafuckup Takeshi," said one. She must have been really drunk. "Youcan'tbelyingonsomechick."

"Your girlfriend is going to, like, flip out," said another.

"Hey," the third said, "Do you think, like, one of us could make a request for NSYNC? This music is so repetitive. What the fuck is it?"

"Idon'tknowitsucks."

"It's like jackhammers pounding in my head. Who the fuck listens to this robotic shit? Would it kill the DJ to play New Kids? Remember when we all went to that concert in eighth grade? When I asked for 'Hangin' Tough' he put on the Macarena and waved me away. Maybe he just doesn't like girls."

"Maybehe'slike gay."

"Definitely this music is gay. The guy has on necklaces and a wig. Look, maybe we can get Carlie to ask him. She's alternative, right? Or goth? Maybe he'll, like, listen to her."

"No," one reflected in a moment of soberness. "She'll ask for Radiohead, and it'll be, like, super depressing in here."

"Let'sfuckingoIhavetopee!"

I watched them enclose Takeshi and take him away. Takeshi wobbled like an oversized blue rabbit in a circle made of satin and shimmering hair. Out of nowhere, he tried to claw his way through the girls and run back to me.

"Oh my god," one of the girls yelped. Trying to escape, Takeshi had peeled off one of her gloves and thrown it to the floor dramatically. The victim touched her bare arm. "Are you, like, high, Takeshi?"

"You think it's weird he's spending so much time with that weird skater chick?"

The girl bent to pick up her glove and then yanked the top of her red sweetheart neckline dress. "Hell fucking no. Everyone knows she's a dyke."

They linked arms with Takeshi, dragging him off.

"Hey, what d'ya say we get outta here and walk to the beach and look at the moon? How focking rad would that be? Huh? Huh?" Stick Boi said, suddenly beside me. I had never seen Stick Boi grin so big.

"That's a long walk, bro."

"I drrrragged you here and I kno' you hatin' everrry minute, girl."

"I'm wearing heels, dude."

"Baby's in heels. And Takeshi's too wasted to drive. How fekked is that. The world is, like, upside down and shit."

"I could drive," I offered.

"What? You don't even have a licence."

I tapped my lips. "I really need to get on that. Especially since I can parallel better than Takeshi. That parking job he did when we got here was horrific."

"Okay, let's go!"

I sighed, "Fucking Miriam's friends took him."

"Fucking Miriam's friends," echoed Stick Boi. "Fuck fucking Miriam's friends."

Stick Boy shot off like a rocket, arms waving everywhere. He headed straight for the centre of the dance floor. Little Louie Vega was playing. The track, "Deep Inside," sampled Barbara Tucker, which I had heard at the first rave Del ever took me to. The song made you feel like you were sinking into a pool of blue water. I saw him spin Takeshi around and around. Then he encircled his hands around Takeshi's waist and ran toward me screaming, "Run, Baby, run!"

A minute later, the three of us were outside the club, panting hard, deep house pouring out like chianti wine into the streets, rich and strong.

FORTY-SIX

"We gotta go before Madelaine and her crew focking catches him and shit," Stick Boi huffed. He was pushing Takeshi like he was a tire he was rolling up a steep hill. Takeshi was officially more wasted than all of us.

Stick Boi tossed me the keys from Takeshi's pocket. We piled into Takeshi's dad's Mazda. I started the car, and we took off. Stick Boi unrolled a window and howled wildly into the summer night. I headed down to English Bay.

There were tribal ravers in hemp ponchos close to the water's edge, playing bongos and dancing. Drawn to the mysticism of drums and bare feet, tribal ravers were usually white and loved Indian clothing, psychedelics, and earthy dance movements — all preferably experienced outdoors. Admiring them for their freedom, I also kicked off my heels and sat on a log, letting my feet sink into the cool sand next to Takeshi while he kept saying, "Woah, cool man," to no one in particular. I never wanted to wear heels, see ballroom gloves, or hear anyone talk about the New Kids on the Block ever again.

"Oh my god," I said flatly. One of the hippie couples sitting on a log was Jimmy and Del kissing. I could recognize her long, hazel pigtails and rainbow pantsuit anywhere. "That was fast."

"What was?" Stick Boi said from the shoreline. "Shit, Takeshi's lying in the bloody sand, yo."

Just as I was about to suggest we should return Takeshi I saw Del drape a blanket over her shoulders. Fuck. Had she seen me? She stood. It was then I realized this was a woman in her forties holding a picnic basket. I settled back on the driftwood log.

"Hey," said Takeshi, now sitting up abruptly in the sand. "So, for real, where the fuck is the necklace I gave you, Baby."

"It's in my journal." It was such a simple answer. "Come sit here," I said. Stick Boi was busy tossing stones into the ocean.

He pulled himself onto my log. "Sitting next to you always gets me in trouble."

"You're way too serious for your age," I said, nudging him playfully.

"Says the girl who reads more Victorian novels than our English teacher."

"Hey, do you think me being Indian means I should read more Indian authors?"

I realized all the sparks flying from the moon might distract him, being this was his first time on E, but he said something quite lucid, reminding me of Eva in those moments she was really with me. "I think yes, we need to know our histories, but I also think that if Victorian novels are your thing, and you dig 'em, fuck it. Read 'em. Maybe one day you'll find a way to merge it all into just you, you know?"

"Wow, you're wise beyond your years," I said.

"Ya think so?" He smiled, absorbing this, the way people genuinely absorbed compliments when high on E. "Duuuude. If you think that, wait 'til you hear this. Jane Eyre is so pragmatic, right? But she still goes for passion with Mr. Rochester over boring St. John. I think that's ballsy. I should take a lesson from her."

"You read the book?" I was genuinely taken aback. White light rippled over the ocean.

"Um, yeah. You told me it was your favourite book. And you know how boring my girlfriend's parties are?"

"Wow, Takeshi, I'm shocked. But you know what? Jane didn't want a logical love. That was her loss, because if you ask me, I thought Mr. Rochester was a narcissistic prick. You're not like that, you know? You're sweet and loyal."

"You make me sound like a Shih Tzu. Am I being friend-zoned?"

"Asshole, you rejected me."

"I guess I wanted to avoid being hurt by you first."

I decided not to go there. "Well, sweet and loyal is sexy."

"Really?"

"Yeah. I mean, it's what I want. Someone who is going to be there for me and take care of me." I thought of Jie and tried not to cry. "That's way better than some entitled dick. Trust me."

He turned to me. His eyes were glittering with pieces of moonlight. He started to kiss me, tentatively at first. Then, hard, passionate, and insistent. His mouth fit mine in a way that was effortless.

When he broke away, we looked at each other.

"Hey," I said softly, "I'm leaving." My words were carried away in the night.

"You're leaving?"

"Yep. I'm going to London." He looked so confused, I needed to say more. "It should come as no surprise to anyone that I don't have enough credits to graduate. Did you know our graduation was renamed 'school leaving ceremony' so all the burnouts like me could still attend? Before Colleen left our school, she pulled some strings and" — I put on an English accent for these words — "I'm 'redoing the twelfth standard abroad.' That and the principal of our school said I'm never allowed back. Like, ever."

"As if!"

"She was dead serious. Anyway, there's, like, this boarding school for girls out there? I have no choice because apparently, none of the teachers trust me here." I gave him a how-dare-they-not-trust-me pout.

"Well, you could try another school."

"My grandmother's willing to foot the bill if I go. And everyone involved thinks I have bad influences here."

"How the fuck is this even happening?"

"Well, she's a soda factory heiress."

"No, I mean how will you leave Vancouver?"

"I don't have much to leave," I admitted.

I saw his pain then, a mound sitting in front of us. Of losing us before us even started. His face was destroyed. He took off his tux jacket and draped me in it and we just sat, holding hands, feeling everything together. There was a sudden chill, and we both leaned in.

"Hey," I said, my voice very quiet, "I think we both knew our timing was off. Right from the start. We have tonight. My story's got to keep going. And so does yours, you know? I promise I'll keep in touch. And I won't even be mad atcha if you keep dating, err, you know, Melissa."

"You swear you'll stay in touch?"

"Cross my heart."

"I've forgotten my girlfriend's name too," he said, and pulled me close to him so I could smell his salty scent and piña colada candies.

PART 4

FALL 2018

FORTY-SEVEN

Next to my laptop were some of my favourite books. George Eliot's *Middlemarch*. Jane Austen's *Emma* and *Sense and Sensibility*. Charlotte Brontë's *Shirley*. On the nightstand was another pile of books. *The Eustace Diamonds, Villette, Lady Audley's Secret*. I had reclaimed these as my first loves. A long time ago, I was told that I needed to understand the plight of people of colour. I spent years on Chinese, Black, and Indian authors. I became an expert in postcolonial and anticolonial literature.

And then I mixed them. Who I was with what I loved. I wrote in the gothic genre featuring Indian protagonists. Because even though I loved all these classics, if I was going to write a novel, I didn't want to tell some white girl's tale. I wanted to tell mine.

I booked an Airbnb close to the New Westminster pier. Just like Jimmy's building, this place looked aged. But once I was standing outside of it, it glimmered in the sunlight. Glassy children's marbles looked like they were mashed into the rock stucco. This was the sparkle-stucco Eva had once told me about. It was October and the air was crisp, fresh.

"Quincey," I said, turning to my son, "Those are old broken bottles you see there, smashed up in the stones. Isn't it enchanting?" I had adopted the quaintest of British accents, which I could turn on or off in strength like a faucet.

"Yeah, mum, it's fantastic!" he chirped, following behind me.

When I opened the apartment door, a retro lime-green couch caught my eye. The piece hadn't been in any of the Airbnb pictures. Immediately, I was reminded of Eva's jumpsuit. I started a little. There was a matching pastel-green tea kettle on the stove, the colour of her eyes. There had been times in my life I remembered her so clearly, she could have been in the next room. Her white hair pinned back in rhinestone clips. Her wild imagination; her manic energy. A character in my newest novel, *Sugar Mansion,* was based on my old friend.

The apartment's interior was recently renovated with bamboo wooden floors, the walls painted the colour of a pale baby elephant. There were chrome appliances and little green succulents that napped lazily on the windowsills in baby-blue ceramic pots. The chairs in the kitchen looked like they were all made from clear water, formed out of a translucent plastic. Bay windows shaped into cubes gave you a full 3D view of the Fraser River. Below the apartment, next to the wharf, there was a market where you could buy jalapeño or truffle cheese spread, rosemary sea-salted flatbread crackers, or cashew toffee, all on a whim. Even indoors, I could hear the cry of seagulls and waves. In 1996, the only sound coming from Jimmy's apartment had been Everything but the Girl. If I were to walk up Columbia Street, in less than a minute I could hunt down Jimmy's old place and see if he was still there. But no such urge overtook me.

Years ago, I had written my first gothic novel, influenced by the Victorian period but set in a contemporary timeline. My protagonists had Hindu parents and British schooling. The Patel family had inherited wealth from a tea factory (based on my grandmother's soda factory) and lived on a sprawling London estate. I included all the classic Victorian gothic tropes in the book. A haunted house from the 1800s. A lovely garden with giant shrubs. A crew of caretakers. Odd siblings — in this case, twins, both avid stargazers. Rajesh died in a tragic car accident at ten, while his sister, Manisha, was spared. Through the sheer art of believing, Manisha did not accept Rajesh's death and thus Rajesh continued to age as normal mortal humans do, raised by caretakers who also believed he survived. Meanwhile, Mrs. Patel, believing her son was dead, went mad and locked herself in a room and Mr. Patel coped by leaving on long business trips. Just like my own mom and dad behaved when Ravi died, I had the Patel parents withdraw from Manisha Patel.

In my novel, the staff noticed ghostly occurrences. They were confused why Rajesh sleepwalked through the garden, stargazing. Or, why the deceased driver of the other car kept reappearing on the Patel driveway. I based this character on my grandmother, down to her regal Indian outfits. Manisha Patel continued to live in the mansion with Rajesh and the staff, and through the power of faith, Rajesh was eventually able to be seen by the rest of the town once more. I called the novel *Twin Star,* and it was later turned into a series on BBC called *Cursed Twin Star.*

For my second novel, I used one of the Victorian mansions in New Westminster as inspiration. The main characters here were Indian sisters who were well versed in Mary Shelley books and solved local mysteries. I channelled the outrage I had felt when Bryce told me I shouldn't idealize Victorian novels to demonstrate that Indian people didn't have to be spokespeople in saris for the rest of their lives. The publisher thought a book based in this area should be launched here.

I set my suitcase on the oatmeal-coloured sheets in the bedroom. Quincey was off exploring the apartment. I hadn't planned to live in London for so many years; it had simply been easy for me to stay. I fell in love with the buskers at the tube, who in recent days were all doing raspy, reworked versions of Ed Sheeran songs. Or Camden Town's bizarre-gothic-circus tattoo shops and camphor-scented boutiques. In 2000, when the French musician St Germain released the track "Rose Rouge" with its iconic sampling of Marlena Shaw singing about getting together in her bluesy way mixed with jazzy, deep house beats, I had felt nostalgic about my time raving and listening to blues with Jie. But when I married Henry, I decided to become a permanent resident. This meant I never saw my grandmother again. Occasionally, before she passed away, she would send me diaphanous, botanically inspired Carol Brady blouses, so thin they would slip like wings through my hands.

A couple years ago, my father visited me in England. Fully white-haired, he was more cheerful than I remembered. Maybe this was because I had married a sensible man and started behaving as he thought a woman should. Or maybe it was because he had been freed of the burden of having to worry about me. Either way, the past sat between us like a pile of boulders on the table as we ate Pakistani food, just like we had all those years ago. With my son, my father had no past and thus was free to be jovial.

In England, I developed friendships that took the place of family. Danika, my first dormmate from boarding school, became my best friend and I watched her marry her wife, Eliza, last year. Stanley Chow had taken the place of Stick Boi and Takeshi for me. In our twenties, we shredded the UK streets on our boards in our frayed denim trousers littered with patches, flea-market jumpers unravelling at the wrists.

Aside from Colleen, Danika and Eliza were the first people I told about Ravi's ghost. On their urging, I spoke to a therapist. There, I obsessed not over his death, but of Ravi rejecting me at the bus stop. I was told it was my mind that had decided to eject Ravi. I did not believe this. It was no use trying to talk to people who could only see the world as comprised of the living and dead, without any middle ground. I could, however, accept that Ravi's time with me was up, and that now he could exist eternally as characters in my books.

Unpacking my clothing now, I couldn't help noting all of it was Ravi approved: blazers both boxy and tailored, fresh white shirts, ties, and sneakers brought over from my notorious collection. A pair of jeans, cuffs hemmed in a way that Ravi never favoured with his skinny, rockstar style but I felt he would admire nonetheless. After I found them all homes, I strode into my son's rented room to do the same, and I found myself thinking of Henry. Ravi was responsible for us marrying.

From Kensington, Henry was fifteen years older than me. He had a Hugh Grant vibe and a penchant for pairing stylish sports jackets with trainers. One of his main marketing clients was a British winery. Most people thought of France or Italy when it came to wine, but England had some surprisingly good vineyards. Henry was constantly scoping out various wine estates and cellars in Sussex or Kent. We contrasted deeply, but it worked: I wore Sally Ann jeans and skimpy Top Shop shirts, ate a steady diet of street chips, and danced at nightclubs with Danika and Stanley to out-of-date dance chart hits. We'd let off steam spinning to cheesy Abba tunes under the rainbow lights, skateboards stowed safely at the coat check.

Henry and I had met at a pub that reminded me of a wooden church with its nicked oak-bench seating and stained glass windows. It had probably been there over a hundred years. Stanley and I, driven by hunger, pushed open the heavy doors in tattered charity-shop sweaters.

"Loneliness will sit over our roofs with brooding wings." Henry was shaking his fist in the air with theatrical passion. Why was this man quoting Bram Stoker's *Dracula* to the bartender? "People want a national wine."

The bartender, Ollie, grumbled how England could not make a decent wine to save its queen.

"That's an outdated view, mate. England's cooler, wetter climate means grapes ripen with a unique flavour profile," Henry explained. "Our whites are dry, and our reds are fruity. In fact, our wines are perfect for celebrations."

"It's my brother's birthday today. I want to celebrate," I announced.

"Oh," Henry had said, puzzled. "With a fizzy wine, you think?"

"Why not? Loneliness need not sit over my roof."

Ollie, large and stocky, knew full well of my usual theatrics to get free drinks. But he reeled a little when I kept talking. "My brother isn't alive anymore, but like you said, death can be commemorated in a more cheerful manner, don't you think?"

"Well, not exactly my point. But never you mind," Henry said, swallowing down a frown. "Pour us a glass, Mr. Bartender!"

"Cheers, mate," I held up my flute. "I'm a twin, so technically it's my birthday, too."

"Bloody hell. This one is full of plot twists. Hence your visit to the pub!"

"'There are darknesses in life and there are lights, and you are one of the lights, the light of all lights.' To Ravi," I said, swinging back my glass.

"To Ravi," Henry said, a little thrown off I was also quoting his favourite novel. And then, "It is meant be sipped, you know."

Ollie told him fizzy wine was "never fuckin' goin' on the menu, mate." Henry had still bought us drinks that day.

I smiled, remembering this. "Quincey, do you want some biscuits?" I called out, as I opened several cabinet doors to find the one the teacups were housed in.

On a grey day in London, a skater girl and a wine buff had made a connection over *Dracula*. I grew up in our relationship, eventually dressing less like a street hooligan. Stanley made a lot of fun of Henry at our wedding, but he also liked him. Five years after we met, when I was thirty, I had Quincey. By then I'd finished a degree in English Lit and started writing novels.

I dropped a sachet of orange pekoe in a Swedish-designed white mug. Poured boiling water in and watched the water change colour.

A few months ago, Henry had died of a heart attack. No warning signs. By now, I was an expert at having people vanish from my life. A few nights later, I ducked into the pub where Henry and I had first met. Ollie didn't complain when I pulled out a bottle of English sparkling rosé from a brown paper bag. We drank the whole thing, even though it was far too sweet and Ollie thought bubbles belonged in soda pop.

Empty glass in hand, I had told Ollie I was going home to Vancouver.

"Mum, I quite like this place. Are we going to stay?" asked my ten-year-old. He had rushed into the kitchen to snag the shortbread cookies I'd put out. As if I was going to eat every single one without him.

"Let's start with a visit and take it from there," I said, dipping a ridged cookie into my tea.

Which was the same thing I'd told Ollie.

FORTY-EIGHT

The book launch was tonight. On a whim, I looked up Stick Boi on Facebook and sent him an invite. I saw he'd opened a tattoo shop not far from where The Grape Monkeys had been. I hoped Stick Boi would know who I was — my Facebook profile pic was a place rather than a face: Norton Conyers, the house in North Yorkshire which Rochester's Thornfield Hall in *Jane Eyre* had been based on.

When I looked up Jie, I found nothing. Her memory still caused me searing pain. I saw her in my mind, dancing to Etta James in an orchid negligée. I also did not find anything on Del or Jimmy, not that I would have invited either. I hadn't looked up Takeshi. I just couldn't bring myself to reach out to him despite promising him all those years ago that I would.

I did find a Facebook memorial page dedicated to Eva started by her sister. Eva was immortalized as a beauty queen in an organza, teal pageant dress. In the top banner cover photo, Eva was grinning, silver hair pinned back with rhinestone barrettes, palms holding out piles of gold glitter.

Billy Be Good, I saw, was making money touring schools to talk about his experience using heroin; his sleek, black Astro-Boy hair now replaced by a skinny suit and blonde hair. Calista was working with him, but she'd kept her edgy look. I wondered if that made her more popular with teenagers. Bryce had posted a clip of himself being interviewed as a citizen journalist on police brutality in Seattle. Rather than tone down his ideas, he had grown more aggressive, throwing off his interviewer. And JoAnne, I already knew, was living in Ibiza now. Long ago I had read a magazine article featuring her and then started hearing her signature house tracks being played at chic London boutiques. But now she had a fan page followed by nearly a million people. When I saw that Lady Gaga was one of them, I raised my glass to my lovely friend.

When I looked up Carlie, I saw she now had a little girl named Tabatha. There were pictures from Disneyland. I stopped at one of a pumpkin pie bordered with gold leaves. Carlie had captioned the photo *Thanksgiving at Nana and Poppop's* and typed a follow-up comment: "Mom roasts the pumpkins the night before for this pie. The filling goes in her homemade pâte brisée pastry, and she makes maple syrup whipped cream to go with it! Lucky meeeee!" *What?* I thought to myself. But I suppose Denise had always surprised us with her culinary talents, even in her macaroni-and-dill-pickle-casserole days. I saw her and Bill as homely grandparents now, perhaps putting on a little Rolling Stones and Zeppelin for old times' sake.

Pulling myself out of the social media daze, I looked in the mirror. I had asked my stylist to shave the sides of my head into a proper French fade. I styled the top. I was dressed in a tapered black suit with a white button-up shirt. Sleek, svelte. Instead of giving my characters witch-like dresses made of crumpled brocade, I also dressed them in classic wardrobes of trench coats or streamlined masculine suits. All I had on my face was a serum made from oranges. Despite my experimentation with glitter and fake eyelashes, I'd always be the person who had walked into Burger King and met Delilah, fresh-faced and stripped of pretense. But I wasn't ready for the world back then the way I was now.

"Quincey," I said. On my wrist, I caught a glimpse of The Big Dipper I had tattooed after my first book was published. I cocked my neck, adjusting my watch. For one second, in the reflection I saw myself as a blue-haired teen. "Grandad'll you pick you up soon, mm'kay?"

Dark-haired like me but fair-skinned like Henry, Quincey scowled. Like his namesake from Henry's favourite vampire novel, Quincey liked to tell twisted tales and had a furious interest in weapons.

He was currently engaged with the PS4 system that had come with the Airbnb, fascinated with some game that had guns. He was the same age now as I had been when I lost Ravi, and I was relieved to see him grow up without a sense he was missing his other half.

Autumn was the perfect season to release a gothic novel; leaves fell into a cinnamon pile on the ground, still crisp enough to crunch underfoot. My father had already picked up Quincey by the time my car arrived. Glancing now out at the New Westminster streets, all built on steep hills like San Francisco, I thought about the girl who had boldly driven Del's car. The car whisked me downtown under a cotton-candy sky of pink flossy clouds set against a blue background.

The car stopped at a light. Jie and I would have once flipped out at the idea of a private car driving us anywhere. We'd walked down these very Vancouver streets, where she'd always, out of the corner of her eye, looked for Cynthia. Much like I was looking for Jie now. The traffic light changed. My chest tightened.

On West Hastings, the car pulled to the curb. I stared at the engraved outer stonework and ionic columns on the eighteenth-century-style Birks building, lit up now by cerulean lights. The glittering picture-window boxes featured pear-cut diamonds, beckoning for people to peek at the promise of a lifestyle they would never have. The launch was taking place in one of the skyscrapers here, on the top floor. Funnily enough, my British publisher had tried to sell Vancouver's beauty to me. But no view could have beaten the one I once saw with Ravi, lying flat on a running track, plotting stars.

I entered a building with old-fashioned brassy elevators set in a modern-day lobby with veiny marble flooring. Stepping off on the highest floor, I was inside Midnight restaurant. Immediately, I was hit with a panoramic view of Vancouver. From this vantage point, the horizon was a sliver of pomegranate. This would have been the exact street Del and I once trudged along. I thought of the pasta restaurant we had snaked our way through, the smell of garlic, olive oil, and tomatoes hitting us on the way down to the illegal warehouse party.

Sophie, the woman who worked for my British publisher in Vancouver, greeted me. She had ash-blonde hair and wore a beige one-shoulder dress. I'd met her so many times on Zoom calls that it felt like we'd already met. A table in the front of the restaurant featured my books. In the back, near that endless window encircling the whole restaurant, sat rose-coloured wine and pastel macarons resembling flower petals. Chairs had been set in front of the bar, the nucleus of the restaurant, their direction angled toward the windows where, presumedly, I would give my talk. Champagne glasses sat on the bar.

Many people had already claimed a chair. A smaller venue created the illusion of the crowd being larger than it was. I thought back to my bookstore appearances in the early days of *Twin Star*. I remembered going up to perfect strangers, book in hand, peddling my novel like a car salesman.

I made my way to the podium Sophie had set up.

FORTY NINE

"Ravi did come to see me, and he was realer to me than the stars in the sky," I said, echoing the thoughts of my seventeen-year-old self. "In fact, I used one of his visits with me, when Gastown turned into a Charles Dickens novel before my eyes, to help me create one of the most haunting scenes in my new novel."

People raised their hands.

One lady in the back asked, "Do you think you were drawn to gothic novels because you saw Ravi as a ghost?"

"I don't know," I said honestly. "Ravi grew up with me as he should have. The idea of him not being planted in soil and being burned instead had stunted me as a child, and so, I took on many of his traits to save his soul."

"What author would you most want to meet. Living or dead?" It was Sophie who asked this, surprising me.

"Henry James," I said without hesitation. "At the end of his 1898 gothic horror novella featuring two charges that are looked after by a governess, one of the children, Miles, dies because his heart stops. But as soon as I put the book down, I pictured his heart restarting. I imagined he grew up and went back to the manor to tell the story to the audience, many years later. However, when I looked it up, all academic literature written on *The Turn of the Screw* agrees that it is an anonymous guest that tells the tale, and there is zero speculation that this is Miles. But, just like how no one else in my past seemed to recognize my visions of Ravi were real, I felt readers also failed to see the possibilities there were for Miles. So, I would ask Henry James, have I solved a mystery?"

The crowd hummed, taking this in.

I decided to add a bit more to this. "When Henry wrote *The Turn of the Screw,* he'd lost his friend Fenimore to suicide. He'd also lost his mother, father, and … his brother. Authors in the gothic genre have often suffered tremendous loss. Writing becomes a place of refuge, and conversely, a place where fantastic horrors are given a chance to be expressed."

"Do you like contemporary gothic writers?" A man jotting notes asked.

"Yes," I said. "*The Thirteenth Tale* by Diane Setterfield expertly weaves in all the classic Victorian gothic tropes but indulges in fire and incest as well, something my books have avoided. I love her old-world style of narration. And while *The Goldfinch* by Donna Tartt doesn't fall into the genre we are discussing, warm-hearted Hobie in Tartt's book reminds me of Setterfield's character, Aurelius, in *The Thirteenth Tale.*" I decided not to admit that both characters reminded me of Henry.

After the questions, Sophie settled me down to sign books. A young Indian woman stopped to chat with me as the line dwindled.

"My first passageway into gothic horror was V.C. Andrews books," she confided. "Those dark, haunting book covers with black roses and midnight mansions really sucked me in at thirteen."

I nodded. "People often think the gothic genre is vampires, witches, the occult, or dark fantasy. And these things can, of course, overlap. But children locked away in attics and siblings falling in love are classic psychological horror."

"True." She was wearing a faded old baseball T-shirt and jeans — the very outfit I had worn to my mother's *shraadh,* a lifetime ago. "Gothic horror is a very white space … I'm trying to read more South Asian literature."

I bent over the table to sign her book. "I get that, but I wish Indo-Canadian literature wasn't only about arranged marriages and immigration. I would love to see Indians explore representation and genre."

"Exactly! I can let go of the lack of diversity in *Harry Potter* because that was written, like, twenty years ago, but things have to change."

A tall man approached the table, interrupting the girl. He looked around to make sure there were no more patrons, and then, satisfied, he tapped one hand on the cloth as if to test that there really was wood underneath the linen. I raised my eyebrow at this odd gesture. He had black waves of hair, a fitted leather jacket, and light crinkles under his eyes. He seemed a little uncertain in his step, like he wasn't sure he should be there at all.

"So, look, man," he said, his voice taking me back to 1996, "I just bought this book," he held up a copy of *Sugar Mansion*. "And I'm just wondering, what does one have to do to get a signature around here, yo?"

FIFTY

"Takeshi?" I ran my palms down the front of my slim-fit men's slacks. Before I could think twice, I stood up and threw my arms around him, nearly knocking him over.

"Wow," he said, his uncertainty easing immediately. After he regained his footing he stepped back, holding me at arm's length. "You look good, Baby. Grew up. Turned English, too."

"How did you …" I tried to force any British out of my voice but was failing at this. Unable to find words, I flipped to the title page of my book, and scrawled:

> *To my dearest old friend, Takeshi.*
> *From Sugar Kids to Sugar Mansion. We grew up.*
>
> *— B. Ambani-Walsh*

"Stick Boi told me to come," Takeshi said, watching me fan the page dry with one hand. "He's in LA at a tattoo convention. He wants me to ask you why your profile pic is, and I quote, 'an ol'-ass farmhouse.' Gotta love that guy. Seen him recently?"

"No! I just got here."

"Good old Stick Boi. That guy was always good and pissed at you." Takeshi shoved his hands in his leather jacket pockets.

"Stick Boi was madder at me in high school than my own dad, for fuck's sake."

Takeshi laughed. "Stick Boi's name is sort of ironic now because he's gained a lot of muscle, dude. He's a gym rat. Inked head to toe.

And duuuude," Takeshi paused, gathering himself. "He wears skinny jeans now."

"Noooo."

"Yaap. True story," Takeshi thrust one hand against his heart to convey earnestness. "And it don't stop there. He's got a hipster beard and only drinks craft beer."

"That little fucker couldn't coax a single hair out of his chin in high school. Did he really open up a tattoo shop?" I shook my head, trying hard to picture this transformation of my anemic friend. "I saw that part on Facebook."

"Yeah, the place is like a teenage boy's lair. He started out at as an apprentice, and I guess some investor guy took a chance on him. People come to drink some gourmet coffee that that punk makes. He turned the broom closet into a comic book library. 'Member how he used to draw cartoons in high school? Now my man publishes a comic series called *The Purple Lynx* on the Internet and has a legit underground fanbase. People request tattoos from it, like, all the time."

"I totally remember! He designed one for me in high school."

"Yeah." Takeshi looked the same and different at once. Sexy in a new way, charming in the old.

"And you," I managed to force out, gesturing at him.

"Me? Yeah, man. Well, I, uh, recently got engaged." I followed his gaze to a beautiful Asian woman drinking champagne by the door. She was wearing the female version of Takeshi's leather jacket paired with black satin pants.

I swallowed.

"Her name is Carrie Liu," Takeshi traced his thumb along his angular jaw. "My grandparents reeled over the Chinese bit for a while, but they got over it pretty fast after getting to know Carrie. She's a chef, and she makes better *onigiri* than my mom, no lie. And," he pointed to himself. "Funny thing … people call me Takeshi full time now. Dr. Takeshi. I guess I can officially give up on Jed."

I raised my eyebrow.

"I'm a history professor. Specializing in Japanese internment camps from World War II. I teach at UBC. Do a lot of work with the Japanese Society of Vancouver."

My hand went instinctively to my throat. "Oh my gosh. I'm sorry about your locket. I really meant for you to have it back. Maybe Carrie wants it …"

"What? No, I wanted you to have it." He looked a little startled I had brought this up.

"But it was your grandmother's." I could feel his quizzical eyes upon me. "Takeshi, I saw a picture of your grandmother in the school project. I know the locket is a family heirloom."

Something passed over his face. Confusion? Amusement? "Oh, fuck," he said, now pulling lightly at the collars of his leather jacket. "I said the woman in the photo was my grandmother in that school heritage project so I wouldn't have to interview my own family. I didn't want this Japanese woman and her family's war-era photos to end up in the garbage can, so I took them home from the giveaway box at the auction place. And I gave the necklace with the young woman's photo in it to you. Judging from the letters included in the box, that girl had died young. I thought the necklace could, I don't know, protect you, or something."

"Oh," I said, a little surprised. All those years, that locket had been the one thing besides my journal that had meant something to me. "I," I said, feeling it was only fair that I also share, "have a ten-year-old son. My husband passed away last year."

"Oh, wow. I'm so sorry. But I'm glad you found some happiness," he said. I saw something, ever so minor, flash in his eyes. He lowered his voice. "This is hard for me to say, Baby, but I was kind of a mess when you left. You promised me you were going to keep in touch, and you fucking disappeared on me. Took me two whole years and a flight to Europe looking for you and not finding you, by the way, to finally get over you."

"You came looking for me?"

"I got your grandmother's address from the school office. They weren't keen to give it to me, but apparently you had, like, a million overdue library books and maybe some 'borrowed' ones you never remembered to check out and walked away with? I promised to try and get those back in exchange for the info."

I rolled my eyes at this.

"Anyway, I went to your grandma's house, and she begrudgingly gave me your whereabouts. She figured I'd just write you letters and had felt pretty good about herself when she got to tell some blue-haired Japanese kid that her granddaughter was in another country. But I had a bunch of money saved up from working when we were in high school. When I got to your dorm in London, the people living next door to you said you'd gone to stay at some girl's family's house for the holidays. I think someone named Denny? Nika? After that, my trail ran dry, and my ticket date was up. I decided to travel all of Europe as part of my grand campaign to forget you."

"Oh yeah, Danika," I mumbled. I imagined what it would have been like to see Takeshi in Britain. "I didn't reject you, Takeshi. I moved. Still, I know it must have been hard —"

"I saw Spain, Italy, Paris, Amsterdam. But, no," his voice was thick with emotion, "no, you don't actually fucking know, Baby. You walked away and didn't look back."

"There's a reason I was like that." I checked for Carrie. She was at the appetizer table, lychee macaron in hand. Takeshi's fiancé, I sensed, didn't want to be anywhere near me. I remembered Carlie's crew and how they had a similar aversion to me; it was something you could pick up in the air, like when rain was coming. "It wasn't you. I had things I needed to learn about myself."

"It's okay," he said, holding his hand up. "Because of you, with Carrie, I dove off the highest fucking diving board and just went for it."

"Well, travelling Europe and snagging a hottie fiancé are some pretty cool things to be partially responsible for," I said, trying to lighten the mood.

He didn't laugh. "Honestly, if you weren't my homie, I'd have never come here tonight. But you know what the good thing about Carrie is?" He broke off for a second to look at his fiancé. "I don't feel like Carrie is going to disappear."

"Love shouldn't feel like you never quite have your footing. But, hey, it probably shouldn't feel like you're wearing sweaters, drinking chamomile tea, and baking cookies all day long either." I couldn't help but smile faintly as I said this, conjuring up an image of Henry and I literally doing this. "Look," I said, putting a hand on Takeshi's shoulder, "remember when you read *Jane Eyre*? You said you admired that Jane had the guts to go for the Mr. Rochester kind of love, and I said I'd choose St. John? I always told you I preferred practicality over passion."

"Yeah," he said, looking a little impatient.

Takeshi had shared so many things it was important that I was just as honest. "With Henry I chose St. John."

"Right."

"But I reread that book after Henry died. And I realized the deepest connection Jane had was with her childhood friend Helen. Later, Jane had this same bond with Diana Rivers. Diana taught Jane to speak German and recognized Jane's thirst for life. They really got each other, right? And do you know what I thought?"

Takeshi shook his head, finally making eye contact again.

"I thought," I looked squarely at Takeshi, "that she should have chosen Diana. Fuck St. John and fuck Mr. Rochester."

Takeshi laughed. "What?" he said, perplexed. "That wasn't even a choice, though."

"Exactly. Back then I didn't think it was a choice for me, either. I think men can be attractive and interesting. But I shut my feelings off when it comes to them. In high school I took up skateboarding.

I didn't have a group of female friends. I was lost. And while none of those things demonstrates anyone is queer …" I swallowed, fiddling with my cropped hair, "I'm someone who connects romantically better with women."

Takeshi looked shell-shocked. "'Someone who connects romantically better with women.'" He sounded like a robot reading from a dating website.

"I felt like when my twin died, he became a part of me. Like I swallowed his masculinity or something. Maybe I was exposed to more testosterone at birth; that was one of the theories that kept coming up when I researched fraternal twins. Or maybe none of that is real. Maybe I just like being with women more and would like it no matter what. I was so scared the world would think of me as a dyke, especially my dad and my grandmother and maybe our whole school, that I did everything I could to be straight. Trust me, I did everything I could. All I know is at my age, I'm really fucking tired of fighting it."

He was taking me in. I straightened my posture, ready for his reaction. Suddenly, he saw it, what people today would see in an instant, what his past experiences with me had skewed for him.

"I get it, Baby. Stick Boi will, too." Takeshi was the same accepting person he had always been. Even at forty years old, he looked extremely like his former seventeen-year-old self. It was hard not to see him with a board in hand, jeans slung low on his waist, skate T-shirt hanging off his lean frame. I half expected Stick Boi to come racing around the book table to tell us to hit the road already and stop fucking the fuck around.

I made a face. "That guy better be smoking whole-ass cigarettes by now."

"He fucking does hookah or some shit now at a lounge. Meets me smelling like grapes and ambrosia. And hey," he said, "We all knew you were going to do this whole writing thing. Hell, you even managed to put yourself through some kind of time machine, looking like a character out of *Jane Eyre*."

"Ha," I said, looking down at myself. "I don't think women wore suits back then, but I'll take the compliment. And, by the way, remember your old girlfriend, Marsha? Her friends seemed to know crystal clear I was queer at grad. Said so themselves when they dragged you off to go dance to the house music they apparently hated."

"Who is Marsha?" And then his face lit up. "You mean Miranda? Funny story, those chicks ended up becoming the biggest ravers in the early 2000s. Every weekend they'd go to the Plaza of Nations in these plastic skimpy outfits with glow stick necklaces wrapped around their over-tanned necks and get super wasted and make out with each other. Now they're all married and pretend it never happened."

Carrie, I noticed, was picking up a new flute of champagne at the bar. She really did look lovely sipping that drink. Exposed long neck, beautiful bones, wavy hair hitting her jacket. Her eyes were enhanced with lashes and black smoky shadow. Takeshi and I both watched her for a moment, transfixed. Then he turned to me. "Chicks are not easy to date, dude. Don't be fooled by all the flash. Stick Boi and I might need to help you navigate the waters."

I leaned in close to him, "Well, shiiit, you kinda owe me."

He cracked a smile. "Don't think now 'cause you all in a suit and what not, we'll let you off the hook with the whole board thing, though, Baby. Yo, you are not getting off that easy. And I know those ain't your regular sneaks; all fucking polished and scuff-free. *Fuck that shit.* I hope you can still fucking pick up a board, Baby. Don't go telling your boy you forgot to skate."

"You need me to wear beat-up shoes to prove I'm not a poser?"

I had a vision of Stanley Chow and I then, cruising the streets of London on our boards, seamlessly winding down footpaths and roads, our view punctuated by red double-decker busses and shops that all touched each other in that old village way. I had not realized how much I had missed flying down concrete until that moment. I almost wanted to go off with Takeshi right there and then. Ruin these prettyboy shoes in under one minute flat.

Takeshi gave me a little salute before plucking my book from the table and slipping it under his arm, "Those sneakers are giving me a Rufus vibe, just saying."

"Rufus with the white tracksuits from high school? That Rufus?" I said, astonished.

"If the shoe fits."

"Fuck off, Takeshi. Seriously."

He dodged a punch. "Look, I better check on my fiancé."

"You mean your dead sexy fiancé," I corrected.

He laughed, full bodied and unrestrained. "You're all right, you know that, Baby?"

I held up my hand to signify a goodbye, sure Takeshi was seeing the seventeen-year-old me. For much of my marriage, I was worried Henry would see me as cold and distant, perhaps sensing that I would never fully be able to give myself over to him passionately. We spent our time visiting places like the Brontë sisters' home in Haworth and Shakespeare's reconstructed house in Stratford-upon-Avon. Our relationship was built on comforting walks through pastoral backwoods, cheese-and-wine-dates, and tea picnics. We had lengthy discussions about the emergence of psychoanalysts into the gothic genre. Henry had loved Freud's 1919 essay, "The Uncanny." And while I had preferred tamer, more romantic gothic literature, Henry loved the darker, more horror-driven side of the genre. His all-time favourites were *The Strange case of Dr. Jekyll and Mr. Hide* by Robert Louis Stevenson, *The Haunting of Hill House* by Shirley Jackson, *Frankenstein* by Mary Shelley, and *The Castle of Otranto* by Horace Walpole. He was obsessed with the mad, the murderous, the monstrous. It was no wonder that we had bonded over *Dracula*. Later, I learned that it was never the love story that had fascinated him in *Jane Eyre*; rather it was Mr. Rochester's deranged wife who was locked away in the mansion. And this, I believe, is the reason I never shortchanged Henry in our marriage, because of his love of the untameable.

Lost in my thoughts, I had wandered all the way to the last of the windows. This one was separated from the rest, a little circular cutout that belonged on a boat. A string of white lights framed the curved glass, holding in the inky purple Vancouver skyline like a gallery painting.

"Hey," said Sophie, bringing me back to the present time.

I hopped in place a little. "Hey," I said, my word rebounding off hers.

"Do you want me to put a little music on?" Sophie's face was illuminated with her phone screen as she tapped in her password using alternating thumbs.

I could see the table of confections cleared out by the wait staff now, baby-blue and lemon macarons piled onto a silver tray using tongs. Pistachio, mango, vanilla bean, espresso, and pink passionfruit ones, too. Someone had put on coffee, and the rich smell of roasted beans wafted through the room like a lazy river.

"Yeah, sure."

"'Kay." She sighed. "We can just listen to music and unwind. Stevie isn't expecting me back right away anyhow." I peeked over Sophie's rhinestone-embedded phone case to look at her Spotify playlist. Kanye West, Kendrick Lamar, Travis Scott, Lil Uzi Vert.

"Really, Soph? Like, really and truly?"

She laughed, blocking my view. "It's how I relax, okay?"

"Before you go straight hood to unwind, how about some Etta James?"

"Actually, that sounds perfect. You want me to choose a certain song?"

"'Anything to Say You're Mine.'" I could already hear the words in my head. That melancholy voice singing about never hearing back from the person they treasured.

"Okay. I gotta figure out how to connect to the Bluetooth speakers," Sophie said. "Do you want a tame drink, or do you just want to go in for the hard stuff? Oh, and hey, before I forget, there's a woman at the door that says she knows you."

"I'm thinking a whiskey sour."

"Ooh, legendary."

But I wasn't looking at Sophie anymore. I was staring at the woman standing all the way at the entrance.

"Uh, Soph? Just bring me two whiskeys, neat."

"Look at your face. That's someone important, huh? I'll grab your drinks."

I heard Sophie's words, but they were barely being absorbed. I stared at the periwinkle satin dress with the peekaboo lace bustier. Colourful tattoos wound from her shoulders all the way down to her wrists in designs of cherry blossoms, dragons, watercolour irises, and things I couldn't make out. Her face was round and full, black glasses perched halfway down her nose. Thick, black roots sprouted into green hair laced with turquoise accents, all arranged in a messy updo.

Something inside me jumped.

In her hand was a promotional poster of tonight's literary event, which had been placed at all the local bookshops and universities Sophie could think of. I had never been more grateful at Sophie's insistence that independent bookshops were the best places to promote my book.

I made my way toward Jie, my feet falling into sand.

AFTERWORD

Raving was — and is — a global phenomenon. It is my great hope that readers have their own memories of some of the music in this book, or, for those of you who never lived through these epic times, are given a taste of the acid house era. *Sugar Kids* looks specifically at the Vancouver rave scene during the mid-nineties, featuring club nights with fine West Coast DJs, visual effects teams, local boutiques, and record shops. I sprinkled in some goodies for you veterans: some of you might have seen Mark Farina play or gotten into a Sol night in Graceland for free with a well-worn beer coaster. To fit with the timespan of the book, I made up rave names (but locations may be familiar) and stretched reality to include some quintessential tracks and artists. You can still have brunch at the Templeton or buy shirts at the Rock Shop on Granville (where my eldest son recently just bought Slayer memorabilia), but you will only find Jimmy's surf shop in this book. Like Baby, I had a shoebox full of rave flyers and experiences to help shape ideas. All the characters in this book, however, are fictional. This includes the fabulous Li'l Miss Thang and DJ MouseCat.

    Raving, while an awakening time for many of us, also had a dark side. In writing *Sugar Kids,* I wanted to explore substance use in and around the techno scene. Baby, unable to process many of her emotions after losing her twin brother and mother, is undoubtedly drawn to this subculture. She is also prone to hallucinations and shaking episodes alongside her affinity for MDMA. All are coping mechanisms for her. In fact, many years after Colleen and Baby have their talks, Oliver Sacks would write a book about hallucinations and how they can be shaped by depression, migraines, stress, blindness, or taking drugs. Sacks would declare that hallucinations are a fantastic phenomenon not to be ignored but rather nurtured, like Lewis Caroll's characters do in *Alice in Wonderland*. Colleen, however, tries to help Baby find ways to suppress Ravi from visiting her by trying to fix her mental state so she wouldn't need to find solace in the company of someone who doesn't live in this world. How different would life have been for Baby if Ravi were to continue visiting her?

In *Sugar Kids*, Baby finds herself adopting a skater persona and a love for Victorian gothic novels. In part, this is to help elevate her acceptance in the mostly white spaces she occupies. She can't relate to her Hindu customs, particularly after her twin brother is cremated. Later in the book, she is challenged for liking "white-people books" and told to read books by people of colour. Baby, who relates to Jane Eyre, finds herself both emancipated and restricted by this advice. Sometimes it serves her well to hide her Indian identity behind a raver or skater persona, but conversely Baby is shocked when she realizes she can't always hide behind a subculture to disguise her Brownness. *Sugar Kids* thus explores whether it is fair for people of colour to be relegated to being spokespeople for their race their entire lives, and if it is their duty to represent their cultural heritage in everything they do. Can Indian people write about books that do not involve chai and saris? Can they be experts in Western topics?

The rave scene was inclusive of many sexual identities, making it a perfect setting for Baby's journey toward accepting her queerness. Her statement to Takeshi at the end is therefore meant to be less of a surprise confession than it is a documentation of Baby becoming herself. Baby's Indian identity makes this journey more difficult. How does the intersectionality of Baby's race and gender play in her coming-out story? It should come as no surprise that our 2SLGBTQIA+ youth are overrepresented in the homeless population. Baby was also close to living on the streets, and in the book, she often notices the gross inequities of Vancouver's Downtown Eastside. This is a reality that sadly still resonates with Vancouverites. Readers will also perhaps be able to make links to today's fentanyl and homelessness crises.

A special thanks to Mark Boheim (DJ Markem) for putting up with my questions about Vancouver DJs and the rave days. In the nineties, DJ Markem was a regular feature at Graceland on Thursday nights. His sets were legendary. I've given Mark a little cameo in the novel. Once upon a time, I'd rush to hang out in Mark's glass DJ den, which was always covered in candles. Today, he and his wife make homemade candles as a side business, and he works as producer/director for ABC in Washington, DC.

If you want to listen along to some of the old-school bangers mentioned in this book, search YouTube for the book title and my name. I made a playlist for you.

ACKNOWLEDGEMENTS

Usually, at the end of my books, I include a list of sources that readers can refer to if they want to expand on their knowledge. However, in this case, the novel serves as its own guide. If you want to deep dive into Victorian gothic fiction, house music, or works by psychoanalysts, please try Baby's choices.

Thanks to my nineties crew: Calvin Bill (for mysterious places), Shawn Ayres (for ONE), Dawne Schabler (my warehouse rave partner), Elizabeth Dylke (for Mark Farina and matching wigs), Jolene Boyd (for vintage boutiques), Keleah Strack (for Stanley Park), and Amber Warnat (for Squamish/Whistler). Finally, for Mike McDevitt who gave me my first skateboard.

Thanks: Vince Preap, Nihan Sevinç, Jennifer (Quynh Le Dang) and Leonardo Ngo (In Loving Memory), Christine Lai, Jessica Curtis, Cyndy Curtis, Dawn Chan, Annie Rodgers, Anson Tong, Michelle Helland, Emma Parhar and family, Harmeen Kainth, Paul Allinger, Ajan Khera, Michelle Aguasin-Ustaris, Dr. Lisa Smith, Anita Brown, Tasleem Rajwani, Karen Wu, Manav and Emily Bhardwaj, Sari Nobell, Ayla Mellios, Víctor Manuel Monterroso-Miranda, Kat Tuason, Stacey Kumar, Curran Faris, Brenda Conroy, Amber Heard, Jessica Herdman, Jennifer Schaefer, Allison Flannagan (and your lovely mother!), Nadine Kelln, Dr. Huamei Han, Dr. Habiba Zaman, Sandra McIntyre, Claudia Hernandez, Jason Starr, Alisa Lvin, Robin Maggs, Darrel Yurychuk, David McKee, Leanne Sherwood, Paul Toth, Jodie Haraga, Maddi Wilson, Dino A. Poloni, Deborah MacKenzie, Kevin Rey, Dr. Sean Ashey, Tami Storey-Cooper, Sothea Puth, Samone Kennedy, Nathaniel Roy, Francisco Garcia, Noriko Hagiwara, Raquel Lahrizi,

David Vosper, Elisha Ramstad, Alba Naharro, Inder Singh, Karen Lim, Maria Carr, Negar Saberi, Heather Greenlay, Emily Carpenter, Tatsuya Kawai, Helena (Jun Jie) Luo and Christopher (Rui-Da Deng) Luo, Daniela Alexandra Abasi, Ryan and Karen West, Gagun Chhina, Pawan Chhina, Candice Montgomery, İbrahim Sencer Özer, Gleb Krotkiy, Aneeta Dastoor-Oblette and Jean-Michel Oblette, Demi De Boer, Elizabeth Bydon, Elizaveta Nesgorova, Vielda Morris, Maria Paula Acosta Estrada, Gabby Galindo, Joshwar George, Elena Stojanovksa, Madeline de Shield, Alex and Kylee Carreño, Surindra Sugrim, Simon Johnston, Rishma Johal and family, Sonali Pandya, Jind Singh, Roger Chen, Kathyrn O'Neill, Jana Wall, Sean Witzke, Philippa Joy, Braden and Jamie Eguia and family, Kayle Grace, Alnoor Gova, Savannah D'Mello, Jessica Felix, Mike, Marie, and Madison Kennedy, Emily Deegan, Vic Herr, Beaker, Dave Pottinger and crew (Maggie, Maya, and Lincoln), and Eileen Palmer (In Loving Memory).

To Rosemary Winks, Maureen Kihika, Anthony Ndirangu, Lucas Wozniak, and Giuliana Alayo Casa, for believing.

To the Khoja community, Samba Fusion (especially Carine Carroll and Halie Scaletta), Ocean View Library, Guildford Library, Book Warehouse, and the Douglas College Department of Anthropology and Sociology, for support.

To everyone at Roseway Publishing! Beverley Rach (publishing), Sanna Wanni (publicity and truffle fries), Kristen Darch (copy editing and partner in obsession), Lauren Jeanneau (production and design coordinator), Tania Craan (cover design), and Anumeha Gokhale (marketing, sales, and distribution). A special thank you to Fazeela Jiwa (development editing) who helped give *Sugar Kids* just the right ambience and vibe.

To Pam Dhanju, Renu Thapar, and Sagar Singh, who helped with translations and Hindu cultural details. Shrey Grover, who has previously helped me with Hindi pronunciations for audio book purposes. And Barbara Mantini and Nisha Ahuja for bringing audio books to life!

To the Japanese society in Vancouver, for sharing their stories with me in Japanese.

To Ashvinder Lamba, for hosting me for the Toronto Super Conference.

To Michelle Koebke (from Diamond's Edge Photography), who is the *most* talented photographer I know, for always showing up. I appreciate you.

To my family: Aleksandra and Kazimierz Burkowicz, Farah Asaria, Shirin and Amir Suleman, Mumtaz, Zishan, Shaif, Shabir, and Khalisa Hemraj. Fatim and brousin, Ali Hemraj. In loving memory of Rizwan Hemraj and Mohammed Hemraj. And to Naseem Sherif, Zahoor Sherif, and Nishat Sherif who suffered through the rave years and put up with my craziness.

Finally, thanks to my husband, Jakub Burkowicz, who spent our sixteenth wedding anniversary eating macarons (find them in the book) in a café while I edited. And to our sons, Anjay, Alek, and Augustyn Burkowicz, who inspired the star gazing segments in this novel. Alek's library books helped us plot stars when we went out for late night runs during Covid, helping me form ideas for Ravi. Anjay helped me decide on the rap music and artists in Baby and Jie's jamming out section. And Augustyn provided cuddles through all my writing stages.

And finally, to all the ravers who made up the nineties scene: for the times we danced together, spun in a field together, and thought we couldn't imagine tomorrow without each other.

—TB xxx

ABOUT THE AUTHOR

Taslim Burkowicz's work is inspired by her Indo-Canadian heritage. Favouring a sensory rich writing style while exploring social justice issues, Burkowicz has a bachelor's degree in political science and education from Simon Fraser University, and resides with her husband and three boys in Vancouver, BC, where she runs, dances, reads, and is chased by deadlines.

PREVIOUS PUBLICATIONS

Burkowicz has written three previous novels with Roseway, and her works have appeared on CBC's new fiction lists. Her novel, *Ruby Red Skies*, appeared on *Shrapnel Magazine*'s "Fall Favourites of '22."

RUBY RED SKIES (2022)

> "A deftly crafted novel that expands the historical echoes and cultural geographies of Canadian literature."
>
> — DR. MARIAM PURBHAI, author of *Isolated Incident*

Ruby used to be a fiery, sexy, musical genius. But when she got pregnant as a teenager in the 90s, her life took a turn into banality. Now a middle-aged Indo-Canadian woman, she feels unseen and unheard by her white husband and struggles to communicate with her mixed-race daughter. When she discovers her husband cheating, she embarks on a quest to unearth exciting secrets from her past. To find what she needs, she drives straight into B.C.'s raging wildfires, accompanied only by the fantastical stories her mother used to tell about their ancient Mughal ancestry — a dancer named Rubina who lived in the concubine quarters of the great Agra Fort. This book is at once historical fiction and political romance, deftly navigating themes of mixed-race relationships, climate change, motherhood, body shame, death and the passage of time

— For more on this title, visit *fernwoodpublishing.ca/book/ruby-red-skies*

THE DESIRABLE SISTER (2020)

> *"Like a beautifully woven sari, this novel brings together a range of strands to create a remarkable final piece."*
> — WINNIPEG FREE PRESS

Gia and Serena Pirji are sisters, but as the first-generation born in Canada to immigrant parents, their lives play out in different ways because of their skin tone. Gia's fair skin grants her membership to cliques of white kids as a teen, while Serena's dark skin means treated as inferior. This superficial difference, imposed by a society obsessed with skin colour and hierarchy, sets the sisters into a dynamic that plays out throughout their lives. In a world where white skin is preferable, the sisters are pitted against each other through acts of revenge and competition as they experience adultery, ruined friendships, domestic abuse, infertility and motherhood.

— For more on this title, visit *fernwoodpublishing.ca/book/the-desirable-sister*

CHOCOLATE CHERRY CHAI (2017)

> *"A moving contribution to the fictional writings about migrants and racialized women across transnational borders.... profoundly touching."*
> — HABIBA ZAMAN, author of *Asian Immigrants in "Two Canadas"*

Young, free-spirited Maya Mubeen leaves behind the pressures of family, marriage and tradition for a life of experience and adventure — proving to herself, and her mother, that she is anything but a typical Indian girl. After diving with sharks in the Philippines and a sordid breakup amidst the bustling nightlife of Tokyo, Maya's sense of who she is — and where home is — starts to falter. An ancient chai-making ritual holds the key to Maya's past and present, unlocking the secret lives of her matriarchal ancestors. Traversing the globe and historical eras, *Chocolate Cherry Chai* binds together themes of familial pressures, the immigrant experience, motherhood, love and loss into a poetic narrative.

— For more on this title, visit *fernwoodpublishing.ca/book/chocolate-cherry-chai*